THOUGH THE ICE

AN ENEMIES TO LOVERS ROMANCE

CENTRAL STATE HOCKEY
BOOK 1

JAQUELINE SNOWE

Published by: Jaqueline Snowe
Copyright 2024, Jaqueline Snowe
Cover Design: Star Child Designs
Editing: Katherine McIntyre

This is a work of fiction. The characters, incidents, dialogue, and description are of the author's imagination and are not to be constructed as real. Any resemblance to actual events or persons, living or dead, is completely coincidental.

To nurses—our society wouldn't be where we are without you. A huge hug to Tina, Rachel, Tessa, and the NICU nurses who helped us IMMENSELY...there aren't enough words of thanks to everything you all do.

CONTENT WARNING

Dear reader,

This story talks about some things that may be triggering or upsetting. Through the Ice deals with the loss of a parent due to cancer, an emotionally abusive parent, a parent who suffered a stroke and is recovering, and a few scenes take place in a hospital.

Please take care of yourself and do what's right for you.

BLURB

The last person nursing student Audrey Hawthorne wants to be paired with for her senior clinicals is Theo Sanders. The hockey star responsible for her brother's season-ending injury, so she's branded him as enemy number one. Yet when they're assigned to the same ICU team, Audrey can't avoid him.

Theo, known for his easy smiles and sunny disposition, has always been misunderstood. Behind his cheerful facade lies a man struggling with heavy responsibilities—he's been the main caretaker for his siblings ever since his mother's stroke. When he learns he'll be working alongside Audrey, he sees it as a chance to prove he's not the villain she thinks he is.

Forced proximity in the high-stakes environment of the ICU makes it impossible for Audrey to maintain her grudge. She discovers Theo's life off the ice is as complex and demanding as her own, filled with sacrifices and care for those he loves. Theo starts to break through her defenses, where they begin relying on each other for everything. But as their relationship deepens, can Audrey risk alienating the only family she has left?

1

Audrey

My favorite part about living on campus was the smell of the quad. The landscape always had fresh flowers, and the trees were a hundred years old. My dad and I used to find gardens to explore, where he'd bring a journal to write down the different plants we saw. I smiled as I walked by snapdragons. Before my father became sick, he'd always give me twenty dollars to pick my favorite flower, and we'd plant them in the backyard. Man, he'd be so proud of me entering my senior year of nursing school. Whenever life got hard, I'd think about his kind smile and reassuring hugs.

You can do hard things, Auds. With a brain like yours, nothing is impossible.

So much had changed since he passed. My mom sold our childhood home and moved a few hours away to heal. My brother Quentin and I both attended Central State and hung out once a week, but everything was complicated. I loved my family, but... the familiar weight grew behind my ribcage, making each breath harder than the last.

No. I shook away the stress. I couldn't worry about it now. We were assigned a group project for one of our classes about community health, and we agreed to meet on a Monday night to begin. That was one thing I was adamant about: getting all As. I had to for my scholarship, and with the pressure of finances, I couldn't lose a penny.

My team agreed to meet on the second floor of the library, and as I made my way to the stairs, my phone buzzed. *Mom.*

The same conflicting feelings went to war in my gut: dread and relief. Every time she called, I was glad she was still alive. But the dread... *she needs more money.* My throat closed as I stared at my phone. I could call her back later, but she'd just keep trying. It'd be better to get it over with now. "Hi, Mom."

"I haven't received any payment from you," she barked out.

No hellos or how are yous or I missed yous. I swallowed the ball of emotion and clenched my fist to keep my fingers from shaking. "I sent you a hundred bucks last week."

"That didn't cover what I need." She coughed, and it sounded gross.

"Are you sick, Mom?" My stomach bottomed out. One of the reasons I wanted to be a nurse was due to how many family members had gotten sick while I'd grown up. We spent a lot of time in hospitals with my grandma, aunt, then dad. I thought nurses were superheroes.

But hearing my mom cough made me go on high alert. "You should call a doctor."

"That would require money, Audrey, obviously."

"You have insurance though. With Dad's life insurance poli-cy..." I couldn't finish the sentence. While I was grieving my father, I had to be the one in charge of everything. The funeral, the costs, the insurance... my mom gave up then, and four years later, nothing had changed.

"I still have some copay or something. Look, I know you're studying or whatever, but when can you send more money?"

"I don't know." I squeezed my eyes shut, hating the guilt and anger twisting together into a tornado of emotions. "I can try to pick up more tutoring hours this week."

"Do that. You don't want your mom going hungry, do you? I always told your father you were selfish."

Knife to the ribs.

"What? No, that's—" I leaned against the stair railing, using it as support as my mom hung up. I'd gone through the cycle of feelings with her from anger to sadness to guilt to denial. But none of them mattered. The last thing my dad said to me was to make sure our family was okay. I was the only one strong enough to protect them, and every time my mom asked for money, I wondered if this was what my dad meant. I gave myself five seconds to be fucking angry at my mom, then I pushed the bitterness away. I stood taller, took a deep breath, and made eye contact with the last person I wanted to see. Theo Sanders.

The guy who could've ruined everything when he injured my brother on the ice last year. Quentin was here on a scholarship, and if he wasn't healed soon, he could lose it. Guess who'd have to find a way to pay for his school? Me. I could barely afford life right now, so yeah, I hated Theo Sanders.

He stared at me from across the lobby, his brows furrowed, and I shook my head. No. I could only handle one emotional crisis at a time. My heart raced, and my palms sweated, but I found my way toward the table with the girls from my class.

"Hey, Auds," Lily said, smiling at me before her grin fell. "You alright? You look stressed."

I nodded. She was my closest friend in the program. We weren't the happy-hour-type-friends, but we liked studying together and partnering up. "I'll be okay. Sorry I'm late. My mom called."

I sat next to Jessica, who stared at her laptop. She was not my favorite person in our cohort, but at least Lily was in the group.

"How are we going to develop a community outreach program about mental health? This should be a professional's job." Jessica chewed the end of her pen as she sighed. "Like we're going to be able to make any difference with this when social media is the reason we're all depressed."

My eye twitched. I needed this project to go well.

"Don't think like that." Lily frowned. "It's worth exploring, and we need this grade."

"Being a realist?" Jessica rolled her eyes and cracked open an energy drink. The familiar smell of Red Bull filled the air as she guzzled it. I really didn't like Jessica. She was obnoxious and careless about people around her. She slurped loudly before continuing, "We can do this bullshit assignment and pass. I don't have time to dive into this. I don't know where I'm placed for this semesters clinicals, but I better not have to drive far. Have you two heard anything yet?"

Lily shook her head, but her eyes lit up. "No. Professor Reid told us we'd hear tomorrow. I'm honestly so excited."

Jessica grinned. "I am too. It'll be so good to not just read books and learn the real shit that goes on. My sister went through a similar program and pretty much said that her time at clinicals was where she learned everything, not the books or projects. These just seem like a waste of time, to be honest. I'd rather be doing the real shit."

While I often disagreed with Jessica most of the time, I did understand what she meant. "I know what you mean," I said, my voice a little shakier than I wanted. The call from my mom had rattled me. "It'll be nice to have real life scenarios and get our hands dirty."

"See, Audrey gets it." Jessica sipped her drink and pointed to her computer. "Okay, let's get this over with."

I scanned the project outline on our course website. There was a research phase, design phase, implementation, and evaluation of the plan. The muscle in my neck throbbed just thinking about managing the group dynamics, the project itself, and ensuring I got an A while picking up more tutoring hours. The stress headache was coming on fast and furious. Rubbing my forehead, I took a few calming breaths and pushed the worry about my mom and Quentin to the back of my mind. I couldn't do anything about them *right now,* so I had to focus on what I could control. Like kicking ass at this project.

"Oh, hello there." Jessica whistled as she nodded toward the front of the library. Almost on cue, whispers picked up across the study room. Slowly, heads spun toward the entrance, and even my own gaze moved from Jessica toward the cause of the commotion.

Theo Sanders.

Damn it. *Why is he here?*

A surge of heat—all from anger—raced from my head to the tips of my fingers. I tightened my grip on my water bottle as the rare urge to throw something overtook me. He had no idea about the financial pressures we lived with, and why the hell would he? But that rationale didn't stop the hate I had toward him. His actions had changed my brother for the worse.

"My god, he is hot as hell. He's on the hockey team this year, right?" Jessica twirled her hair with her finger as her cheeks pinkened. "Oh, he looked at me. Shit. He's coming over here."

Lily shifted in her seat as I stared at my laptop, avoiding looking at him. I had nothing to say to him. From the little I knew about him, Theo Sanders was a jerk, on and off the ice. The bastard played for our rival for three years before transferring here. To Central State. And Coach Reiner just let him after what he did to Quentin. I never understood it. I didn't care that his stats were great. He *smiled* after he took Quentin down in that game, and that was unforgiveable.

Jessica and Lily giggled at how attractive he was. Which, sure. The fact he was gorgeous had no effect on me. It made me dislike him more. Someone that devilish should have horns or red eyes or something to warn people away.

The way Quentin screamed on the ice... I cringed at the memory. It seemed disloyal, unfair, and rude that Coach Reiner was allowing Sanders to wear a Central State Wolves jersey. The guys were expected to pass the puck to him? Cover for him?

No.

I hated him. Quentin hated him. The team should hate the guy.

Why is he walking toward us?

"Hey there. You're new here, right? I'm Jessica James. It's a pleasure to meet you." She beamed at him.

Hockey guys were pretty legendary here, and it seemed Theo would be no different. I rolled my eyes.

"I am new this year, yeah." He cleared his throat and tapped the table a few inches from my hand. "Hey, you're Audrey, right?"

I nodded but couldn't make myself speak. My stomach twisted with worry as I was forced to glance at him and regretted it. Theo had dark blue eyes and long lashes, chiseled cheekbones and a wicked jawline. The mop of messy blond hair looked like he'd just run a hand through it. *It's a shame he's so beautiful. He's still a jerk though.*

"I was hoping to speak with you. It shouldn't take more than a few minutes." He smiled and rocked back on his heels. He seemed casual, excited even.

My mind raced with reasons he'd want to talk *to me.* Was this a prank? Did he want to rub in my face what he'd done to

Quentin? That seemed unlikely, but there was no reason for the hockey star to speak to me. "Uh, no?" I mumbled.

"Girl, if a guy who looked like that wanted to talk to me, I sure would." Jessica nudged me with too much force. It knocked my water bottle over, spilling the contents across my notebook. "Shit!"

I jumped up, grabbing my laptop so no water would get on it. I'd splurged and got a MacBook freshmen year, and I couldn't afford another right now. Tears prickled my eyes at the thought of needing another device my final year. I'd have to borrow or come here. *Damn Theo caused this...*

"I'm sorry!" Jessica frantically grabbed a paper from her notebook to try to dry it. "Okay, this isn't working."

"I'll run and get napkins in the bathroom!" Lily took off.

"I'll see if there's a towel or something." Jessica went in the opposite direction as water pooled on the table and spilled onto the floor.

Drip.

Drip.

Drip.

"Did anything important get wet?" He cussed and picked up a few of my books and neatly stacked them. His gaze landed on me, and the intensity in his eyes had me sucking in a breath. It was almost like he was looking for vulnerabilities.

"No." Despite the relief flooding through me at not being out money, his proximity had me on edge. My heart pounded against my ribcage to the point of pain as I broke eye contact.

"That's good," he said, his voice deep and commanding.

"Uh, yeah." I swore my skin flushed as red as my folder. My brain couldn't figure out why he was here, speaking to me. I tried picking up my notebook, but I fumbled with it.

"Here, let me." His fingers brushed mine as he took my

laptop, notebook, folder, and phone out of my hands. He set them on a chair nearby and picked up the girls' things too.

"No, it's fine," I said, annoyed.

Why were Lily and Jessica taking so long? I didn't want to be alone with Theo Sanders. Not when my body was about to have a meltdown.

"Why are you—" I started.

"Can I please speak with you about Professor Aldridge?" He swallowed hard, and his throat moved in a very distracting way.

"What about her?"

I adored Professor Aldridge. She reminded me a lot of who my mom used to be before Dad got diagnosed with cancer. Before she only called me when she needed money or told me I was selfish.

The kind, fun, supportive version of my mom was long gone.

Professor A was all energy and questions and challenging us to think outside the box. She was the reason I helped tutor younger students once a week. She believed in giving back, whether it was energy, time, what have you, so if he wanted to talk to me about her... I'd listen. If he had something negative to say, I'd snap at him. Ha, not really. I couldn't snap at anyone if I tried. My thoughts were aggressive, but my actions weren't. Quentin used to make fun of me for it, but the angrier or ruder he became, the quieter and more inward I did.

Theo gripped the back of his neck and shifted his weight from one foot to the other. I hated that I noticed his body. Sure, he was toned. And wore gray shorts that showcased his thighs and a Wolves T-shirt that hugged his chest. Big whoop.

"She told me I could find you here." He flashed a smile, and his blue eyes warmed. I didn't like seeing that kindness on his face. It didn't fit. He was too rugged, too big, too... *hockey* to have a kind face.

"She said you were the best person to speak to about the

nursing program here and that you'd be willing to help me this first week." He shrugged. "I can buy you coffee as a bribe. She might've mentioned you have a weakness for cold brews."

My face flushed even more as I stared at the way his lips curved. He had one dimple on his left side. Not on the other. I couldn't help but notice this. I studied human bodies for a living. *Not the point.* If Professor A had mentioned my name... "Why do you need any information on the nursing program?"

"Ah, well, because I'm in it?" He laughed, but his cheeks reddened, and he looked away. "I'd love to have a quick tour."

"Tour? I can definitely give you a tour. What are you wanting to see?" Jessica appeared fast, her pulse racing at her neck. It was like she'd run back here.

I didn't want to give Theo Sanders any of my time, but I also didn't care for Jessica doing it either. Analyzing *why* I felt that would be a terrible idea. So, I didn't. I blurted out, "Tomorrow, eight am."

He smiled wide, still only one dimple appearing. "Deal. Anything in the cold brew?"

I shook my head. "Just caffeine."

He chuckled before shoving his hands in his pockets. The gesture was sexy for some silly reason, and I forced myself to think about taxes.

"Should we meet outside the student union?" he asked, half a smile on his lips.

"Oh. You're going to give it?" Jessica tossed a towel on the table, missing the spot that was wet. "I can join too."

"I appreciate that," Theo said, his smile widening. "Another time, for sure. Professor Aldridge suggested I meet with Audrey, and despite being a rough hockey player, I like to follow a professor's suggestion."

Then he winked.

Jessica giggled and leaned closer to him. The whole thing

was so familiar, and it clicked. I knew why I offered to help him. It wasn't my fierce loyalty to Professor A. It was the fact that girls like Jessica were always trying to seek clout or fame or *something* from athletes. I might hate Theo, but I'd seen enough people like Jessica to want to protect him from it.

She'd use him, and while I didn't want the jerk to experience joy until Quentin was back on the ice, I didn't want his entire life ruined. My feelings were...complicated.

"I'll catch you ladies later." He tapped his fingers on the table. "I'm sure we'll have some classes together, yeah?"

"You're in nursing?" Jessica's voice went nuclear. "Oh my god. Do you have your clinical assignment yet? What if we're together?"

Theo cleared his throat and met my gaze for a second before I focused on my hangnail. I didn't like the way he looked to *me* for help. I didn't want to be paired with him either.

He shrugged his broad shoulders. "It could happen. Have a good night, and I'll see you tomorrow, Audrey."

I nodded but refused to look at him as he departed. He wasn't even out of earshot before Lily returned, and Jessica hit my arm. "How did you score that?"

"Score what?" Lily asked, patting the table dry. Her attention moved toward Theo, but he'd already left the common area.

"Theo Sanders asked *Audrey* to give him a tour tomorrow. And he's in our cohort. I'd sell a kidney to be paired with him."

Lily couldn't hide her smile. "She should. She's the best in our class."

Jessica glared. "I'm right here, Lilith."

"I stand by what I said."

I blushed at the compliment. I put all my time and energy into being the best, so to hear a friend say it meant a lot. It wasn't like my family was offering up compliments to me and my love life—ha, my lack of love life—was almost comical. "Should we try to get some work done or reschedule for another night?" I asked, hoping to bring us back to why we were at the library.

If we were calling the work session, I could spend tonight trying to find tutoring opportunities to send my mom some cash. That would keep me busy instead of overthinking about giving Theo Sanders a tour. I wanted to stay far away from that guy, even if he was handsome and caused my stomach to flutter. He was a constant reminder of how fragile our family was, and all I wanted to do was escape my reality. Yeah, I'd give him the tour and avoid him the rest of the year. Totally possible.

2

Theo

"WHY ARE YOU SMILING? It looks weird."

I arched a brow at my teenage sister, Emily. She was seventeen and had every ounce of attitude one could at that age. I honestly loved messing with her. It brought me endless amusement. "Does my joy bother you?" I grinned wider, to the point it hurt my face. "What about now?"

"God, you're the worst." She rolled her eyes, but a small smirk crossed her face. I considered that a victory. Life had been tough lately, and any earned smile was a point.

"Are you coming home tonight? Can I hang at Jace's house?"

I grunted. Jace was her *super serious* boyfriend who smelled weird. He also stared at her a little too long, and he had a very punchable face. Some people just did. Maybe his eyes were too close together? I wasn't sure, but my hand itched whenever he was around. "I won't be home until seven. Can you stay here until then?"

"Will my curfew be midnight then?"

I laughed and hit the table, causing the glass of orange juice to wiggle. "Cute. But that's a hell no."

"What is the point of you being my cool older brother if you don't make the rules better?"

"Can't help you there, Em." I finished my bagel just as my younger brother Daniel dragged his ass into the kitchen. The kid was nine and a mess. Just complete disaster. It was strange how the three of us were so different. I was organized and studious, a clean freak. Emily was messy but particular. Daniel was a disaster.

"Hi, bud." I ruffled his hair. "Can I get you breakfast?"

"Pop-Tarts." He went to the pantry and pulled them out, ripping open the package and spilling crumbs everywhere. Even seeing the mess had me jumping from my chair to grab the small broom.

I swept them up as he plopped down onto the couch. A small throb started in the back of my head, but I took a few deep breaths, and it passed. I knew they were tension headaches. I'd gotten them since our mom had a stroke and moved into a rehabilitation facility a year ago. My dad used work to escape, and with her gone... no one was here anymore. My parents couldn't handle Emily and Daniel and Penny.

Oh, did I mention Penny? She was my hellion five-year-old sister. Sass on wheels. More attitude than me on the ice. She had fire red hair and a face of freckles. I smiled just thinking about her. She was my buddy, but I was her brother, not her dad, and it was hard navigating that line.

"Okay, plan for the day, team." I placed my hands on my hips and waited for the two older ones to look at me. "I'll be at school this morning for class and come home to pick you all up. Then back for hockey practice. Then return for the night."

"Sure thing, coach." Emily went back to her phone. "Then I'm going to Jace's house."

"If you do schoolwork." I pointed at her.

"Ugh, you used to be fun. I miss that Theo."

That comment stung. Yeah. I missed him too. I was still that guy, but my family needed me. My parents were my heroes and to see them struggle? I couldn't handle it. I asked for a transfer for senior year to be near home, and I had no regrets about it. Not one.

Yet...when my dad blitzed through the house to leave for work, not bothering to ask if I could take my siblings to school or when he wouldn't come home until nine and assumed I'd be here... that grated on me.

I'd have my whole life for hockey, but my mom having a stroke freaked me out. She wasn't invincible anymore, and it was hard to deal with. She was my favorite person, and guilt stabbed me in the chest when I thought about how long it'd been since I'd gone to see her. It was hard to watch her be a shell of who she was. She'd forget who I was, fall asleep mid-conversation, but all of that was improvement. For the first few months, she couldn't even talk.

So yeah, I didn't party. I didn't do crazy shit. Every minute of every day was school, hockey, or family. It was exhausting, but I didn't have a choice.

No one would believe me if I told them that. My reputation on the ice overtook any truth. They called me aggressive, fun. I'd chirp at our opponents and make them look bad. I'd push the line and laugh about it. But hockey was my escape. It was how I coped with life. The ice was the only place I felt like me anymore.

I wasn't like that off the ice at all.

"Tee Tee!"

I spun as Penny jumped onto me after hammering down the stairs. She was loud and fast. "Hey, Pen."

"Can we listen to Country Roads again and again and again?"

I chuckled. I played Country Roads one time for them, and Penny became obsessed. She now knew every word and shouted MOONSHINE at the top of her lungs. It wouldn't be surprising if she got a note home from her preschool class. "Em is taking you to school today, but I'll play it when I pick you up, deal?"

"Deal."

Penny had handled the shift the best. She was showered with love and probably the favorite of the family. She gave me a high five as I marched out of the house. The drive to campus was only twenty minutes, and I was grateful I'd actually bought a parking pass. I didn't want to out of pure spite, but it allowed me to park closer to the quad.

Back at my other school in Indiana, I'd leave my truck in the garage most days and walk to campus. The rink was close to my apartment with my guys—ugh. An uncomfortable lump formed in my throat. I missed my team. I missed the guys, my space, my life there. They reached out, but I didn't have the emotional energy to respond. Texts stacked up until they eventually stopped coming. My bandwidth was at max capacity these days, and taking on anything more would make me snap.

Central State was great, but it wasn't my home. Also didn't help that the team hated me. The head coach, Michael Reiner, was a solid dude. I liked his style, but the guys had a chip against me for a solid reason. I stopped at the café near the quad and grabbed a cold brew for Audrey, my mind still on hockey.

Indiana had a better record last year, and there was the altercation with Hawthorne. Speaking of Hawthorne...

Wait.

I smacked my forehead as I made my way in front of the student union. There was no way Audrey Hawthorne, that beautiful, shy, and kinda grumpy woman was related to Quentin Hawthorne. What were the odds?

That explains why she looked at me like she hated me...

Fuck.

I ran a hand through my hair, pulling the ends a bit as I glanced around for her. A part of me enjoyed her attitude. I wasn't used to it. It might sound ridiculous, but people were generally kind or over-the-top with me. Like the other girl with her, Jessica-something.

At least in Indiana, a hockey player was just short of celebrity. Audrey wanted nothing to do with me, but if it was because of the injury to her brother last year, that was harder to overcome. She was supposed to be the best nursing student to get help from. I exhaled, the initial excitement of seeing her dying down a little with nerves. Professor Aldridge said Audrey would help me get acclimated and that befriending her would be the best for my growth and success, but how could I do that when she hated my guts?

"You made it."

Damn. I squinted against the August sun and smiled at the figure approaching me. Audrey had a unique, throaty voice that reminded me of podcasters. She spoke without emotion, and it made me want to push her buttons. Just to see her reaction. It was a wild thing to think about after meeting *one* time before.

She seemed annoyed to be here, and while it was refreshing, I still didn't like knowing I was the cause of it. "Is Quentin related to you?"

"Ah, put it together, did you?" She flexed her jaw as she adjusted the straps of her bag. Her high-waisted jeans and tight tank top fit her well. I hadn't realized she was so curvy yesterday. It did me no good to think of her that way, not with needing her help with nursing and trying to form some relationship with the hockey team. Plus, there were daggers shooting out of her eyes at me.

It didn't matter if I was the best on the ice. If the guys and I didn't vibe as a team, we were doomed. I clicked my tongue and studied her. She didn't strike me as similar to Quentin. He had lighter hair, a rounder face. But the nose was the same... probably the eyes. "He your brother, cousin?"

"Brother." Her eyes flashed. "And you ruined his NHL dreams by having him sit out a season. You had a cheap shot, and you know it. So let me make this clear: we will never be friends. I'm only doing this because I respect Professor A too much to let her down. Do not try to be funny, don't smile or joke with me. I will answer your questions, and we can beg the Quad gods that we aren't paired together for clinicals. Am I clear?"

"Did you practice that on the way here?" I grinned, a flicker of irritation dancing along my spine. She didn't know that her brother was a punk ass on the ice, always playing dirty and going after others. He thought he was hot shit and went after the wrong dude. He deserved my shot at him, and *everyone* fucking knew it. But she made her opinion known, and it wasn't worth the effort to show her otherwise. Hell, what time did I have to go into making her believe me? I barely had a free hour to sleep.

She rolled her eyes and crossed her arms. "Don't start with me, Sanders."

"Using my last name is a little flirty," I fired back, unable to stop myself. There was something about her. The way she held her shoulders, the way she glared at me... there was a familiar air to her I didn't want to explore. When I saw her on the stairs yesterday, gripping the railing for support, my heart lurched for her. She was going through *something,* but I'd never know and didn't care to. However, I could mess with her. That was always on the table.

"I'm *not* flirting. I would never flirt with you. Now ask your questions."

"Here's your drink." I handed it to her. "I only spat in it twice."

"Great." She took it and closed her eyes at the first sip. "I hate you, but thank you."

"Anytime." I fought a smile again. "Now, give me your five-star tour, and I'll give you a tip."

She slow-blinked me before opening and closing her mouth. She seemed confused if I was joking or not, and the adrenaline rush returned. I hadn't felt this type of rush in years. Excitement and a challenge.

"The nursing building is all the way down there, on the left side." She pointed. "You could use your brain, if yours still works, and look that up online, but I'm so glad I was able to help point you to a large building."

"You're incredible. Your bedside manner must be top-notch." I snorted. "Please, continue. I wouldn't survive without you."

"Our health sciences library and simulation labs are a little harder to find. There is a separate building between our UGL and Thompkins Hall."

"UGL?"

"Underground library. We're known for having it half in the ground, half out. But the simulation labs are in the basement of a neighboring building. And they aren't marked well. It's part of the superstition and legacy. Apparently, someone died in the building like fifty years ago, and the story behind why is a little shady, so there are ghosts." Her lips curved up as she spoke, like she was enjoying herself. The sun hit her face just right, and for the second time, I thought she was pretty.

"Oh, that's fun." I loved a good ghost story.

"Our health services building also matters. You might have to put in volunteer hours there twice a week. It depends on if your prior school—" she cringed "—made you do that. I don't think Indiana has a great nursing program."

"Don't be elitist." I arched a brow. "You can talk shit about their hockey team but not their school."

She pressed her lips together. "You're right. That won't happen again. I'll hate you in a more respectful way."

"Perfect. Okay, so simulation labs, health services, our main building. Aldridge said you were the go-to for success, so what should I do?" I gripped the straps of my bag and studied Audrey.

She was about a foot shorter than me and had no wrinkles or lines on her face. My mom always said wrinkles were a sign of laughter, so it made me feel bad for half a second that she didn't laugh a lot.

That wasn't my problem, but it made me wonder why she was so prickly.

"What's the secret sauce?" I asked again.

She sipped her coffee and started walking down the side-walk. I joined her, obviously, and caught a whiff of her perfume. It was damn delightful. Peachy and flowery and pleasant.

"You need a good study group. Jessica and Lily are not mine, usually. They're great in their own way, but my regular group is different. We meet once a week. Sometimes it's to vent or cry, but they're the reason we're successful. Finding a cohort makes the difference because this degree is demanding. Now, can I ask a question that's direct?"

"You told me you hated me. Figured that kinda crossed the line already. Ask me what you want, Hawthorne."

Her eyes flared, but I wasn't sure if it was in annoyance or amusement. I was gonna vote amusement.

"Why are you in nursing? That's a very hard field, and you're on the hockey team. You probably won't be able to keep up."

My chest tightened at her question. She didn't understand my life and clearly had no interest in doing so. "That answer would require some friendship, and we're not friends, nor will be, as you pointed out. I'll manage, and that's my business."

She frowned. "Most hockey guys are drafted and don't care about degrees."

"Stereotyping me already." I jutted my chin toward the union, slightly annoyed and hurt at her attitude. She didn't know how hard I worked or how much was on the line. I'd seen so much change in our life because my mom's stroke. I couldn't rely on a sport for my future, for my family. Plus, I promised my mom I'd finish my degree. I'd never break a promise to her. "I think I'm good for the tour. Thanks, Hawthorne. I'll pray to the gods tonight that we aren't paired up for clinicals."

Her frown deepened as I walked away from her, but I didn't care. She didn't know, or care to know, that her brother deserved what happened to him. I had no regrets for hitting him hard.

Audrey might have sway in the nursing program, but I worked my ass off and was dependable as fuck. I'd prove my worth here, just like on the team. One day at a time.

Plus, I didn't need friends. I was here a year, that was it. I had my family and the ice, and most days, that was all I needed. Screw Audrey Hawthorne and her judgmental attitude. I didn't have time for it.

3

———

Audrey

My brother and I met for breakfast the following morning, and I hated the chink in my armor. It remained with me all yesterday, knowing that I'd upset Theo. It was clear with the tight shoulders and the way his smile fell off his face. Just, totally melted off as I'd stereotyped him and insulted him.

I hated him for hurting my brother, but I wasn't cruel. I could be decent toward him without intentionally jabbing him. It didn't help that Quentin moaned all yesterday about how his life was over, and he was in a low place, so it made me channel my anger onto Theo.

If Quentin didn't have his scholarship, I'd be screwed financially. For him though, he needed a way to take out his energy and aggression. He'd always been that way, needing a release to deal with the stress of us losing our dad. Without a way to burn it off, he'd been a hot mess the last few months. Every time he'd be upset or worry about money, I'd get angry, and seeing Theo just made all the anger come back.

And I'd taken it out on Theo. That was beneath me. It was

becoming more challenging to shove everything away, to brush it aside and be better and hold it together. I felt like... I was a bursting at the seams with emotions. There was no outlet for me. There was yoga and TV, school, studying, repeat.

"You figure out your placement yet?" Quentin asked, shoving a piece of toast in his mouth.

"No. We hear today at our afternoon lecture." I sipped the coffee and shoved the eggs around on my plate. They didn't taste good anymore. The texture annoyed me. Plus, my stomach soured the more I thought about my behavior. I didn't let anyone in, but I was never mean.

"I hope it's somewhere close so you don't have to drive too far. You look exhausted, Aud. Are you sleeping okay?"

My eyes almost welled up. It had been so long since my brother was kind to me and asked how I was, so it almost undid me. "I am. This senior year is just a lot already. So many assignments, and I snapped at someone yesterday I shouldn't have."

"Audrey." Quentin leaned forward onto the table, staring at me hard. "You never snap at people. What's going on?"

My throat closed up. I didn't want to worry him and tell him about Theo, especially if it'd piss him off. Two months ago, I mentioned the incident, and he shut down. I needed him focused on positives, healing and getting back to playing. So, I shrugged and waved a hand in the air. "I let my impatience get the best of me. It's no big deal. How's the team? How's your rehab?"

And just like that, I deflected. Quentin cared about me, I knew that, but I could get him to stop worrying about me if I asked about him. He preferred to talk about himself the most.

"I'm getting all movement back and am feeling confident, but Coach won't let me on the ice with the guys yet. If I keep on pattern, I can be out there in a few weeks." He rolled his eyes. "It's been interesting having Sanders with us."

My stomach fell out of my butt at the mention of his name. "Yeah," I said, my throat scratchy. "Is that going okay?"

"I mean, the guy is a dick. He's no fun. He just works out, practices, doesn't talk to anyone. He fucking ruined my NHL run last year. I still don't get why Reiner allowed him to come, but he's good on the ice. He could help us win, which I guess is more important. But I hate the guy. He's an asshole."

"He's not mean to you right?" If he was, then I'd stop feeling bad about hurting him. He'd deserve my wrath if he hurt my brother, again.

"No." Quentin scoffed. "He doesn't say anything to anyone. The guy is a huge shit-talker on the ice, but I haven't seen any of that yet. It's weird." He gripped his neck and sighed. "We haven't started our real practices yet. Once I'm on the ice, it'll be different. I know it. I'm bigger now, and he'll get his ass handed to him."

A beige flag went off in my mind. My brother was going to get revenge on Theo? That sounded out of character, and despite me being the sister, I blurred into the mom role from time to time. "Are you sure that's what you want? Can't you just get healed and focus on your stats to get drafted?"

"Yeah, sis, that's the goal, but Sanders fucked me up. I wanna repay the favor."

"Quentin Hawthorne." I lowered my voice. "I don't like hearing you say this. We're on the same team here."

"I'm not talking about injuring him, Auds, settle down. I meant, mess with him. Trip him. Not do him harm. I'm not like that. Come on, you know that." He laughed it off, but I saw a dark look cross his face.

It was also interesting seeing how my brother had changed the last half a year. It was hard to admit, but I didn't like all the new sides of him. Like the revenge-seeking part of him. *That's hypocritical since you were mean to Theo for the same reason.* Quentin used brute force, and I used words.

"How about we forget all about Sanders and enjoy this brunch? Tell me about the party last weekend."

Quentin went into a tale of foolishness, where him and his buddies dared each other to eat weird concoctions of food, but it had us both laughing, and we were back to normal. It wasn't long before I made my way to class. I didn't have a dream location for clinicals, but I did want somewhere close, so it wasn't a long drive. There was a pediatric hospital, hospice care, ICU, and basic medical units within the area. There were a hundred of us in our senior cohort, and there used to be almost two hundred. People dropped out because it was such a challenge, and I felt pride walking into my fourth year.

I made it.

The hall smelled like pencils and metal, also with a familiar cologne I couldn't place. It was beachy and piney and *shit.* Theo Sanders stood at the end of the row, smiling at me with mischief in his eyes. Almost like he knew something I didn't.

My stomach swooped as he neared me, and the apology I wanted to say got lost as he flashed a full smile. He had great teeth. Objectively.

"Guess who're buddies this semester, Hawthorne. You and me, girl. We're paired up at the Jefferson ICU."

The blood drained from my face, the prickly feeling of shock making its way from my neck to my arms and fingers. His words made sense. They were grammatically correct. But paired. Him and me. All semester.

I...assumed I'd be solo. Professor Aldridge knew I hoped for ICU because I wanted the challenge of the urgency and acuity. Plus, it was a specialized field and would be easier to find a job. It sounded weird to others, but I craved to be the best nurse possible for patients in tough situations. I wanted to be trained and ready as best I could, and that meant working in the place where things were always hectic and slightly unpredictable. I just didn't realize I'd have a buddy.

"Wow, I take your absolute silence as you're so happy you can't even speak. I feel the same way. I'm overcome with emotion. Bursting." He placed a hand on his heart, closed his eyes, and went, "Mm, so amazing."

A million thoughts raced through my brain, each one trying to be dominant, but they blurred together, and the only thing that came out was, "But we hate each other."

Theo's eyes flew open, and his gaze moved from my eyes to my mouth, then back up. He pressed his lips together before sighing. "No. *You* hate me. Don't put your negativity energy on me. I can't afford that."

Then, Theo Sanders walked away.

This was the second time guilt stabbed at my chest. Why was I the bad guy here when he was the one who'd hurt Quentin? Why did I keep upsetting him?

I just needed my feet to move to talk to him, to explain this wasn't me. I didn't hurt people intentionally, yet I had with him twice now. I just...ugh. Confrontation was my biggest fear. It paralyzed me, made me want to vomit. My stomach twisted and knotted as I lost sight of Theo. He wasn't hard to miss with his hair and size, but he blended in with the rest of the students. This lecture hall was large for just a hundred or so students, but there were so many people in here today.

Why?

"He is so hot, and he's in nursing? My god. A smart jock. I'm in love."

"Who got paired with him? Can we shank her?" Giggles followed that comment. My stomach bottomed out. I wasn't used to hearing anyone say something like that about me. I liked being invisible.

"Sanders as a nurse. I think I'm feeling faint... what if I fell?"

I shoved the voices out of my head and made my way down the aisle. This was no different than with Quentin. People talked about him all the time. He was a starting freshman and had great stats. People never put us together as siblings, which was fine with me. I hated being used for clout for him. Using me to get to him never worked.

At no point in my life would I ever go to my baby brother with a girl interested in him.

My heart raced at the potential confrontation with Theo. My palms sweated, and every part of my body fought the urge to talk to him, to apologize. My comfort zone was calming others down, like patients, while remaining strong and consistent. I didn't say sorry. That meant having relationships with people, and I just didn't have those.

But my gut told me saying sorry to him was the right move. I'd still talk to Professor Aldridge to see if we could switch partners or if I could go solo, but I could rectify my wrongs to Theo.

It took a minute, but I found him sitting in the front row, smiling at his phone.

People stared at him from every direction, but he didn't care or notice.

"You," I said, gripping my bag tighter to channel some of his positive energy.

"What an opening, Hawthorne. I can already tell we're gonna fall madly in love." He smirked and put his phone in his pocket. "Here to declare your feelings?"

"Why are you so..." I waved my hand over him, not able to find the correct word. His carefree attitude was contagious and made me hate him less. It was distracting and captivating.

"You're ridiculous," I sputtered.

"Thank you." He grinned, that dang dimple popping out

again. "Now, are you gonna sit by me, or are you afraid I'll bite you?"

I couldn't back down from his dare. It was juvenile, but the guy was so extra. The knowing smirk all the time, like he was one second away from cracking a joke. He was too smug. Huffing, I sat in the chair next to him, which caused our legs to touch. Heat spread through my thigh, and instead of moving away, he let his leg remain there.

His thigh touched mine, and my face heated.

I jerked my leg away, out of survival, but he definitely noticed.

"We're gonna see some shit working together, Hawthorne. You'll have to get used to me somehow."

"I came to apologize to you," I blurted out. When everyone else learned how to be cool and charismatic, I was either too busy taking care of my sick family or reading a book. Quentin could verbally spar with the best of them, where I turned inward and grew too awkward.

He tilted his head to the side, his soft blue eyes curious. He then spun all the way to face me, every ounce of his attention on me. "Oh, this is interesting. Let's hear it then."

I felt under the microscope. The way he stared was almost unnerving, like he truly listened or cared what I said. Most people saw through me or just asked what they needed before moving on. But no, not him.

"I didn't mean to stereotype you."

"Yeah, you did." He shrugged yet kept his attention on me. "You definitely did. I'm a hockey jerk, right?"

Swallowing down the urge to run, I kept firm. "I'm sorry I did."

"That's a better apology." He offered a quick smile. "Forgiven."

"Wait." I blinked, prepared to say more. "That was fast."

"Yeah. The world is too complicated and tough as it is. Why hold onto the small stuff for longer than you need to? We'd never enjoy life then." He tapped his pen against the side of the chair a few times before he grinned for real. "Why do you look like you're about to pass out?"

"I don't." I sat back and ran a hand over my face. Embarrassment flooded my cheeks, and I kinda wished the auditorium chair would fold in half and take me with it. "Okay, maybe a little."

"Do you need me to take your vitals, just to be sure?"

Damn. His voice dropped an octave, and my breath caught in my throat. He was teasing me. I knew that, yet the slight variation had me blushing even harder. I cleared my throat.

"I'm messing with you, Hawthorne. It's too easy. Probably because you hate me, but I can give you shit without really worrying about it. Its freeing, tbh."

He finally faced the stage. My whole body relaxed without his stare, and I caught my breath. There was something about Theo that unnerved me. The way he oozed charm, the fact my entire opinion of him felt wrong after meeting him, or the way he actually saw me. The combination of all three made me dizzy, yet instead of walling myself off more, I wanted to explain it to him.

"Confrontation makes me insanely nervous. My pulse races, and my stomach cramps, and I didn't like that I hurt your feelings yesterday. I wanted to apologize for that, but then I said we hated each other, and you seemed upset again. I'm not used to being an asshole." There. I said it. I stared at a spot near the lectern that had a smudge from a shoe, even though I could feel Theo's attention on my face. "Then you forgave me so easily it threw me off guard."

"Do you need me to be madder at you?"

"Yes, I deserve it."

"Well, in that case, fuck you, Hawthorne."

I snorted. It was a honking sound that escaped before I could stop it. I covered my mouth with my hand, chuckling at the unexpected comment from Theo. His grin matched mine, and he nudged my elbow with his.

"It's nice seeing you laugh. Super sexy snort, by the way."

Damn it. I laughed again. "No, you can't be funny. It's not allowed."

"Ah, didn't realize. Sorry, I'll work on that. I'll add it to my list right now. *Be less funny because Hawthorn snorts like a hyena.*"

My stomach did another weird flip thing, this time a little more pleasant than the others. Theo was charming.

"Dude, Sanders! I can't believe you're on our hockey team now. I am obsessed with college hockey, and your stats are sick! I know people will have feelings about Quentin being out, but dude, you are better." Peter, one of the fellow classmates in our cohort, put his hand on Theo's shoulder on the other side.

And snap. There went any medium-warm feelings I had toward Theo. *Better than Quentin.* What the hell?

The rush returned to my ears. I couldn't sit here and listen to them talk hockey when my brother was miserable and off the ice and I had to work twice as many jobs to save up just in case he lost his scholarship. Because of Theo fucking Sanders.

I wasn't super religious, but I had to piss off a god somewhere to be paired with him. For the whole semester? Yeah. No.

I grabbed my bag and got up, needing distance from him. I found a spot three rows up, and I ignored any tingling feelings that he watched me. He could stare all he wanted. Peter had reminded me of the truth. Theo had gone after my brother during a game and intentionally hurt him.

That wasn't anyone I could associate with.

Fired up, I emailed Professor Aldridge to see if there was any chance of changing partners for clinicals. There wasn't really a professional way to beg, so I kept it short and to the point. She knew me. She also understood my relationship with my brother and what his injury had done to me.

I cracked my knuckles and barely paid attention to the professor going over the clinical schedule. We'd receive them in email and blah, blah. I'd been ready for this year since I started. I just wanted to learn and not have to deal with all the complications of Theo Sanders.

Not even fifteen minutes went by before Professor A emailed me back.

Audrey,

You and Theo are suited perfectly to be paired. Trust me on this. Looking forward to our coffee chat next week—hope week one has been fun.

--A

Well, there went my last hope. She never changed her mind. I glanced up to glare at Theo and found him staring back at me, the line between his brows deepening in concern. How dare *he* look concerned?

No. I shook my head and avoided his face the entire lecture. We'd only speak when at the ICU together, and that was it. And if he ever mentioned my brother, I'd punch him in the throat.

4

Theo

I was gonna be late. Nothing worked me up more than missing a deadline. Whether it be an appointment, an assignment, or an oil change, being even a few minutes late stressed me the fuck out.

And this wasn't any of those things. The meeting was with Coach Reiner. He set up a time to talk after a workout the follow day, but Penny needed to be picked up, along with Daniel, and Em was at her part-time job. By some heroic feat, I had my siblings in the back of my truck as I sped toward the rink.

"You're driving too fast." Daniel tapped the window. "Dad would be mad."

"Dad has other things to worry about," I said through gritted teeth. Like, avoiding me and his other children, pretending to work, making me the parent. *Three minutes until the meeting.*

Why did he have to schedule it last minute? Fuck. We were a mile out at least, and parking and the walk... I ran a hand through my hair, frustrated as hell. It wasn't a good look to be late to a one-on-one. The guys had a hard enough time with me being a rival for three years, but Reiner wanted me on the team.

But to be late?

"I'm hungry." Penny's voice had that watering tone, the one she used before bursting into tears. "Snack, please."

"Pen, I don't have anything with me." I swallowed hard and yanked the wheel down the side street. There was an open spot, but we'd have to run to the rink to make it on time. "Okay, I need an hour, please. Then we can get ice cream or pizza. Whatever you want. Just let me talk to the coach, okay?"

"I'm hungry!"

Fuck me. I pinched my nose, taking a deep breath before going into action. "Daniel, there's a vending machine outside Coach's office. Use my card and get your sister whatever she wants."

"What about me?"

"You too, obviously."

Nine years passed by the time they got out of the damn car. Another decade to get them walking toward the rink. I fired off a quick text saying I was almost there. He could bench me, make me run, skate laps, whatever he wanted. I'd take it.

It was crazy how going through this with my family really did teach me to be more sympathetic toward others. It made me question how kind I was before. Guys who showed up late, who I'd judge harshly, could be going through a million things I'd never know about. Sucked that people had to go through tough moments to grow.

"Okay, let's walk faster, people." I hoisted up Penny on my side and jogged. "Daniel, run."

It was a hot mess, but we got to the rink, and I was only seven minutes past our time. Bad, but not horrible. But I hadn't thought through this part of the plan. Daniel was nine, not a teenager. He couldn't watch Penny thoroughly enough.

"What should we do? Where's my snack?" Penny asked, nervously glancing around the hallway.

"Daniel, you and her need to stay in the hallway until I'm done."

Tick, tick, tick. Another minute late.

"But what about the food?"

"Guys, please." I was about to snap. A flash of resentment burst through me. Why did I have to be the fucking parent to my siblings? Why couldn't I be a normal twenty-one-year-old, focusing on hockey and school? Why did my mom have to have a stroke and my dad essentially left me in charge because he couldn't *handle* it? Life wasn't fucking fair.

"I need food!" Penny yelled and dropped onto the ground. A guy glanced at us down the hall as her cries grew louder.

"Let me talk to my coach, tell him what's going on." I gripped my hair, just as Audrey walked down the hallway. She wore a simple olive-green tank top and cutoff jeans. Her hair was down, and she wore a black hat, and damn. She looked cute, but I wasn't in the mood for her judgement today. And of course, she'd see me at a weak moment. Not that it mattered, but I wished I was working out shirtless or something.

"Snack now!" Penny screamed. "I need food!"

Audrey stopped and frowned at the three of us, but her expression shifted immediately. Not ice queen or timid. She almost seemed concerned. "What kind of food do you like?"

Penny sniffed. "Crackers."

"Oh, dang. I don't have crackers, but I have some Pop-Tarts. They are my favorite thing ever. Do you like them?"

"I do." Daniel chimed in.

"Audrey," I said, my voice cracking. "I'm so sorry—you don't, they just—"

"I don't mind." She waved her hand in the air. "Who are you two?"

"I'm Daniel, and this is Penny." Daniel glanced at her, then at the ground. "I'll watch Penny. Go to your meeting."

Fuck me. Twelve minutes late now. "I have to talk with the coach. My siblings... they... it's complicated."

"Hey." Audrey swallowed and met my gaze. "I'll hang with them. How long do you think your meeting will last?"

"I have no idea. You don't—please don't—"

"Go. If you're late, you're screwed." She jutted her chin. "I promise it's okay."

She had no reason to offer this. None. A small part of me thought she'd do it to mess with me, but her face softened when she stared at my siblings. I had a million questions. A billion, actually. Like why, for one, did she offer this?

"Theo, *go*."

"Right." I took off toward Reiner's office and paused outside the door. Nerves gripped me. We'd talked before, we had to before the transfer, but this was the first meeting he'd requested, and I was fifteen minutes past. I knocked, mentally preparing myself for the consequences.

"Come in."

Here went nothing.

I twisted the handle and kept my face neutral. Coaches didn't want apologies for being late, nor did they want excuses. "I'll take whatever consequences you provide, Coach. I know I'm fifteen minutes late."

Coach Reiner nodded as he crossed his arms. The dude had a sleeve of tattoos that made him look badass, but compliments were worthless. "Why were you late?"

"Excuses don't matter, Coach," I intoned.

"Sure. I agree with you, but I asked you a question." He leaned against the front of his desk, not quite sitting on it but also not standing. He also spoke in a consistent tone, not giving anything away.

"I didn't plan accordingly to make the meeting time."

"Dude." Another voice came from the corner of the office.

I snapped my attention toward him, unaware there was even another person in the room. Jonah Daniels, the new assistant coach stood there. He looked like he was about to smile. I nodded at him. "Coach Daniels."

"JD, please. I've always been JD on the ice." He pushed off the wall and jutted his chin toward Reiner. "You'll learn how Reiner works this year, but he is legit asking why you're late. He's an annoying millennial and cares. You'll get used to it."

"Jonah," Reiner warned.

"You hired me as your assistant, so you get my shit talking."

Okay, I fought a snort but wouldn't dare laugh. I focused on the puck sitting on his desk.

"Anyway, Theo, JD is right. If its time management, we'll work on it. If it's something else, I want to know. I'm about entire player development, not just what happens on the ice. You're already drafted to the Acorns. You have the talent, so it's my job to home in on that and prepare you in whatever way you need."

"I appreciate that." I cleared my throat. "I take care of my siblings because my parents can't right now. You know my mom had a stroke, but she's not getting better, and if I wouldn't have driven, my brother and sister wouldn't have been picked up from school."

"Shit," JD muttered.

"Where are they now?"

"Currently in the hallway. Audrey Hawthorne offered to sit with them, but that makes me a little nervous because she hates my guts."

Reiner snorted. "You and her have something in common. Despite being two years older, she basically raised her brother."

What? I glanced at Reiner, the urge to know every detail bubbling up. "What do you mean?"

"Not my story." He waved his hand. "I wanted to talk to you about that, actually. How have guys on the team been?"

"How you would imagine."

Most of the guys were dicks or didn't acknowledge me. Two in particular, Price Charming and Jaxon Beers, were decent. But everyone else seemed team Quentin. Their goalie Alex Hannigan or their defensive star Liam Levers were probably my favorite teammates so far. They were quiet, focused, and pushed me to be better in the gym.

But Quentin's crew, they were trouble.

"You ready to address what happened with Hawthorne yet?"

"Is that what this meeting is about?" I didn't want to discuss that night or that play. It wouldn't help anyone.

"Please, have a seat. You're too uptight right now, and it's stressing me out."

I moved toward the chair as him and JD sat too. They seemed relaxed and at ease. I forgot what that felt like. "I'm not uptight sir, I just would rather not talk about that injury, it wouldn't help anything."

"But we both know the truth of that night." His eyes flashed. "And yes, I'm talking about the fact Quentin deserved what you did."

"Fun fact about Reiner, he likes pet projects." JD hit my shoulder.

"JD, Jesus."

"What? Theo's not the problem, you know this. We lost the senior leadership last year, and the guys are too young and not disciplined enough. Q reminds me of Cal Holt a bit, before he grew up."

"I forgot Cal Holt went here." I smiled. "He's having a hell of a career right now in California."

"He's coming to visit in a few weeks, actually. Let me know if you want to chat with him separately. Might be nice to hear about the pros." Reiner tapped his fingers together and leaned forward. "When you approached me about wanting to transfer here, two things came to mind. The first—I want you to elevate the guys we have. They are rough and need a strong role model. That is you. Secondly, I have some guys who I need to have an intervention with, and they are Q and his crew."

"And I help with that?"

"Yes. Quentin is a dirty player. We both see it. But he's young and can change. You're assigned as his mentor this season."

"Jesus." I ran a hand over my face. First Audrey, then him. "Are you sure?"

"Yes."

"Okay." I pinched my nose and met his gaze. "I'll do it. It won't be easy. I also feel like I should admit that I'm also paired with his sister for clinicals. That's a lot of Hawthornes."

Reiner winced. "Shit. I didn't know that."

"Yeah, this could go terribly," JD said, hitting the side of the desk. "Might fail entirely."

"Would you shut up?" Reiner glared at his assistant before meeting my eyes again. "I'm having regrets hiring my brother-in-law."

"That's on you," I said without thinking.

He tossed his head back and laughed. "This is gonna work out great. I'm going to announce the pairs next week, and I'll continue to check in with you. I'm also naming you captain. This team needs a shift, and you're going to lead it."

Captain.

Clinicals.

Mentoring the guy I injured.

Audrey.

My siblings.

I wasn't sure I could hold it all together, but I nodded. "You got it."

"Be here fifteen minutes early to do gassers before next practice. If you're leading the team, you gotta lead by example."

I nodded and shook his hand. I also shook JD's before leaving. That was a trip, and I needed to process what the hell just happened. That was... not what I expected.

I didn't realize others knew Quentin played dirty and crossed the line. He was a punk ass freshman who thought too highly of himself, and I just happened to be the force to knock him out. Reiner saw it though, which changed things.

One thing remained the same. Audrey didn't realize what kind of player her brother was, and it wasn't my place to tell her. If they were as close as Reiner made it seem, then I would never do that to her.

The meeting only lasted fifteen minutes, thank god, so I jogged back toward the entrance, but they weren't there. Fuck.

Laughter caught my attention, and I jogged down the hall to find Daniel and Penny with Audrey playing a game with Cheez-Its.

"Okay, slide it through the goal and you get a point." Audrey made a temporary goal with her fingers as Penny slid a Cheez-It on the table. "Goal!"

"Yay!" Penny danced, and as she spun, she saw me. "Theo! Audrey taught us a new game with snacks!"

"Yeah?" I ruffled her hair and studied my new buddy, the sister of the guy who I injured, and one I had to mentor. Our lives couldn't be more complicated. It made my stomach twist. An incorrect move could blow everything up. My whole goal this year was to graduate, make sure my siblings were okay, and get better on the ice to go to the pros next year. That was all.

"It's simple. Nothing, really." Audrey stood and scooped up the crumbs and tossed them in the trash. "Your brother and sister are wonderful. Daniel told me about the zoo trip he just took. He wants to be a zookeeper."

Yeah, I didn't even know that. He'd always loved animals, and I was glad he opened up to someone, even if it was Audrey.

"You'd be great at it, especially dealing with this monkey." I picked Penny up, and she cackled.

Daniel smiled. "You hear that, Penny? You're a monkey!"

Penny howled and made an *oo oo* sound that echoed around the small room. For one second, barely even a whole one, Audrey and I shared a smile. Her face softened, and she didn't seem like the uptight, judgmental woman who glared at me. She was pretty and fun. When her full lips curved up on the sides, her entire face transformed, and it hit me how beautiful she actually was. Weird.

I shook that compliment out of my mind because it served no purpose.

"We can head back home now. I'll drop you off." I pointed toward the mess on the table. "Let's clean this up before we go."

"I don't mind." Audrey stood, all traces of our shared moment gone. "Go on. I'll clean this up. This is easy."

"I can help you!" Daniel jumped from his chair so fast, it knocked over even more crackers. "Oh no."

"It's alright." Audrey smiled and immediately got on the floor to pick up the mess. "Easy fix."

"Yeah." Daniel sighed, but the tips of his ears were pink. It was fascinating to see him blush, first off. Secondly, Audrey was being ridiculously chill about this. I didn't trust it. They picked up the mess within a few minutes, and my siblings and I were at the doorframe, Audrey remaining at the chair with a thoughtful look on her face.

"Thanks," I mumbled, my throat feeling thicker than normal. "That was nice of you."

"Of course." Her gaze moved from my siblings, the smile falling as she focused on me again. "See you around, Sanders."

Yeah. She would be. And I didn't like the fact I owed her one.

5

WE HAD ORIENTATION TODAY. Our weekly schedule would be Tuesdays and Thursdays, but the head nurse planned for us to do the orientation the Friday before so she could also pass on some studies she wanted us to familiarize ourselves with. There was no reason for the firework of nerves exploding deep in my gut, at least not for meeting with Marcy Rumble. I'd asked other students who worked with her at this ICU, and she was known for being blunt, to the point, safe, and exceptional.

It was the fact Theo stood in his scrubs, a half-smile on his face, leaning on the wall outside the hospital as I approached. The afternoon sun hit his hair just right, the shades of blond and brown combining together. He had thick hair, messy, but kept professional, and it was unfair how good it looked on him.

It was hard to accept Theo Sanders, an asshole on the ice, aggressive, and a shit-talker, was the same guy who cared for his siblings. He obviously loved them, and it annoyed me that I found it admirable. I didn't want to think anything kind about the dude. We could stick to being professional at clinicals, and that was it. Nothing more.

The scrubs clung to his arms and chest, his muscles defined and chiseled in a way that made my pulse elevate slightly. I swallowed and hoped he wouldn't see me, but I didn't get another two steps before he glanced up from his phone and smiled.

"Hey, Auds." He waved and pocketed his phone.

Auds. He wasn't my brother or my friend. I frowned, hating the catch in my throat at hearing him say that nickname.

"I hoped I'd catch you so we could walk in together. Hey, we should exchange numbers."

I pressed my lips together, determined to dislike him. "I don't know if we need to do that."

His jaw flexed before he shrugged. "Okay." He shoved his hands in his pockets and jutted his jaw toward the entrance. "Ready? I almost couldn't sleep last night I was so anxious. Heard horror stories about working the ICU."

"It's a great way to prepare us for life post-graduation," I said, cringing at how robotic I sounded. Why couldn't I just say I felt the same? Nerves hit me too, but admitting any weaknesses to him could be used later.

He rolled his eyes, his lips quirking up. "Oh, I didn't realize that. Thank you. Geez, that's such good information to learn."

Damn it. I fought a smile. "You're sarcastic."

He covered his chest with a hand and grinned. "Me? No."

A snort escaped before I could stop it. Theo's eyes lit up as he walked close enough for our arms to brush together. With one small touch of his elbow grazing mine, my skin burned with awareness. His freshly showered scent also hit me, a pleasant clean smell.

"Ah, you do have a sense of humor. I wasn't sure at first, but I'm glad it's there. I liked the sound of that weird little snort."

"It wasn't weird," I quipped, mentally scolding myself. "Okay, yeah, it was. Sorry."

"Nah, I liked it. It's no cackle, but I'll get you to cackle someday. I'm sure of it. Operation Auds Laughter is underway."

My lips parted, and my stomach swooped in an unfamiliar, dangerous way. He was being too nice to me. Why? I didn't deserve it or understand it. His genuine demeanor freaked me out because everything was a contradiction with him.

"Why are you—" I started, about to ask the very question but stopped when we approached the nurses' station. Marcy stood there in her purple scrubs and her hair pulled back tight in a ponytail. She didn't smile, but her body shifted as she greeted us.

"Ms. Hawthorne, Mr. Sanders, welcome." She shook my hand, then Theo's. "Let's not waste time. Today I'm going to give you a tour to learn where to find our essential equipment, patient rooms, emergency exits, and restocking areas. Memorize it. I need you both understanding the physical layout in the event of an emergency."

She handed both Theo and I a folder. "In there, you'll find our protocols and procedures. There's nothing too crazy, but please familiarize yourself with our infection control practices, patient privacy laws, and emergency response procedures. Once your shift starts with me, there are moments where we won't have time to discuss procedures. Seconds matter here. They could be the difference between life and death."

I gulped down the rush of adrenaline. My grandpa died in an ICU after a car crash when I was eight, and I never forgot the sounds and smells of the hospital. They said the crash did all the damage, but what if someone could've stopped the bleeding five seconds earlier? Would it have mattered?

I'd never know, but I took Marcy very seriously. I refused to be the reason someone didn't make it out of the ICU. Theo's gaze landed on me, his eyes solemn and serious. No evidence of the goofy guy who was there five minutes earlier. Something warm landed on my pinky finger, and I sucked in a breath when I traced the reason.

Theo locked our pinkies together and squeezed for two seconds and let go. That touch sent flurries of emotions in my chest to the point it ached. That one little gesture reassured me and flustered me within seconds.

What the hell was that?

I swallowed hard and jerked my hand away from him. His jaw flexed, but that was the only sign he reacted to my quick movements.

"Any questions yet?" Marcy asked, her tone brisk.

We shook our heads. My questions had nothing to do with the orientation and everything to do with the giant next to me.

"Okay, after we do the layout tour and protocols, we'll get into safety procedures and an equipment overview. You need to know how to handle disposal of sharps and hazardous substances."

Marcy didn't wait a beat before moving into the tour. She pointed out the essential locations, only pausing every ten minutes or so to see if we had a question. The hour went by in a blur. It was pure adrenaline and excitement but a blur, none-theless.

This place would be my second home this semester. It smelled like chemicals and the memories of losing people I cared about, but it fueled me to be here. If I could somehow learn all the tricks, I could keep Quentin safe. Or help others return home to their families.

In the sixty minutes we were there, there had been one code blue and one critical response. Everyone understood their role and responsibility during that time, and it was fascinating to see everyone remain under control. There had been no loss of life in that moment, and I knew that wasn't always the case.

My pulse raced the entire time, and my body went into survival mode. I'd been through so much loss I could shut out the worry and focus on the task.

"Okay, Theo, Audrey," Marcy said after we told her to use our first names. "I have a few things for you to read this weekend. This semester isn't just about observing. You must *learn*. I want you prepared enough to take the job after month one. That means reading, discussing, and applying. The studies I referenced in your folder are about pharmacology and pathophysiology. You need to deeply understand the medications commonly used here and how they interact with other medicines, as well as conditions commonly seen here. Learn and understand the disease process, potential complications, and rationale around treatments. Also, communication is essential in a code blue. You'll need to anticipate needs before they're said. I'll see you both Tuesday morning."

With that, she left us as the station where we entered, and she was out of sight within a few seconds.

Theo nodded twice before whistling. "This is going to be an experience, that's for damn sure."

Out of nowhere, a ball of emotion caught in my throat. I hated showing feelings. They were exhausting, and I didn't have time for them, but shit. My hands shook, probably from adrenaline, and I sniffed to avoid letting my stress show. It had to be an adrenaline crash of sorts. There was no reason to be sad or stressed. I'd found an extra session to tutor and sent my mom a hundred bucks. Sure, she'd call again, but my racing heart had no place right now. I cleared my throat, scolding myself for having any weaknesses. "I'll see you Tuesday."

With my head down, I marched out the automatic doors. It was only five pm, so I could grab some food and start reading whatever Marcy laid out. I had a ton of other assignments to work on, but this had to come first. I could busy myself with tasks.

"Audrey, hey, wait up."

"What do you want, Theo?" My voice was scratchy. "Don't you have hockey to play?"

"It's a Friday night, so no. I already worked out with the team." He caught up to me and gently touched my upper arm, stopping me.

The same unfamiliar and intoxicating heat spread through me from having his bare fingers on my skin. He let go the second I tensed and held his hands in the air. "Why are you upset?"

"I'm not." I crossed my arms and prayed he wouldn't call me on my lie.

"You are."

Okay, that didn't work. He arched a brow in challenge before his expression softened in understanding. I hated that his face was so readable, so kind.

"I have an idea, and I'm gonna need you to say yes to it."

"That's a terrible way of asking."

"I'm not asking a thing." He flashed a quick grin. "It's been pissing me off all week that I'm in debt to you—"

"For what? No, you're not."

"You watched my siblings for a bit, which you didn't have to do at all. So yeah, I owe you." He shook his head. "I never got to thank you properly for that—"

"No need."

"Would you stop talking for one second?" He laughed and put a hand on my shoulder, squeezing it for one long heartbeat. "Are you always such a pain in the ass, or is this special for me?"

"Don't take too much credit, I'm generally like this."

"Noted." His eyes danced with amusement. "Now, if you keep quiet for one minute and let me propose my idea, I think you'll agree."

I opened my mouth, but he held up a finger, stopping me.

"Ah, no, shh." He smirked. "I'm taking you for ice cream. You're not getting out of it for two reasons. Three, actually!" He held up his massive hands and counted down. "You're upset, and I'd be a shitty *classmate* to let you walk off by yourself without checking on you. We're gonna experience some wild shit in there, and I'd rather we have each other's backs. Secondly, I owe you for helping me out the other day. I'm a gentleman most of the time, so it's the least I can do. And thirdly, I glanced at one of those studies we have to read, and what the fuck? They are hard, and I want us to buddy read. I read one, you the other, then we share notes. I don't have time to read both this weekend, so yeah, that's my proposal."

If it weren't Theo Sanders the hockey guy, I'd agree to all of this instantly. Yet, it was him, and I needed to make sure that wall was up before saying yes. "We still don't like each other though."

"Oh, yeah, no way. You're the worst." He made a goofy face, clearly joking, but the sentiment landed with me.

"Okay. As long as we don't become friends."

"You've made it clear that would never happen, Audi 5000. Now, let me buy you some dessert and then we can cry about how intense Marcy is."

"Audi 5000?"

Theo chuckled. "It's super fitting for you. You're always trying to leave a conversation, and your name is Audrey. It's perfect. So, Auds, you an ice cream kinda gal or a cake kind of lady?"

"Uh, whatever you want." I swallowed, nerves prickling along my skin from how near he stood by me. Heat radiated from him, and he smelled way too good for being on shift all day.

"I'm asking you though." He ran a hand over his jaw, the movement causing the ripples in his forearm to clench.

Clinically speaking, he had wonderful forearms.

"Whatever is near us."

"Audrey." His tone changed. He was more serious.

I frowned but met his penetrating stare. The colors of his eyes clashed with the sky around us, but they were easy to get lost in. Way too easy. "What?"

"When was the last time you went on a date? Did you pick a spot or just say *whatever* is near?"

"I don't date, Theo." My face heated, and my insides tightened. He was super experienced, obviously. With his looks and hockey status, he probably dated all the time.

I just never had time. It was always working, saving money, helping Quentin, keeping my academic scholarship. Dating didn't fit that mold, and yeah, I'd missed out on a lot of moments. I never had the big kiss-in the-rain scene or the hot date to prom or losing my virginity or falling in love. But I took care of my family the best I could. Even if I didn't like them much right now.

I was too busy, too focused on surviving, that any relationship, or attraction, fell to the wayside. "No time."

"Hm, I call—"

"Ice cream. I want ice cream," I blurted out. I couldn't be sure if I wanted to stop the dating conversation or if I really craved ice cream. It had been so long since someone asked what I wanted that I'd forgotten how to answer. How pathetic. "Mint chocolate chip. In a waffle bowl with sprinkles."

"Whoa, settle down there, party animal. Sprinkles? Don't go too wild."

He was teasing me, but by the warmth and kindness in his voice, I didn't mind. If anything, my lips quirked slightly as I glanced at him.

"Saw that, Audi. Saw your little smile. That's a point to me."

6

T heo
        Audrey sucked the spoon in her mouth, her round, full lips covering the utensil like she was on some OnlyFans account. The thing was, she wasn't trying to be sexy. She had some ice cream on her chin and a trail of drops on the table, yet watching her relax was intoxicating to the point I wondered if I was all right myself.

She was makeup-less, wore scrubs, had her hair pulled back tight and yet she looked good. Good enough to question why I was so adamant about keeping her at a distance. Besides the whole brother thing. That was clear. I didn't need a reminder about that because when I thought about her punk ass brother for more than a second, I wanted to walk away from any friend-ship with her.

"I can't believe you convinced me to do this. It's been years since I've eaten here and had this." She held up her large waffle cone as her large jade eyes softened. Her entire face shifted from that gesture, and I liked it.

Audrey was tough, but when her gaze went all warm like that, she was stunning. Her button nose scrunched a bit, and her almost too large green eyes stood out even more. Her face was smooth, and I had the weirdest urge to run a finger down it. My chest warmed as I stared at her, and I took a small bite from my one-scoop cone. She called me basic getting vanilla, but I argued it was a classic. A staple. Dependable.

"Well, what I think I hear you saying is thank you. So, you're welcome." I held up my spoon, and she clinked her spoon. Holy shit, that was the cutest thing.

She smiled. It was brief, like a flash of lightning, but shit. Audrey had a killer grin. I'd only seen it twice, ever, but it was memorable. "Thank you," she said, her voice dropping an octave. "For the ice cream and for pulling me out of my head."

"Care to share where you went?" I took another bite and ignored the urge to not enjoy the sweets. With training and the season starting in a month, I shouldn't go off the meal plan, but I was weak when it came to desserts. I had no restraint. They were the way to my heart and soul. I could decline any other vice, but ice cream was the worst. I'd eat an entire pint in one sitting if I had the option. Probably two of them.

Audrey stared off toward the window of the ice cream shop, her gaze unfocused. "I've always wanted to be a nurse to help others, but it hit me today how dangerous it could be. How much our choices, and our decisions matter. We have to know every routine and step and make tough calls within half a second." She gulped.

I understood that look. My stomach twisted with worry that there was more to her than met the eye. No one carried the weight of the world on their shoulders without a reason. Audrey and I might have that in common.

"I can't be the reason someone doesn't go home to their family." She took another bite, her eyes returning to normal. "I don't feel prepared enough. I need to study more, read more. I could call previous students—"

"Hey." I covered her hand with my free one. She sucked in a breath and stared at our connection with wide eyes. She'd reacted that way every time we'd touched. "We're not going to be the reason. Not right now, not our first job. These places have protocols in place so new and inexperienced staff are never on their own."

"I can't mess up. I refuse to. I had a bad experience when I was a kid." She let the words trail before her eyes widened, and she shook her head. "I've worked so hard for this, to fulfill my dream, and I'm worried. Isn't that stupid?" She rubbed her fingers over her forehead so hard there were little indents there.

"Then do it nervous." I kept my palm on the top of her hand, enjoying the softness of her skin. It was nice holding someone else, even if the person hated me and was pricklier than a cactus. "I'm sorry about whatever you went through. I want to ask questions but also respect your wishes. Someday, I might tell you about my family too."

"Like why you care for your siblings?"

I nodded. "But that would require us being friends, and you told me that won't happen."

She chewed her lip, a frown line appearing between her brows, and I regretted my dry joke. I nudged her knee with mine, getting her to look at me again. "That was a joke, Auds. We can form a truce even without being friends."

"Why do you watch your siblings though? How are you going to handle that and hockey and these clinicals? Do you have other help?"

And pop. There went the nice bubble I was enjoying. My life outside of this moment was nothing but stress. She was a distraction, a fun, unexpected one, but I didn't want to think about all waiting for me. Like the fact my dad needed a *night away for the third time this week,* so I had to be home with my family on a Friday night. Instead of answering her question and having her derail the evening, I spun the question around on her. Bantering with her was slowly becoming my own form of amusement. "It sounds like you might care about my health and sanity a little bit."

"What?" She shook her head. "No, of course not. You could have the shits right now, and I wouldn't care at all."

I barked out a laugh. Her answer was so unexpected I wanted another one from her. "Okay, then why ask about how I'm balancing three very stressful things if you don't care?"

She sucked her teeth and shrugged. "Don't want to have to carry the team in the ICU."

"You wouldn't. Lie better."

She rolled her eyes, her lips quirking for half a second before she stared at me. "That's a lot to take on. I wouldn't wish all that on my worst enemy."

"And am I your worst enemy, Audrey?" Damn, my voice dropped low, almost like I was flirting with her. Which I sure as hell wasn't. Did I need to list the reasons why that would be foolishly stupid? Unforgivably stupid?

Brother. Teammate. Captain. Clinicals. Injury. No time.

There, that stopped me.

"No, my enemy's name is Penelope Bloomsberry."

Another unexpected answer. I fought a grin. "And who is she?"

"My nemesis. Enough questions. Your ice cream is melting, and we have things to read this weekend."

I took her cue and stopped teasing her about hating me. It was obvious she didn't, and she struggled with it. I wanted her to struggle with judging me, but I was also not naïve enough to think we'd ever be real friends. While I wasn't ready to share my story with her, it was clear she wasn't prepared either because Reiner's comment remained in the back of my head the last few days. She'd raised her brother. How? Why?

It made me think of my siblings and if anyone injured them, preventing them from doing the thing they loved for a year... I wasn't sure I'd ever be able to move on. Even if they deserved what happened to them.

If she'd raised Quentin, then she'd truly never forgive or understand why he got injured that game. Disappointment clouded my entire mood, the reality of the situation hitting me. I wanted to be friends with her. I didn't want her to hate me. I'd always been able to get along with everyone, but I hadn't found a real friend here at Central State yet, and it sucked. It took a lot to anger me, and life generally had so many bright sides. But I'd seen the looks she'd given me. She'd never accept me as anything but the guy who injured her brother.

Defeat didn't sit well with me. When I'd lose a game, it'd take days to recover from, so after spending time with her and realizing I wanted to be friends, it hurt to know we couldn't be. With such limited time I had, it was wasteful to put energy into a one-sided relationship.

"You seem stressed." She took another long lick of her spoon. "Is it clinicals or all the other stuff I mentioned?"

"Doesn't matter." I sighed and took a bite. "Thanks for letting me treat you to ice cream, but I think I'm heading out."

"Wait, already?" She frowned, her lips pouting on her heart-shaped face. It was almost like she didn't want me to leave, but the momentary display of emotion zapped from her face the next second. "Of course, yeah. I'll see you Tuesday."

"We're doing the buddy-reading, right?"

"I'll read both anyway." She didn't look at me. She stared at the center of the white table, where a bunch of sprinkles had fallen over. "I can share notes with you. What's your email?"

I wrote down my email on a napkin. Not my number, because she refused, but my stupid email so she could share her detailed notes. If that didn't scream never-friends, nothing else did. "I'll ask around to see if anyone else got assigned those studies so I can buddy ready with them."

"I don't mind sharing with you." That frown line appeared between her brows again. "I said that, right?"

"Sure, but the point is for us to save time, and if you're going to do it anyway, it's not the same." I waved a hand in the air, itching to get out. I had an hour left of free time before my dad needed me at the house. I'd be a good partner during clinicals, but that was it. Being a solid teammate made all the difference, so I'd focus on that next week instead of trying to form a friendship with someone so reluctant. "Have a good weekend, Audrey."

"Yeah, you too." Her voice seemed distant, off even, but I didn't let myself stress about it. I didn't have the capacity to worry about her. Sure, she seemed sad as we walked out of the hospital, and I wasn't a jerk. But my investment in her had to stop now. I was one papercut away from losing it, and Audrey was nothing but stress.

EM WAS in her room with the windows locked. Daniel had fallen asleep, and Penny was out like a light an hour ago. My dad was in another town again so that left me alone. Finally.

Exhaustion wore me like an accessory, and the season hadn't even started yet. That would happen in four weeks, which would add another layer to the stress-meter that was ready to blow. Man, I missed my mom so much. The facility she stayed at was about twenty minutes from here, and I hadn't gone to see her in a while. Guilt ate at me, but it was so damn hard to see her now. She wasn't the same mom who raised me, and fuck, it gutted me. Being the only one awake in my childhood home had nostalgia hitting me left and right, and I needed to do something to distract myself. *Make lists.* I had so damn much to do, and it would push away the horrible thoughts.

Lists helped me stay on track and not spiral out of control too much. So, I wrote down everything I needed accomplish and tried not to have a freak-out. The studies Marcy assigned would take hours, time I didn't have. It was already eleven, and I had practice in the morning, a shit-ton of homework, a team event with Coach, then back home. I had three hours on Sunday, if that, to do it.

Fuck. I slid into bed and fired up my laptop, determined to read half of the first one about pharmacology. It focused on the effects and management of vasopressors in septic shock patients. It had a detailed analysis of the use of drugs and indications for use, dosages, and titration, and side effects. Then we had to answer the question: In a patient with septic shock, what are the main focuses of the nurse during the early stages of treatment?

My brain melted into my pillow. I'd vowed to get my degree and not assume that hockey would provide the life we all needed. Hell, if I wasn't focused on getting my degree, I could get my signing bonus now and hire a full-time nurse for my mom to move home and a nanny for my siblings. But I'd promised my mom I'd finish. It was her dream for me to become a nurse and have a backup plan.

I had to finish for her in the event she became herself again. She'd always loved me and was proud of me, but this felt like more. I had to make her proud, and that meant powering through this regardless of how hard it was.

Just thinking about my mom motivated me in a way that was hard to describe. She knew why I couldn't visit her, or at least I hoped she did. It gave me the boost I needed to get some work done, but before I got started, an email popped open from AHawthorne.

I clicked.

Hi, Theo,

I read the first study and found it fascinating. The challenge question at the end really had me thinking, so I found a few books at the library, and wow, we have so much to learn! It was honestly fun exploring the stacks for it. I included a detailed synopsis for you below, along with a few scaffolded explanations to the challenge question. I hope it helps you somehow.

I've been thinking about Penny and Daniel. If you have to choose between hanging out with them or reading, pick them. I'll read all the stuff for both of us.

I'm going to the library tomorrow afternoon for the pathophysiology study. I'll send more notes for you then.

Thank you again for the ice cream. I can't recall the last time I did that with anyone. I'm sure my face didn't show it, but I really enjoyed it.

Best wishes,

Audrey Hawthorne

I SCANNED the notes she sent and exhaled so hard I choked on my own breath. Her notes were so detailed, so helpful. She'd scanned her own handwritten notes, and my god, her handwriting was beautiful. Was that weird? Did people think that about handwriting? I did though. It was her own font. *Hawthorne.* That sounded like a font people would choose. It was better than Comic Sans by a landslide.

Her comment about my siblings made me think she was lonely and then guilt hit me for not even trying to win her over. "Fuck." I rubbed my face with my hands, an itchy, unpleasant feeling dancing down my spine.

This was the second time she'd done something unexpected

and nice for me after claiming to hate me. It didn't add up. It sent mixed signals, and I didn't know what to do.

I could at least respond.

Hi, Audi 5000,
   Thank you for the notes. You're a lifesaver.
   I'll owe you more ice cream then.
   T

There. That was quick.
   Oh shit. She responded instantly.

You don't owe me anything.

Yes, I do. These are the best notes I've ever seen, and I'm exhausted. I read that challenge question, and my brain almost fell out of my skull.

Theo, that's not possible. And you're dramatic for a hockey guy.

For a hockey guy? I smiled as I emailed back. Her responses were so unpredictable I honestly enjoyed it. My life was chaos, but each day was like dropping a deck of cards. My issues would be one of the fifty-two options, but it would follow a pattern. Her though?

   Wild card.

   Yes, for a hockey guy. You should know better being a nursing student.

. . .

You're no fun.

Theo,
    I hope you get some rest this weekend. See you Tuesday.
    Audrey

Damn. Her email had a finality to it. I read it again, and my shoulders tensed at the formality of it again. Had my comment upset her? I was teasing her via email. Sure, not the best route, but she didn't think I meant anything negative about being no fun, yeah?
    Audrey,
    I was joking with my last email. What time are you going to the library tomorrow? I'll join you and help.
    I could picture her frown and her eyebrows drawing together, and that didn't sit well. From what I knew about her, she was all studies and work. She didn't have a lot of friends, and hell, if she was like me, she wanted to have fun but couldn't. An idea struck, but it required my dad to actually help out. Unease flowed in my gut as I typed out a text to him. I hated the relationship we had now, where it was all stress and anger. I knew he was struggling, but so was I. He escaped the feelings and left me here to pick up the mess. Chewing my hangnail, I typed out my text.
    Theo: Something came up at school, and I have to study. Can you be home?
    Dad: Can't you study at home? Plus, you're drafted. Who cares about the grades?
    Theo: Dad. I can't watch your children tomorrow.
    Dad: Your siblings need you, Theo. I'm not sure I can be home.
    Theo: I'm leaving the house at noon. Find someone else then.

Damn. It felt *good* to send those words to him. We'd argued once after my mom had her stroke, where he told me to drop out and move home until we figured things out, and I refused. He didn't think my schooling was important anymore, not when I could go straight to the Acorns and receive money—even though that would mean he would have to parent. He was delusional. He wanted me to skip class and handle everything at home so he could work.

I refused.

I silenced my phone after Audrey responded with *I'm there all day, mostly.*

Audrey was becoming an interesting distraction from my shitshow of a life at home. I'd find her, convince her she was fun, and complete my half of the project. It was the least I could do. The girl who swore she hated me kept doing kind things for me, and I wanted to do something nice for her.

7

Audrey

Quentin and my weekly get-togethers used to be my favorite part of the week, but disappointment wedged its way into my neck. No matter which way I twisted, my shoulders pinched with stress.

Quentin was late. Again.

It was only ten minutes, but he hadn't responded to my text. I had a tight study schedule today, tutoring slots for more cash, along with meeting for our group project, but my plans never mattered to Quentin. My studies always came second to his hockey. I didn't mind it in high school as he was working on getting a full-ride scholarship, but that happened, and me prioritizing him just never stopped.

I worked my ass off to get straight A's and receive semester scholarships to save money. Quentin didn't realize that I tutored all summer or on Sundays so he could have spending money. He didn't know mom hit me up every other week for cash so she could buy food and live the life dad wanted for her. I hid all of it from Quentin so he could have somewhat of a normal life. I was the one to carry the scars and burden, not him, so his dismissal of my feelings hurt.

It did even more as my mom's text from last night flashed in my mind. Despite sending her a hundred bucks, she wanted more. She *had* to have more.

Ugh.

I didn't even want to be in this family anymore, but then my dad's voice would say *people struggle in different ways. Have you tried breaking through to them?*

I tried, Dad. I really did.

I hated feeling this bitterness creep up. I tried so hard, hoped to find a full-time job nearby and start my life. Would my mom be begging for money my whole life? Would Quentin always need me to help him behind the scenes? My future wasn't as exciting even more with those unknowns. How sad was that?

Getting straight A's, making sure Quentin was good, and finding a nursing job were all I'd cared about for so many years. I lost myself along the way, and my brother didn't even respect me enough to text.

Audrey: I'm leaving. Text me if you ever want to get lunch again.

I fired off the text, letting my temper get the best of me. Quentin had always been emotional, and this injury had really set him back. He was more demanding, pouty, and only focused on the negatives instead of the positives.

My phone buzzed. Quentin called me.

"Hi, Quentin," I said, letting my irritation boil over.

"You're so dramatic." He laughed, and something muffled came over the phone. "I was caught up with something for the team. Plus, you're just going to the library anyway, right? Sorry I didn't text you. I figured it'd be okay. I didn't mean to leave you hanging, Audrey. Promise."

Quentin always toyed with the line of right and wrong. He said the words *sorry* and *I didn't mean to,* but they didn't ring with

genuineness. His usual aggressive voice shifted to kinder, a sign
he wasn't lying. But my feelings were hurt, and he wouldn't care.
He'd joke it off, and I wasn't prepared to handle that today.

"Alright." I shifted in my seat at the coffee shop. "Hope the
team stuff went well."

"It did, thanks, yeah." His voice softened. "My guys are
helping me deal with the fact Sanders is on the team. Coach is
having him mentor me, which is ridiculous. The fucking nerve
of Reiner doing that. I have a plan though, don't worry. Sanders
is gonna regret ever coming to this school."

"I need to go." My voice cracked, and my stomach dropped
in a horrible, falling-through-frozen-lake bad way. Hearing him
be so cruel about Theo physically hurt me. My brother had no
idea Theo had siblings depending on him.

I still didn't know why he was taking care of his siblings, but
I saw the love between them. The trust. How could Quentin
think about retaliation? That was what his anger was about,
wasn't it?

"Don't be mad, Auds. I'll make it up to you, I promise. Want
me to find you at the library?"

"No. I have plans. I need to go, Quentin." I hung up, rubbed
my temple, and took a few deep breaths. I loved my brother. I
did. It was just us for so many years, and he was achieving his
dream, minus the whole injury thing. It was easier to remain
quiet and let Quentin enjoy being young, while I was forced to
deal with the aftermath of sickness and death. If I had to be an
adult and I could protect my brother, I'd do it in a heartbeat.

Yet, his behavior was worsening, and confronting him wasn't
something I'd ever do. He'd twist my words or guilt trip me, and
it would further deepen the divide between us. How could I
isolate myself even more? If I truly lost Quentin, I'd have no one
left. That devastated me.

I chewed my lip, the horrible, lonely feeling weighing me

down to the point I slid in my chair. These moments would come fast and hard but only linger for a few minutes. I'd let myself wallow before snapping out of it.

Yes, I envisioned a different life. I used to dream about having a group of best friends and a family that smiled and laughed together. But that wasn't the hand I'd been dealt, so I had to stick to the plan, or I'd completely derail. Exhaling, I silenced my phone even though no one would call me.

I had a few study buddies who'd agreed to meet tomorrow evening, so it was me and my thoughts and my homework keeping my company. My favorite table in the library was tucked back in the corner, out of view and pretty quiet. I liked the scents here, old books and coffee. The combination reminded me of going to a diner with my dad. We'd do our daddy-daughter time there where he'd let me try coffee without telling mom, and we'd eat dessert for lunch. He'd be proud of me right now. He'd encourage me to keep going. He'd know I was doing my best with Quentin and Mom.

"Audrey?"

A familiar, deep voice pulled me from my memory. My stomach somersaulted at the interruption and at the fact Theo stood in front of me with a plate of cookies.

"Hey." Theo smiled, the gesture familiar and pleasant. He brushed his hair off his forehead as he jutted his chin toward the chair across form me. "Can I join you?"

"Sure, yeah, okay." My words blurred together as surprise took over. Theo was at the library, in my spot. Seeing him caused a flurry of weird feelings in my chest and stomach as I thought about his emails.

He hadn't meant the comment, cruelly at least, about me being no fun, but he was correct. I wasn't. Yet, there was some-thing about him that pulled me toward him, wanting to dig deeper and ask questions.

"These are *thank you* cookies. I wasn't sure what your favorite was, so my siblings and I made four different types. Not from scratch though. I'm not that talented." He chuckled, but the tips of his ears reddened, almost like he was self-conscious.

Why would Theo be embarrassed at all?

"Thank you," I mumbled, my own face heating as he slid the plate over. No one in my entire life brought me dessert, except for my dad. Man, two memories of him in such a short time. I missed him so much it hurt to breathe sometimes. I had to get my emotions under wraps. "You didn't have to do this—"

"Yes, I did." His tone had a bossy edge to it. His intense hazel eyes bore into mine, and I wished, probably for the first time ever, to know what he was thinking. If he saw me as a dork in a library, who was no fun at all.

"You see, you continue doing nice things for me yet are determined to keep me at a distance. I get why. I injured your brother." His jaw flexed, and his gaze moved toward the left instead of my face.

My stomach dropped just thinking about Quentin and his comment to me. It was the ultimate betrayal to tell Theo my brother was planning something. Yet, I could warn him. Somehow. Without breaking Quentin's trust. "Uh, are you and uh, Quentin okay?"

He barked out a humorless laugh. The muscles along his forearm flexed as he met my eyes. This time, there was no softness present. "Do you think we are? No. Of course we aren't. The dude is determined to get me back for taking him out. And Reiner not only named me captain this year, but he wants me to mentor your brother."

I winced. That was a terrible idea for so many reasons. "What?"

"Yeah." He pressed his lips together and reached for a

cookie. "I'm digging into the sugar cookie. Pen chose the sprinkles, but stop me now if you want this one."

I shook my head, watching the way his teeth came down on the dessert. He had great teeth. White, straight, probably had braces when he was younger. I expected a missing tooth or something from all the roughhousing he did on the ice, but no, Theo had a great smile with no missing teeth.

"Do I have something on my face?"

"Oh. No." I swallowed, my skin buzzing from getting caught mid-stare.

"Then why are you staring at my mouth like that?" His tone held no accusations or innuendo, just curiosity. I mean hell, why would Theo ever think I'd look at him with anything but disdain?

"You have perfect teeth."

He chomped them down with a vampire-grin. "Thanks, grew them myself."

A snort escaped before I could stop it. Then it shifted into a full chuckle. "You're an idiot."

"Yeah, but I like making you laugh." He shrugged and pointed to the book I had open. "Auds, are you starting the second study already? You told me later this evening."

"I needed to distract myself." I twirled a highlighter in my fingers and blushed under the way he stared at me, almost like I was a specimen, and he was determined to figure me out. "The easiest way to engross myself is reading. Full nerd status."

"Why do you need a distraction? Isn't your life busy enough as is?" He smiled, taking another bite of the cookie.

It was a weird, gross feeling to be jealous of cookie, but I was pretty sure I was. He held it with his large hand, his fingers wrapping around it and bringing it up to his very full lips. Seriously. There had to be a study to read about why I was so focused on his mouth.

His question hung in the air, lingering between us. He'd brought me cookies. He'd taken me to ice cream. I helped with his siblings and notes. Maybe, just maybe, we could figure out this colleague, friend thing. I read that nurses had to have friends at work to get through the dark moments, so maybe it would be best for my career to befriend him in a professional, healthy way. That meant opening up.

"My dad passed away when I was in high school after a long, horrible battle with cancer. My mom hasn't been the same since, and I was missing him today, how simple our life used to be before all the sickness." I inhaled the fresh scent of coffee from the café near us. "This place reminds me of him."

"I'm so sorry, Audrey." Theo's entire face softened as he sighed. "I'm sure that put you in a really tough situation of taking care of your mom and your brother. I know how hard that can be, truly. You're suddenly expected to be a grown-up when you're a kid yourself, and it's... exhausting."

"Yes." I nodded, hard. He understood it. He got it. Swallowing the lump in my throat, I continued, "I want to make the best choices, but the stress overwhelms me all the time. What even is the right choice? We had a plan before he was sick, but it's different now, and I wonder if I'm making everyone's lives worse." I spoke in riddles because I couldn't complain about Quentin to him. That would be messed up.

"My mom had a stroke a year ago." Theo's voice hardened, his eyes filling with sadness and turmoil as he stared at me.

My gut fell, sympathy for him gripping me.

"Penny was three and a half, and suddenly my dad had to put my mom in a care facility because she needed so much help. We don't have good insurance, so the cost is ungodly, and my dad is working all the damn time. I'm suddenly the parent to my siblings." Theo ran a hand over his face. "I know what you mean, Auds. I fucking understand all of it. It's numbing at times.

It paralyzes me. How am I qualified to help Penny at school? Or tell Daniel the right advice about bullies?"

"Theo," I whispered, the urge to crawl across the table and hug him so strong my hands twitched. I couldn't even finish the sentence. Saying *sorry* was pointless. I hated hearing it over after losing my dad. It didn't help. Sometimes, just listening and being there was enough.

He shrugged and ran a hand through his hair, pulling on the ends and causing it to stick up in weird angles. It was absolutely endearing. "Is it better or worse to lose someone you love completely, like your dad? Or to watch someone you love never be themselves again? My mom is my favorite person alive, but she's not herself. Because of the severity of her stroke, her speech and entire left side were affected. Even with all the therapies, the chances are slim that she'll ever be the mom we all need again. We don't know what the future holds for her."

Tears welled up and spilled down my face, and Theo saw it. "Oh, Auds." He moved out of his chair and kneeled in front of me, his hands coming up to wipe the tears off my <u>face</u>. Him touching me crossed so many lines in my head at how close he was to me, how near his lips were to mine, and how good he smelled, but none of that mattered when he pulled me into a hug.

"I should've asked if you wanted a hug, but I'm selfish and need one myself." He spoke into my shoulder, his face completely buried against me. His hair tickled my chin, and I could hardly breathe with him pressed up against me. His arms came around my middle, squeezing me. His touch was a comfort and a flame. Parts of my body that had lain dormant for years came to life. My thighs tingled, heat spread to my core, and even my nipples tightened with want. My pulse raced, and my breath quickened as I returned Theo Sanders's hug, and holy shit, I liked it.

His back was so thick and strong, and his cologne was like an evergreen tree and leather had a baby. I breathed him in as he cupped the back of my neck and held me against him.

His large fingers dug into my scalp, as he said, "Fuck, I needed this. Thank you."

Then, he released me and returned to his seat, a small smile playing on his lips. His eyes seemed lighter as he leaned back in his chair with a sigh. "Fun fact about me, my love language is touch. A good hug can reset me and give me all the endorphins I need, and damn, Auds, you're a great person to hug."

My world was spiraling out of control. Gravity stopped working, and I floated in the library archives. It was wild how no one saw me just hanging out in the air as I tried to connect back to my body. That hug changed my life. I wanted it again. I felt safe and excited and comforted and turned on all from his hug, and it didn't matter that it was Theo Sanders. He understood what I lived with such clarity that it was addictive. I wanted more of it.

"Yeah, uh, that was…" My voice trailed off as my entire face heated like a firepit. I nervously pushed my hair behind my ears, unsure what to do with my hands. They trembled. "Thank you," I managed to whisper. "I needed that too."

"Okay, so do you have something else to work on today?"

How did he go right back to his cheery, annoyingly upbeat self? My whole body was in panic mode, trying to figure out what was right and wrong, and he was just so happy. Ugh. Unfair.

"Uh, yes." I sounded like an imbecile, unable to form full sentences or speak more than a few words. He stared at me, and I immediately focused on the plate of cookies.

"Perfect. I vote you focus on whatever else you need to do, and I'll do the reading for the second study and try to provide the same detailed notes you did. Those were amazing, Auds. Also, can we talk about your handwriting?"

"What about it?"

"It's amazing." He smiled and pointed to my notebook. "Look at your letters. Seriously, you could sell this as a font online or something. Pretty sure people do that."

"Thank you." My skin warmed for the millionth time from his compliment. "Never thought about going that far with it, but good to know."

"Always solid to have a backup plan." He winked.

That simple gesture rattled me. It was playful and flirty and fun. All the things I wasn't. I pressed my lips together. I needed a distraction from *him*. "You can send the notes to me whenever you get them done."

"Sure will, but it sounds like you're kicking me out? I hoped I could hang here with you for a few hours." He frowned and cracked his knuckles on his left hand. "I might've assumed you'd be down for that, so I apologize. You probably want space. Mm, yeah, okay. I can go—"

"No!" I blurted out. "I don't want you to go."

"Huh." He grinned wide, the playful spark coming back. "You sure?"

I nodded. "I like the company."

"Whoa, Auds. That's a big move for us. Alert the media."

My lips quirked. "Stop. Don't be annoying. You're not horrible to be around."

"Okay, you're gonna declare your love for me soon. Could you scale it back?"

Damn. I smiled before I could stop it. Theo's face changed as he stared at me, his lips parting and his eyes widening. His nostrils even flared. "What is it?"

"You have a fucking beautiful smile." He pursed his lips and shook his head before letting out a little laugh. "Seriously, it's a good thing you don't flash that around all the time. It'd cause car accidents."

He was teasing. That was a joke. There was no way he thought my smile was beautiful. Yet, my voice caught in the back of my throat, and my skin felt too tight on my body. *You have a fucking beautiful smile.* No one in my life had said those words to me. They made me feel... alive in ways I forgot existed. A blush crept down my neck, and I rubbed it, willing the flush away, when I realized I hadn't responded. "Thank you for saying that. That was very kind."

"It's the truth, Auds." His gaze zeroed in on my mouth again. "I'd never be foolish enough to tell you to smile more. Fuck those weird men who say that, but just know that I'll remember every time you do. That's for damn sure."

I sucked in a breath as fire licked my skin, starting at my head and neck all the way down to my toes. His words had a way of affecting me so much it alarmed me. I knew what attraction was, as I'd read about it. But to experience it like this, with him? Overwhelming. It had to be a fluke. A weird byproduct of my mood.

Yeah.

I wouldn't feel this again, I was positive. So, I focused on my studies and not Theo the rest of the afternoon. I'd use the next two days to get this weird blip out of my system. Crushing on Theo, the guy who hurt Quentin, would only complicate my mess of feelings.

And I couldn't afford any more distractions.

8

Theo

It was Monday afternoon, and it was weird to be dreading one interaction with a Hawthorne and anticipating one with the other. I was meeting Quentin in ten minutes to talk about our *mentorship* and then I'd see Audrey tomorrow at our first all-day clinical.

Had I thought about her a thousand times since the library? Yup. Probably even more. The way she embraced the hug like no one had hugged her in years or how she blushed hard any time I was decent to her. Or the fact we'd both experienced something many didn't: being the oldest sibling and the role you had if tragedy hit your family. Maybe it was the fact we had that in common that had me interested in her. Not in *that way* because yeah, that wouldn't work. Even though her pillow lips and long eyelashes were my weakness.

I cleared my throat and leaned back on the bleachers, forcing thoughts of her away. Meeting with her brother while thinking about how hot she was would be a terrible choice on my part. And I could still control my mind enough to make it obey.

The door to the rink slammed open, and Quentin walked in, causing a damn scene. He wore a boot on his left leg and a scowl mad enough to start a war. The kid was all energy, reckless aggression, and anger. He channeled it to the wrong things, yet he refused to listen to anyone. It made me question why Reiner put him on the team, but from the research I did, Reiner enjoyed pet projects. He liked taking guys who were a little rough but super fucking talented and reforming them to be the best versions of themselves. I admired it about him but didn't love the fact I was part of the plan.

"Thanks for meeting here," I said, drawing his attention. He rolled his eyes like the child he was and plopped down ten seats from me. "Oh, cool, let me just pick up and move to you. It's your world, right?"

"It's the least you can do since you ruined my fucking career, you piece of shit."

Nice. He was spicy today. I grabbed my coffee and patience, took a huge swig of both, and neared him. He looked like shit, actually. Dark circles under his eyes, messy hair. My first thought was irrational: why the fuck was he worn-out when he wasn't working himself to the bone like his sister? He had no reason to be tired.

"Look, you can be pissed all you want. Won't change a thing. You can tell whatever lies you want to everyone else, Quentin, but we both know you deserved my hit last year. You play dirty and think rules don't apply to you, and you got your ass handed to you by a more skilled player. That sucks, but—"

"That's not true!" he yelled, his eyes bulging out of his head. "You're not better than me."

"That's your takeaway here? Dude. I've already signed with a team. I'm going pro after this year. What offers do you have? Zero. And want to know why? Because you're a bad teammate on the ice." I stared at the ceiling, not loving my approach so far.

I just didn't have enough energy to be gentle with him. I already knew I'd spend the night regretting this whole interaction, but I couldn't stop myself.

"How am I a bad teammate? How did I start freshmen year if I was so terrible then, huh? Just because you have an offer doesn't mean shit. You probably bribed your way in."

"Do you hear yourself?" I laughed and stood up. "I respect Reiner, so I agreed to mentor you and be named captain."

Quentin paled at that. Good. He didn't know that news. I liked surprising him.

"But you need to pull your head out of your ass. You're entitled, and I don't understand why. You're not the fastest or the biggest or the toughest on this team. If you think you are, you'll never play anywhere but this rink again. You have all the right skills, but you're not mature enough to grow."

"Who the fuck do you think you are saying that to me when you took me out for a season? Do you know how hard I worked to get here? How much I needed this place to escape the hell at home?"

"We all have our own versions of hell, Quentin, and the day you realize it's not a competition of who had it tougher will be the day you make real friends." I shook my head. "I know you think you're gonna get revenge on me somehow, but injuring me won't help you in the slightest. You should be focusing on improving your game and grades. Do you have a backup plan if hockey doesn't pan out?"

"I don't need a backup plan."

"There's another error on your part. Injuries happen all the time in this sport. I could be taken out game one, and I still have a life waiting for me."

"Yeah, being a *nurse* is a real life." He rolled his eyes, like the jab was meant for me.

"Speak like that again about your fucking sister, and I'll

break your other ankle." My voice came out quiet, somehow the threat more than a yell. Quentin paled and held up his hands.

"This has nothing to do with Audrey! I'd never—"

"You made fun of nurses, who are the backbone of our health care system. Your sister is the best in the cohort, so when you talk shit about them, you talk shit about her."

He blinked, his dumb mouth parting as his brows furrowed, but I kept going. "I'd think with what happened to your dad, you'd have more respect for nurses. Unless your insult was just about a male being a nurse because if so, we're done. And you might imagine the team will have your back, but my stats speak for themselves. I'm a good teammate, and after one game with me, they'll all turn on you. Now, if Reiner asks, our first mentoring session is over."

Ooo boy.

My hands shook from adrenaline, and I needed to go for a jog to get rid of the weirdness from that chat. Fuck. That was not how I envisioned being a mentor to a punk ass kid, but he was so ungrateful and full of himself. How was Audrey so kind and selfless and Quentin the opposite? I rubbed my temples, regret clogging my throat as I thought about the fallout. Reiner would be pissed. Audrey would be upset. Even though I was looking forward to seeing her tomorrow, I'd just have to prepare myself for Audrey to be cold to me again. After seeing her smiles and jokes, I really didn't want to go back to indifference.

AUDREY STOOD outside the hospital holding two cups of coffee. Her hair was pulled back, out of her face, and her light blue scrubs were tucked in. She looked like a real nurse, and she seemed happy. Her version of happy though. Her eyes were wide, and her gaze kept darting as workers walked in. Fifteen minutes before seven meant a lot of shift changes.

"Theo, hi," she said, her lips curving up on the sides. "I brought you coffee. Uh, I didn't know what type."

Shit. Was she blushing? She clearly had no idea what happened with her brother, but I really liked how she stared at me. "Coffee for me? Auds. Get outta here. You must've poisoned it."

"What? No." She blinked.

"I'm teasing." I winked, and our fingers slid together as she handed me the to-go cup. "Figured you were so jealous of how I looked in scrubs, you wanted to take out the competition."

She scoffed, but her gaze softened. "I wouldn't be that obvious, Sanders."

A warm, pleasant sensation formed in my belly when she looked at me like that and had that snarky tone. Audrey had snark to her, and I appreciated it. We walked toward the door when it hit me. "You were waiting for me?"

She stared at the floor and shrugged one shoulder. "Yeah. Figured if we're partners it would be nice to walk in together."

"So sweet." I nudged my hip against hers. "Never let anyone tell you that you're not the sweetest, kindest—"

"Enough." She snorted. "I already regret it."

A bubble of anticipation flowed through me as we neared the head nursing station to check in. I wished I could text my mom for encouragement or hear her joke around about all the shit I'd see. Literally. Despite having my whole hockey career set out for me, the thought of making a difference like this mattered so much to me.

"We got this, Sanders." Her tone turned serious.

"Yeah, we do." I sipped the coffee as our eyes met, and her nerves were clearer now. Was I nervous? Hell yeah. But I had pre-game jitters for a decade and knew to embrace the chaos, welcome the flutters. Audrey might not have that to fall back on, and I set the cup down with the intent to grab her hand but stopped myself. She might hate that even though I wanted to feel her skin.

"Use the nerves to your advantage. Those flutters in your gut? That means your body is paying attention. Your senses are heightened. You see things differently. It means we're alive."

She sucked in a breath, her eyes widening as she stared at me, and I said to hell with it. I squeezed her hand, her soft skin like a flicker of flames. "You're the best in our class and ask all the right questions. Do that here."

She blinked. "Thank you, Theo. I-I needed that."

I smiled and released her hand, but her fingers hung in the air almost like she didn't want to let go of me. I also didn't want to, but that was a problem for later in the day.

"Good morning." Marcy arrived, her face firm yet welcome. "Finish those drinks, and we'll make our rounds. I'll have you both shadow me for the first half of the day, then you'll split off and start taking vitals and updating charts with the patients' permission. Ask any question that enters your mind. Now, are you ready?"

"Yes, ma'am." I nodded.

"It's Marcy. Not ma'am."

Audrey released a tiny sound, almost like a laugh, but I didn't dare look at her. I liked the fact we had our own inside jokes. It meant Quentin had kept his mouth shut, and for once, I was grateful for his choice.

"With the shift change, we're going to check in on our post-operative patients, ones who've undergone major surgeries, and check for complications. What are the main complications we'll be looking for?"

"Bleeding, infection, organ failure," Audrey answered.

"Correct."

"Okay, let's go." She walked down the hall and approached a shut door. "Patient one is a thirty-five-year-old woman who was brought in from a car crash two days ago. Major surgeries on her stomach, legs, and arms. Multiple wounds to redress and check on." Then Marcy knocked, and we followed her into the room.

"Hi, Bea, I have two nursing students with me observing this morning. Are you alright if they're in the room when we check the surgery site and your vitals?" Marcy's tone shifted from her all-business one to kind, calm, and reassuring.

Bea nodded and offered a sad smile. "Sure. Welcome."

Audrey smiled. "Thank you for letting us be in here, truly. I know it can be uncomfortable."

"Not after you have children." Bea laughed, and Audrey joined her.

It was beautiful and strange to see Audrey's bedside manner shift so much from her day-to-day personality. Despite her nerves earlier, she seemed at ease. *Kind of like me on the ice.*

I should've been watching Marcy check vitals—even though we'd known how to do that since freshmen year—but instead, I admired Audrey and how she seemed to mouth the procedure.

Marcy updated the charts, checked in on pain management, and brought out a breathing machine that helped patients get oxygen into their lungs to prevent any infection there. Audrey bounced up and down.

She did that again in the next room—an older gentleman's appendix had burst and was on the verge of sepsis. Audrey also did it on the third and fourth visits. I wasn't sure why it was so wonderful to see her like this. Maybe it was knowing she worked so hard for so long, that she never had fun.

We had a fifteen-minute break to grab a snack around midmorning, and we stepped outside in a small courtyard.

"This is –"

"You light up in there, Auds." I interrupted her, not meaning to. "You come alive in the patient rooms, and it's beautiful."

I rocked back on my heels, my ears heating at the compliment, but it didn't make it less true. I needed her to know that.

"Uh, thank you." A blush spread from her face and down her neck. "No one... not that you're calling me *that,* but wow, I've never been told anything close. You didn't say I was... but—"

"You are beautiful." I chuckled, honestly kinda charmed by her rambling. She was an ice queen, always holding it together, and I was lucky enough to see her unravel. It made me want to pull at more threads and learn more about Audrey's unraveling. "However, you come to life when interacting with the patients. It reminds me of me on the ice, actually. It's like you were meant to do this. Patients will see that, Auds."

"Why are you being so nice to me?"

"You brought *me* coffee, girl."

"I didn't want to be friends with you, but unfortunately, we might be?" she said the sentence with a question at the end, her face vulnerable like she'd said the wrong thing. She was adorable. Damn. It was a shame so many people didn't see this side of her because it was cute as fuck.

"Seems to be so, bestie."

She laughed. It was fleeting, but the sound was pleasant and caused that same warm sensation in my stomach. Audrey's laugh felt like scoring a goal. Took a lot of work and the timing had to be right, but fuck it felt good.

"Thank you." She swallowed and held my gaze. "It's been a while since I had a friend, and I know we're oddly connected, but it means a lot that you'd be friends with me. I'm not that fun, or—"

"If you're going to insult yourself, I'm gonna have to interrupt you and demand you stop." I shook my head. "Friends aren't defined by *fun*. It's more than that, and you know it."

She pressed her lips together and a small, slow smile replaced it. "I get a sense of how you are when you play. A little fiery, quick to react. Calculating. No wonder you're drafted."

"Okay, too much." I held up my hands. "Too fast. Too many compliments. Quick, insult me."

Another snort. Fuck yeah. That was two and half today.

"We should head back." Audrey pushed through the doors and glanced at me over her shoulder. "Come on, buddy."

Mm, didn't like hearing buddy coming from those lips.

Marcy approached with a half-smile before saying, "Next will be our patients who've suffered an acute stroke. We need to..."

Her voice trailed off as my body tensed from head to toe. Sweat pooled on my forehead as I struggled to breathe. *Stroke* patients.

I... wasn't sure I could handle it.

9

A udrey

Theo changed. The charming, quick-witted guy I was growing annoyingly smitten with was gone. As we shadowed Rachel around the acute stroke recovery rooms, Theo paled and didn't say a word.

His chest moved up and down at a faster rate. He kept wiping his brow as sweat dripped on it, and my chest ached for him. Was seeing stroke victims hard because of his mom? Was this too much for him?

I wish I knew how to help, but there wasn't the right moment. By the time we checked in on the three patients with varying degrees of strokes, we split up. I helped take vitals and update charts for patients on the south wing with another head nurse, Jennifer. I assisted with monitoring infection sites, and there were some gnarly ones, damn. My favorite part of the entire day was talking to them though, putting the patients at ease.

Jennifer had the coolest quote to one of them that would stick with me forever. She said, "You can be scared, but I'm not. I know how to handle this."

The relief in the patient's eyes was immediate. There was an art of showing confidence and kindness that I wanted to emulate. But Theo's words to me at our break? About being beautiful and lighting up? Best compliment I'd ever received in my life. How was this the guy who battered Quentin's dreams? He was so *kind*.

He remained on my mind until the end of our first clinical shift, and an unwanted breath of relief escaped when our gazes met in the hallway. The pale-yellow walls clashed with dark navy scrubs he wore, and maybe it was the fluorescent lights or exhaustion, but Theo was gorgeous. From the thick eyebrows to the cut of his jawline, and the half-smile his lips naturally did... my stomach swooped in a way I hadn't felt in years.

"You both survived your first day." Marcy smiled and nodded in greeting at two doctors who walked by. "I'll see you both Thursday, where we'll do the same thing. Morning is shadowing, then afternoon you'll be leading. Nice work."

She left us, and both Theo and I signed the paper required of us to document hours. It was three in the afternoon, a few hours before I had to be at the library for a study group, and I wished I didn't have to go. My classmates were dry and not warm like Theo. The truth hit me. I wanted to keep hanging out with him. It weirded me out because there were so many reasons I shouldn't want to.

"That was a day." Theo flashed a grin as we walked outside into the sunlight, but it wasn't his usual demeanor. The tension in his shoulders was evident. I wanted to ask why, but it wasn't exactly normal to jump into the topic with someone who was barely a friend. He could shut me down or laugh it off or worse, ignore me. I only kept my interactions with people to classwork, small talk, or hockey. Anything more required getting involved with people.

Yet, a shadow had crossed Theo's face. The least I could do

was make sure he was alright. I should ask if he was okay or tired or if he wanted to hang out. Oh God. I couldn't ask that!

"Was seeing the stroke patients hard for you because of your mom?" I blurted out, my words choppy and too close together. My question wasn't delicate. I smacked myself in the forehead. "I'm sorry, Theo, I meant to be casual and ease into it but then I got in my head, and the worst thing came out."

He twisted his lips before meeting my gaze. His eyes lit up with amusement. "I mean, you're not wrong. Sometimes, the bluntness is appreciated." He gripped the back of his neck as we walked toward the parking lot. I didn't see his truck near us, and how silly was it that I was glad we had to keep walking?

"Are you alright? Your whole body changed, and I thought about you all afternoon." There. That wasn't too much.

"Sweet of you, Hawthorne." He ran a hand up and down his forearm, his strong fingers digging into the thickest part of his skin. The urge to feel how thick he was had me stepping back.

"It brought me back to when the stroke happened and how she's not progressing. We thought, maybe, she'd get her ability to communicate back, but it's barely there." He gritted his teeth, and his jaw flexed. "She can talk, but her memory is gone, and she repeats herself a lot."

He reminded me of *me* in the time between my dad getting sick and passing. What would've helped me would've been an opportunity to not feel any of it. Just, be someone else for a few hours without the weight of everything. "I know what you need."

His beautiful eyes landed on me, curiosity and hope swirling in them. The fact he thought I could actually help him, that he trusted me enough, caused a small flutter in my gut. This was an unfamiliar feeling, and I wanted to bottle it up.

"Mmm, what are you thinking, Auds?"

"Come to a rage room with me." I crossed my arms,

preparing to be rejected. Sweat pooled in between my boobs as I squished them together, and my heart skipped a beat. Asking someone to hang out was horrible. Did friends do this all the time? It was way easier to be alone.

"A rage room?" He arched a brow. "Okay, I'm intrigued. Tell me more."

"Before my dad died, there were two months of unknowns, and all of it became too much. I felt like I was crawling out of my skin, and I didn't have any outlet. You have hockey, so now I feel silly for suggesting this. You don't need an outlet." I deflated. "I just knew I wanted to not be me for a few hours—"

"I'm in." He waited until I looked at him, then he continued, "I'm so in. I just need to shower off today. There was a moment this afternoon." He cringed. "I live about thirty minutes away—"

"You can shower at my place. If you have clothes. I'm five minutes from here."

His brows about disappeared into his hairline. "You sure? That'd be great actually. I have to be home by five so that way we can spend more time in the rage room."

"Yeah." I swallowed down the flock of nerves. It wasn't just a flutter anymore. "Cool."

"Can you text me your address?" He had his phone out, his face hopeful, and I couldn't disappoint him. I rattled off my number, and he sent me a text. I now had Theo's number.

This seemed like a big deal to me. I hadn't made a new friend in years, and now we were going to hang. He planned to use my shower. Wild. "You can park on the side of the dorm. It's free there."

He frowned but nodded. "I'll see you there, Auds."

It took all my willpower to not sprint to my car and fly home. I had no idea if I'd left a pair of underwear on the floor or a sports bra on a chair. I didn't think how embarrassing it was that I lived in a dorm as a senior! It was so much cheaper, and they had meal options that were helpful with my scholarship. He could judge me, or—no. He wouldn't. Theo had proved numerous times he was such a nice guy that he'd never be cruel.

And that was the niggling thought that wouldn't go away. He wasn't mean, so why had he slammed into Quentin so hard it broke his ankle? No. That was a different part of him. Not the Theo I knew.

I parked in my assigned spot and hustled to the dorm door, but Theo parked right freaking there. *I have no time to clean.* My face heated as I leaned against the entrance and watched Theo stroll up with a bag over his shoulder. He ran a hand through his hair as he approached me, his face always a second away from laughing. Damn. My skin prickled with awareness as he wiggled his eyebrows at me.

"Been a while since I've been in a girl's dorm room. This is kinda fun." He chuckled, and the sound wiggled its way all the way to my core.

I huffed out a laugh, trying not to feel jealous of all the girls who had Theo come into their dorm. But the thought of my jealousy was something to explore later, alone. Just because I was a virgin didn't mean I didn't have fantasies, because I definitely did. I just didn't have time to act on anything or spend time exploring that part of my life.

"You gonna let me in or what?"

"Oh. Yeah." I ducked my head and let us in. My room was on the ground floor, straight to the right. "Uh, I have no idea what state my room is in. I didn't clean."

"I'm living with my parents, Auds. I don't care."

"It could be embarrassing." I clicked the lock and snuck a glance at him. His entire expression was soft and kind. He placed a hand on my shoulder and squeezed. The warmth exploded all the way to my toes.

"Quit stalling, girl. I want to experience the rage room."

"Right." I pushed the door open and whipped my head around to check for anything mortifying. It was a large single-dorm room with a bathroom. I was lucky. Nothing stood out as embarrassing, and I relaxed. "Welcome."

He grinned as he spun in a circle. "This is so you. It's crazy."

"Me?"

"Yeah. Organized, color-coded, comfortable." He walked toward my succulents on the windowsill. "Very Audrey of you."

Another compliment I'd save in my heart. Anyone who actually knew me, knew I loved succulents, yet no one cared. Quentin knew, so did my mom, but they were too involved with their own lives that any of my interests besides financials weren't talked about. It wasn't a complaint; it was just my life.

"I'm just glad I didn't have panties on the ground." I forced a chuckle as I set my keys on the desk and leaned against it. "Or a bra."

"I disagree." His eyes twinkled. "I think that would've been very fun for me."

"Shut up." I snorted again. "Go shower. The bathroom is right through that door." I walked by him, trying not to breathe him in. He smelled wonderful even though he'd worked all day. Goose bumps formed on my arms when our forearms brushed by accident. "Let me get you a fresh towel."

"Thank you."

There was a small closet across from the bathroom, and I stood on my tiptoes, hoping to grab a clean towel on the top shelf. It was just an inch out of my reach, not enough to get a chair to help. I was about to jump when a large presence came behind me. Theo's chest pressed into my back as he reached over me to grab the towel. "I got it. No reason for you to strain yourself."

I couldn't even speak. My skin flushed at his nearness. His deep voice was right by my ear, and his breath hit my neck, causing a flurry of feelings to wind and weave through me. My heart beat so hard it was incredible he couldn't physically hear it. "Uh—"

He twisted the handle to the bathroom, the handle emitting a familiar squeak, when he barked out a laugh. "Goddamn, Audrey. Wouldn't have expected that."

What?

I spun around so fast, my ponytail hit my face. One of my bright pink bras sat on the sink. *Shit.* It was sheer and lacy and one of my secret bras that no one ever saw. It was just for me, and now Theo Sanders had seen it.

"Fuck. I'm—that—sorry." I shoved by him and clutched it to my chest, my face on fire. I couldn't look him in the eyes. "Humiliating."

"Audrey, hey," he said, his voice soft. "This isn't a big deal at all. I mean, now that I know you wear sexy bras under those scrubs, I'll have to force myself to not think about it."

"Why would you think about it?"

"Uh, because I'm a dude, and you have boobs." He laughed, but when I didn't, he frowned. "Hey, seriously. This isn't a big deal."

"Because you see bras all the time?"

"No." He fought a grin but made sure to hold my eyes. "Do you want me to make it even?"

"Even?" God, why was I using one-word answers? Why did Theo mention my boobs? Why was I burning up everywhere?

"Yeah. Here." He set his bag down and shoved fabric around until he pulled out black briefs. "These are mine. See? I'm not embarrassed."

"Oh."

His dimple appeared as he set his stuff in my bathroom. "Do you need anything in here before I shower? I'd hate to be in the way."

I shook my head.

"Alright, I'll be quick." He shut the door, and I fell onto my bed. *Shit.*

My scrubs!

I didn't recall touching any weird fluids, but I needed to get in the habit of removing them before touching anything. I stripped out of them immediately, standing in my black underwear and matching bra. This one wasn't as lacy, but it held my breasts tight to my chest and kept them out of the way. I had the same boobs my mom did, which meant they were big for my body and often caused me back pain. I needed thick straps to hold them down.

"Hey, do you—" Theo poked his head out of the bathroom, his gaze moving down my body. It started at my face, then my chest, down my stomach to between my thighs and legs. His lips parted, and his tongue went the side of his mouth, and that little gesture sent moisture between my thighs.

"Shit. I'm sorry." He jerked back and smacked his head against the door. "Fuck. Damnit." Then the door shut.

Holy shit.

I couldn't breathe. I panted for breath, absolutely frozen. Theo Sanders checked me out, that I knew, but me? What? I exhaled and took a few seconds to settle down. My body was out of control. My limbs didn't know what to do with that much attention. Everything went into overdrive. My nipples tightened, the beaded points almost poking through the fabric. My pulse raced, and my mouth watered.

Was this lust? Attraction?

It had been so long I forgot. It wasn't that I'd avoided guys the last five years, but I just didn't have time. I'd made out with my sophomore boyfriend a lot, and he'd grabbed my boobs a few times, but we never did anything more. I was a twenty-one-year-old virgin who decided to have a sexual awakening with Theo Sanders in my dorm room.

This was a terrible moment to suddenly be wondering what it'd feel like to have someone touch me. And *Theo Sanders* of all people. Fuck. I needed to get dressed. Fast.

I found an old pair of ripped jeans and shoved my legs through them, buttoning them before finding a black tank top. It landed an inch above my waistline and showed an inch of skin. It would have to do because the water had shut off.

Did Theo take the fastest shower to mankind? How long had I sat there, thinking about him touching me?

I added a pair of earrings—topaz, the birthstone of my dad —and applied one layer of mascara because...I wanted to. It had nothing to do with Theo being here. Nothing like that.

The door opened, and I braced myself. For what? I wasn't sure, but I gripped the side of my desk and waited. He stepped out, and his wet hair had curls. *Fuck.*

I was doomed. I was wildly attracted to Theo Sanders.

10

T heo
     I deserved an award for surviving the last six minutes of my life. After taking a freezing cold shower to prevent myself from getting hard, I breathed through my mouth to not breathe in all her scents. The soap? Vanilla. It was enticing and made me want to lick the bar.

The way her body looked. Fuck. She had the body of a goddess. I'd meant what I said about her being beautiful earlier, but that was her personality and facial expressions. I had no idea what she hid under her scrubs, but now that I knew, fuck. It had been months since I'd hooked up with someone, and I was struggling.

She stood there, her cheeks red as hell from blushing and her pillow lips parting as she breathed deeply. Each breath caused her chest to rise, drawing my attention to her tits. They stood out now with that sexy top. This was a new development in my relationship with Audrey Hawthorne.

I was fucking attracted to her.

"Ready for the rage room?" I asked, my voice scratchy and throaty. Ugh. It was the lingering buzz I felt around her.

She nodded and pressed her lips together tight, her eyes roaming over my face and hair. "I like your curls."

Her voice was barely a whisper, and I ran a hand through my hair. My hair became curly when wet. It had always been that way since a kid. And knowing she liked it caused my chest to swell with pride. "Yeah?"

She nodded but then cleared her throat and jumped toward her desk. "I'll get my keys."

"Want me to drive? I can drop you off back here before I head home. Only if you're comfortable though."

Yeah, I was selfish and wanted to be near her. She wanted to distract me from my mom, and mission accomplished. I hadn't thought about my mom or her stroke since the second I got in here.

"I'm comfortable with you."

"Then let's go rage it out." A part of me also needed to work through this attraction. Burn off the energy I had around her. If she offered to get naked and distract me that way, let's just say I'd absolutely declare fuck yes.

Rage room would be better for us. Especially with how things were with her brother. This would add fuel to the fire and *zap*. The lust dulled. I couldn't hook up with Quentin's sister. That was an unwritten rule on the ice. Even if I hated the guy, I'd abide by those rules.

She locked up, and I followed her out of the dorm, letting myself admire the curve of her ass in her jeans. She had narrow hips, and her arms were cut. She had muscle, and I kinda dug it.

"This place is about fifteen minutes from here. They have all sorts of things we can hit. And we can pick our weapon of choice." She grinned just as the sunlight hit her, and damn. The brown and green hues of her eyes and the shades of auburn in her hair—she was stunning. *And fucking smart.*

I guided her to my truck and opened the passenger door for

her. There was a large step up, and I held out a hand, not expecting her to take it. But she did. Her fingers landed on mine as she jumped into the cabin, and when I released her, my hand tingled with heat.

This was gonna be a long-ass semester if we spent this much time together. I'd have to fight my attraction off every minute. I ran a hand through my hair, shaking it as I walked to my side of the truck.

We could totally do this. Be friends, nothing more. Maybe it was the fact I hadn't been with someone in months. Hell, maybe half a year. Balancing responsibilities with hockey and my family was a full-time gig, but before my mom's stroke, I used to hook up regularly. Nothing wild like most of the team but enough to take the edge off.

I started the truck as Audrey crossed one leg over the other, then she shifted again. "You good?"

"Are we gonna talk about what happened?"

Fuck. "Mm, do you want to?"

"I-I don't know. I just... you saw me almost naked."

"Pretend it was a swimsuit. I didn't see anything more than that." And now I was thinking about her in a wet suit, water dripping down her body... I shivered. I wanted to drag my tongue up her body. *Okay, settle down.* "I am sorry about opening the door without warning you. That's on me."

"Oh, no it's okay. Don't feel bad." She cleared her throat. "You're right. Swimming suit."

"Yeah."

The silence grew, and I wanted to pull the thoughts from her mind, analyze them like I would post-game film. See what landed well, what could use improvements. Like, should I have said she was hot? Would complimenting her make this less awkward or more?

I swallowed. Were these nerves? I hated them.

"This place requires us to wear a jumpsuit." She let out something like giggle. It was her version of one, and it was cute. "Then we can pick between a sledgehammer, an axe, a bat, or a golf club. Oh man, they have a room of electronics we can just destroy."

"I've always wanted to punch a computer screen." I slid a glance at her, and her lips were curved up, her face softening instead of the worry lines I was familiar with. "Probably shouldn't with the whole hockey thing."

She gasped. "Theo."

"What?" I checked the mirrors. Was there something in the road? My pulse raced. "What is it, Audrey?"

"You can't go to a rage room. Ugh." She covered her face with her hands, groaning. "It's not worth the potential injury. God, I'm the worst. No, let's turn around."

"No, it's totally alright. I'll behave."

"Coach Reiner would be appalled. You can't get injured before senior year, not before you head to the Acorns."

"Injuries can happen at any time," I said, the temperature cooling in the car. I might as well have dumped ice water all over us. The warmth and attraction fizzled out as fast as blowing out a candle. Why had I said that? Why?

"I, uh, that's why I'm finishing my degree in nursing, so if I do have to quit hockey early for any reason, I'll have another career path. I'm not afraid of injuries as much as others."

"Yeah, that's a good plan. Smart." She stared out the window before adjusting her legs again. "Could I try to convince you to go somewhere else? I'd never forgive myself if you even tweaked a finger."

"Nah, you were too excited talking about it. Worst case, I can watch you."

"No! This is for *you*. A diversion from the ICU and home, you know, to get you out of your head for a little bit. I'm okay."

"Being around you is a distraction for me, Auds," I said, my voice barely above a whisper. I probably shouldn't have said that. It showed too much. I ran a hand over my jaw, the regret itching to get out, and I changed the song to some upbeat punk cover. "Anyway—"

"What does that mean? I can't tell if you're being nice or insinuating something more. Not that you would. You know what? That was stupid of me to ask. I shouldn't have. You would never. Okay, yeah turn around and let me out, please."

"You're kinda cute when you're nervous." I smiled, the tension around my shoulder easing. Audrey rambled like I made her nervous, and it felt good to know I wasn't the only one feeling something here. "And a part of me did mean it that way. You're easy to be around, and I'm enjoying learning about you. So yeah, I *would* insinuate more."

"You can't say that to me."

"And why not?"

"Because."

"Oh, is that all?" I teased, checking the left lane before passing a slow car. We were about ten minutes from the rage room, and I'd make sure we saw this thing through. "Great closing argument. You should be a lawyer."

She snorted. "I hate when you're funny. It makes it harder to keep some distance between us. That's my reason, Sanders."

Did I want her keeping distance between us? Nope. I didn't. "Just to make sure I'm hearing you, Auds, you want me to be less funny because you find me so charming and hot that when I make you laugh you have to stop yourself from attacking my mouth?"

"Theo!" She swatted my arm, her brilliant laughter filling the cab of my truck.

My god, I fucking loved that laugh.

"That is not what I said, and you know it. Ugh, you're such a pain in the ass." She said the words with a smile on her face, and I grinned into my fist.

I wasn't sure what I wanted from Audrey and wasn't sure I'd ever figure it out, but right now? There was no other person I wanted to be around, and I'd just enjoy that feeling.

"FUCK YES! TAKE THAT!" Audrey swung a bat over her head and crashed it onto an old television set. The metal cracked, and glass broke into pieces on the floor, the sounds echoing in the large warehouse. "Fuck you."

She hit it again, her eyes wild beneath the goggles. Maybe Audrey needed this release more than me because she was addicting to watch. All those feelings she kept locked up tight exploded around her in colors, and she was a piece of art. Call me ridiculous, but watching Audrey Hawthorne beat the shit out of old electronics was magical and sexy.

"People suck," she yelled, then picked up an old school phone and tossed it across the room until it slammed into the wall. "Theo," she said, her voice breathless. Her chest heaved as she smiled at me, and I swore something shifted in my chest at that grin.

"What, Auds?"

"Try it. It's euphoric." She handed me an old monitor and pointed to the wall. "Don't overextend yourself but toss it. Make it hurt."

"You're a little evil." I winked. "I like it though." I took the device and tossed it, and fuuuuck that felt good. Wrong and therapeutic. I'd been a rule follower for so damn long that destroying something lit a fire in me.

An emotional fire.

Why did my mom have to have a stroke and not my dad?

Why did my dad expect me to stop my life and take care of my siblings?

What was he going to do when I went to the NHL?

Did he want my money for the signing bonus?

Why couldn't Mom get better and tell me I was doing the right thing?

Who would hold Penny when she was sad?

Would my dad keep Em out of trouble with Jace?

Fuck.

My throat tightened as I moved to another piece of equipment, smashing before picking up an axe and destroying a piece of plywood. "Yes!" I smashed item after item, not caring that I sweated more than I did during a workout or that my forearms would be sore. I destroyed and took out my rage.

Why did Quentin have to be related to my fucking clinical partner?

Why did Audrey have to be so fucking pretty? The one person who understood my stress, who saw me for more than a hockey guy or a caretaker? Someone I felt a spark with who I'd never be able to be more than clinical friends with? It was unfair.

Fucking Quentin.

I switched to a golf club and crushed an old lamp. The sound was so satisfying I shuddered.

"I think our time is up, Theo." A soft voice appeared to my left, and Audrey grabbed my arm. "Do you want me to pay for more time?"

I shook my head, my adrenaline coming down hard. My eyes fucking watered, and I didn't even realize it. "I'm good."

She placed her hand on mine, grabbed the golf club, and tossed it over to the side. I kept her touch on me as we left through the entrance. We returned our jumpsuits and goggles, paid, and walked back into the brutal summer sun of central Illinois. It smelled like rain was coming, and I inhaled, taking a moment to collect myself.

That experience... changed me. I needed it and hadn't known it. Closing my eyes, I faced the sun and let the warm rays wash over me. It cleansed me in the weirdest way. I felt less angry about my dad, about my life being unfair. And when I opened my eyes, Audrey stared at me with such a worried expression it took all my effort not to squeeze her in a hug.

This woman had known exactly what to do, and I owed her. "Thank you." I cleared my throat as emotion clogged it. "This was amazing. I needed it."

"Good. I'm glad." She blushed and stared at the corn fields, but that wouldn't do. I closed the distance between us and cupped one side of her face, dragging my thumb over her jawline. She sucked in a breath as her eyes widened. Her breath tickled my face, and the warmth from her made me shiver.

I gently pressed my lips against hers, craving the emotional connection with her more than I cared to admit. It had been so long since I kissed someone just because I was thankful for them. Years, even, since I'd cupped a girl's face and wished I could express how much I cared for them with one gesture. God, her lips were perfect and slightly wet. I wanted to nibble them. I lingered for two seconds, loving the way her soft lips felt against mine, then I pulled back. "Thank you. Seriously. I don't know how to thank you properly, but that's the best I've felt in months. Months, Auds." I shook my head, admiring the freckles on the tip of her nose and the way her skin flushed while looking at me. "Very few people understand me the way you do, and you've only known me a few weeks. Makes me question my teammates."

She chewed her lip, her gaze remaining my mouth. "You did transfer to a team where most of the guys will hate you."

"Couldn't let me live in la-la land for a few more minutes,

eh? Had to bring me down." I forced a laugh and guided her to my car. It wasn't that I meant to kiss her in a sexual "let's get naked" way. I mean hell, I was attracted to her. But my love language was physical touch. Physical and emotional connection were essential for me, and that seemed like the right thing to do. "I'll take you back, Auds. Thank you. You're a good friend."

11

Audrey

Theo had kissed me. Then he called me a good friend.

But he *kissed* me right on the lips.

It was all I could think about. A full day later, I ran my fingers over my mouth and could still smell the mossy field, feel the way the wind and sun touched my skin, the gentle caress of his fingers on my face before his soft lips touched mine. My body heated, and my skin tightened, and my stomach swooped so much I could fall over.

I hadn't been kissed in years, and he woke up a dormant part of me. Caring for someone was too much work, too exhausting and terrifying, but a quick connection? That wouldn't be too bad.

Get it together.

Quentin agreed to meet me at a salad place between classes Wednesday, and I knew better than to think about Theo around him. There were almost two versions of Theo, the horrible hockey guy who I hated for hurting Quentin, and the one I knew from clinicals. The one who watched his siblings to help his parents.

"What up, sis?"

Quentin pushed the door open to the salad place, a boot on his leg and a smirk on his face. He scanned the room and nodded at a few people before he strutted to our table. He always had a gait to him that screamed confidence. It suited him well for hockey, and after we lost our dad, I was glad he still had a spark to him.

"Hey." I cleared my throat as a flicker of anxiety bubbled in my stomach. He told me he had a plan to get back at Theo last time we briefly spoke, and even thinking about it bothered me.

"You get me something already or should I order?"

I shook my head. "Order for yourself."

He narrowed his eyes at me, his head tilting to the side as he studied me. "You alright, Audrey?"

Pressing my lips together, I nodded but avoided his gaze. Quentin was my brother. My only real family left. He'd held me when I sobbed over losing our dad and had taken me to the movies to get my mind off the grief. He made me laugh through those tough years and became my best friend.

We'd talked about our hopes and dreams. He'd opened up about what made him sad, but those moments were years ago.

He wasn't the same person he used to be, and the fact he dismissed me so easily Monday hurt me deeply.

I wiped my sweaty palms on my legs and took a sip of the iced tea, wetting the back of my throat to ease the growing tension. We used to check in with each other, and I'd enjoy the time. I'd learn about his friends, his classes, his teammates. But now? I didn't have anything to ask.

Ask him about Theo's mentorship.

The thought intruded, and I begged it to leave. Theo would be like politics between us: we just didn't talk about it.

"Alright, I'm gonna need like four salads with how hungry I am." He laughed and sat across from me, his familiar scent reminding me of home. He wore the same cologne my dad bought him when he turned sixteen.

"Yeah." I played with my fork, desperate to try to keep normalcy between us. "Make sure you eat enough."

"Why won't you look at me?"

"Hm?" I glanced at his face, keeping mine neutral. My skin heated at his scrutiny.

"What's wrong?"

I shook my head. "I'm fine. Busy. Studying, as you know."

He frowned and ran a hand over his face. "You're mad about Monday still?"

The tone he used had me on edge. He was about to blame me for it. I knew it. There was no apology in his tone or awareness. When had my brother become mean?

It didn't matter. It was easier to diffuse, to deflect. Move on. It hit me then, that I'd done this hundreds of times. Avoided confrontation because it stressed me out and in the process let my own feelings go unnoticed. Like they didn't matter.

"It's fine," I said, keeping my voice neutral. "How's hockey?"

"Ha." He rolled his eyes and leaned back into the chair. He took my words at face value. He always did.

Did I want him to realize that he'd upset me? Yeah. I did. I wanted him to realize it and apologize, but that day would never come.

"Your nursing buddy is such a dick. Told me the team would turn against me once they saw him play. Are you kidding me? Loyalty goes further than skill on the ice. I can't with this dude. Sanders is the fucking worst."

But he wasn't.

I opened my mouth to say that but snapped it shut. Again, confrontation wasn't my style. "You said he's mentoring you?"

His eyes flashed. "Sure. We can call it that. I don't know what Reiner is playing at, but Theo and I meet once a week to talk and learn from each other. What a joke. What do I have to learn from him?"

"He's drafted already, right? You could ask questions—"

"Whose side are you even on, Audrey? Jesus Christ. Just cause he's a fucking nurse like you, you're picking his side? What's the point of family then?" He glared at me, his face containing so much disdain it stole my breath away.

This wasn't the brother I loved. The guy who was my equal, my friend. I wanted to cry with how different he was now, that I'd been blind to it for so long out of fear of confrontation.

"Hey, whoa, I am really sorry about snapping at you." Quentin closed his eyes and leaned into the table, his expression softening at me. "That was shitty. Sorry Audrey. I know you weren't doing that. I'm really struggling with all this shit, okay? I'm lashing out. You're the last person I want to hurt."

"You didn't let me finish my sentence," I whispered.

He nodded. "You're right. Please, can you say what you were going to? I promise not to be a dick."

"Sure." I ran my fingers over the table, grounding myself for a beat. "You want to get drafted, so you could ask him the process of talking to coaches or lawyers, see what he did well?"

He arched one brow before shrugging. "Yeah, I could do that."

"You don't plan to." I deflated.

"It's a good idea, yeah, but I can talk to Reiner about all that." Quentin relaxed into his chair, his expression so familiar it made my chest ache. He looked so much like our dad, and it made me wish for those days when the three of us did trips to the grocery store together. "We're good, right Auds?"

I nodded. "Yeah."

"Okay, so I gotta tell you about the guys and what we did last weekend. It was wild...."

He went on to tell stories of their parties, shenanigans, and I listened the entire time. Not one did he ask about my clinicals or classes. But that was normal. Quentin liked to talk about himself the most.

This was the first time it really bothered me.

I let him think we were good because what choice did I have? Alienate the only real family I had left? That thought was too depressing to follow, so I sat there, shoving away my hurt and pretending everything was all right.

THE ANTICIPATION of seeing Theo died fast when they split us up Thursday. Besides a quick wave, I hadn't seen him all day, and it surprised me that I wanted to talk to him. I wanted to watch his expressions when he listened and his focus when he was tasked with something.

I also really wanted to ask about the kiss, but girls didn't do that, did they? Theo probably kissed women all the time. He was a hockey star going to the NHL. A quick peck on the mouth for him was nothing, a blink of an eye. Yet, it felt special and meaningful and ugh.

My life was out of control.

During our break, Theo didn't come to the outside portion like we did last time, and disappointment hit me right in the chest. It was wild how much I wanted to talk to him. But he could be avoiding me because of the kiss and brother thing. It made sense.

I'd never been anyone's first choice ever and never expected to be. My mom told me during her grief that life was about setting realistic expectations. If I expected to never be a priority, then being chose second or being forgotten wouldn't hurt.

The rest of the shift flew by, a myriad of experiences and questions that made my mind blur. It was all so fascinating, and losing myself in this role felt great. The worry about Quentin or Theo left, and I had a purpose. A real meaning for being here, and damn, that filled me up with hope.

I clocked out and made my way to the exit when a familiar voice called my name.

"Audrey, hey, Auds! Wait up!"

Theo.

My skin flushed as I angled my head toward him. He walk-jogged toward me with a huge grin on his face. Almost like he was *happy* to see me. He'd avoided me earlier, so that didn't add up. "Hello, Theo."

"Hello, Theo?" He raised his brows. "We've raged together, accidentally seen each other in underwear, and you said *hello* like we're stuffy graduate professors? Come on, girl, I get more than a *hello*."

"Hi?"

"Better." He grinned, and his stare felt like a caress as it moved from my hair to my eyes to my mouth. His expression shifted to concern real fast. "What's wrong?"

"What do you mean?" Could this man read minds?

"Did I upset you? I don't... I can't think..." He ran a hand over his hair, his frown stretching across his face as he stared at me. "Fuck. I didn't meet you at break. I'm sorry! It was Marcy—"

"It's okay." I shook my head, my stomach tightening with the conversation. I wanted it to end. It was stupid. It didn't matter that I missed him. "You're busy. You don't owe me anything."

"Audrey." He grabbed my hand and squeezed, a tender expression on his face. "Auds, I promise you it was Marcy. She wanted me to observe this routine procedure with one cardiac patient, and it was fascinating, but I should've texted you."

"No. You shouldn't have. You don't need to explain yourself." It was foolish to think we were more than just casual friends, so there was no reason for my stomach to twist with nerves.

His jaw flexed, and I forced myself to focus on the trees right outside the entrance. We stood there, my hand in his, and I removed it. It was silly that I felt... connected to him. I was one of many for him, and I knew that. It wasn't rude, but it was the truth.

I knew better than to hope for anything. I fucking knew better, but the hurt still worked its way in my chest, and I wanted to be alone. Maybe it was the leftover betrayal of Quentin changing our friendship or not caring about me anymore. It was a one-sided relationship, and it wasn't fair to channel that energy onto Theo.

"How was the procedure?" I asked, moving my legs to force myself to walk. Outside air always felt good after being in here all day. It smelled fresher. Closing my eyes, I took a deep breath and already felt the tension leaving my body. I was okay. I had me, and that had to be enough.

"Audrey, can you pause for a minute, please?"

"Pause?" My heart raced. I didn't want to unpack my hurt. He wouldn't understand. I could never say how I truly felt, ever. Not after my dad got sick because I had to be the tough one for my mom and Quentin.

"You're seconds away from bolting or coming up with a reason why you have to leave, and I'd really like five minutes of your time."

"Okay." I shrugged and shoved my hands in the pockets of my scrubs. "What is it? Was the procedure tough to watch? I've never seen anything cardiac related, but it seems interesting."

"I hurt you." He rubbed his lips together and regret crossed his features. "I'm really sorry. If I was waiting for you, and you didn't show, it'd upset me too."

That annoying, thick emotional feeling formed in my throat again. *No.* I needed it gone. No one ever apologized to me, I didn't even know what to do with it. I pushed it away. "It's okay, Theo. I said that."

"But it's not? You're lying. Your body language gives you away, and I really fucking like our friendship. I'd hate to mess it up."

"You didn't."

"Audrey, you're killing me right now." He placed his hands on his hips and groaned. "Be mad at me. Push back. Tell me what you're thinking."

I couldn't do that. Not really. It didn't matter. Not to him. I tried with my mom, and she accused me of being selfish. I knew better. "There's nothing to push back on. I'm just tired."

His nostrils flared as he studied me before his shoulders sagged. "I hate that you don't let me in. I want you honest with me, that's all. I'll work on being a better friend."

"You're fine—"

"If you say *fine* or *okay* one more time, I'm gonna lose my mind."

We stared, the tension thick as I thought about the kiss again. This was not the right time to remember how his mouth felt against mine, but it happened, and damn.

His phone went off, ruining the moment. "Please don't leave." He grabbed my wrist gently. "We're not done, but this is my sister."

"Hey, Em." He kept his eyes on me, but they widened with worry. "What? Where are you? Is Jace there? What about Penny? Fuck. Okay. Okay. I'll be there. Yeah. Uh, fuck. Text me your location now."

His tone was urgent. Frantic.

His gaze found mine, and panic oozed out of him.

"What is it?" I asked, fight or flight kicking in. "What happened?"

"Em has a flat tire on the side of the freeway. I have the car seat to pick up Penny in thirty minutes in the opposite direction. Daniel needs to be picked up from school in twenty minutes. Em was gonna help but can't. She's freaking out." He gripped his hair. "What the fuck are they gonna do when I'm gone?"

"Hey. One step at a time. What is the most urgent?

"Emily." He swallowed. "She can't change a tire. Doesn't know how."

"Okay. Then we go there with her. You change it for her and get your siblings. I'll stay with her if you want me to. I can drive her back or just be an ear."

"Yeah. Okay. Are you... Audrey, you don't... this isn't your—"

"Let's go. Do you need me to drive?"

Theo's hands fisted for a beat before he shook his head. "No, I need to focus on something."

"Then come on."

Within five minutes, we were on the road, his sister on the car speaker as Theo asked her more questions.

Was she all the way on the shoulder?

Did anyone stop to help her? If so, say no, that help is on the way.

Did she have the car manual from the glove box? Could she get it ready and find the jack?

Watching Theo stress about his seventeen-year-old sister really showed me the person he was. This wasn't the guy who was horrible to Quentin. Theo cared deeply about his family and was intuitive. It wasn't the time to revisit what we were chatting about, but he read my face and refused to let me lie my way out of it.

I was glad he got the call when I was with him. I'd hate to imagine him going through this alone, driving scatterbrained.

"Okay, do you see a green car on the right?" He zoomed to the far right lane of the freeway. Cars were flying by us, and a little fear trickled its way down my spine.

I'd hate to be stranded here. Alone. Young. Hell, even now I wouldn't like it.

"What is the damn speed limit?" he growled.

"There she is." I pointed about half a mile away. "Put your hazards on and start to slow down."

We approached the car, and the physical relief on his face made my heart beat faster. Theo loved his family. A warm, gooey sensation formed in my chest at the thought of having someone care for me that much. My dad had, but he was gone. My mom used me as a bank, and my brother never appreciated anything. Our families couldn't be more different.

"What the fuck is she doing standing this close to the road?" He slammed the car in park and jumped out.

I followed.

"Emily, get to the side of the medium, right now. These cars are flying past you!"

"I'm sorry. I'm sorry, Theo."

Emily had tears streaming down her face. She trembled as she sniffed, and without thinking, I went into nurse mode.

"You're probably in shock. Let's go sit. Do you have water with you?"

She nodded. "I-in the car."

"Theo, open the trunk and find the jack and spare in there. The user manual is right here. Nice job finding it, Emily." I passed it to Theo. "Read through to see if there is anything crazy. If not, we can use the jack to prop it up and take off the flat."

Emily's water bottle was covered in stickers. I snatched it from the cupholder and made my way over to her. She wrapped her arms around her knees, gravel sticking to the undersides of her legs. "Th-thank you."

"Take a few sips, then a few deep breaths." I sat next to her, not caring about the rocks or garbage surrounding us. "What happened?"

"I was going the speed limit because I hate driving on the highway. Cars go so damn fast. Sorry, uh dang." She hung her head. "I heard this horrible sound, and the car jerked. I thought I was going to die."

"Hey." I put a hand on her shoulder, squeezing it. "You didn't. You're here. You're safe. You did the right thing. Be proud of that."

She swallowed as a wave of sobs hit her. "I can't stop sh-shaking."

"That's adrenaline. It's your body's fight or flight system. It means you made the right choices to protect yourself, but it can be scary when it needs to work its way out."

"Cars honked at me, and people yelled. I thought... I thought one was gonna crash into me. Then, a guy stopped, asking to help, and he terrified me. He was double my size, but when I screamed, he drove away."

"He was probably trying to help, but that would've scared me too." I took her hand and squeezed it. "You're okay now."

"Audrey, can you help me get the lugs off?"

"Are you okay here? Can I help your brother for a minute?"

She nodded and gave me a watery smile. "Thank you. Daniel told me about you. You're nice."

"You have some damn good siblings."

Theo had the car propped on the jack, but the position required him to keep hold on the car to balance it. "Can you take that wrench and get them off?"

"Yes." I had to stand directly in front of him, so my butt almost touched his crotch as I bent to remove the parts. It was unsexy, super unromantic, but I couldn't help but feel a buzz from his heat radiating to me. His spicy cologne wafted toward me, and it took all my effort to not close my eyes and inhale.

The thing about attraction was that it wasn't up to us. Even though I knew we'd never *be anything* I could still be attracted to him.

"Nice muscles, Hawthorne. You know your way around a wrench."

"My dad made sure to teach me the basic things to survive on my own." I loosened them all before undoing them with my fingers. "He showed me how to change a flat, fix drywall, do basic plumbing, and how to seed a lawn. The last one hasn't been that life-changing."

"Not yet at least. You never know when you'll have a nice big yard with kids and dogs running around."

"Maybe." I shrugged as I gripped the wheel and took it off. "That's not really my vision for the future."

"What is?" he asked, his voice gentle as he stared at me with the same open expression that had my knees weakening.

"Just a nice condo. Exposed brick, maybe a patio for succulents and herbs." My life would be at the hospital, working, and I'd just need a place to sleep and relax on off days. I didn't have fantasies about houses or pets or kids. That wasn't in the cards for me. My parents did that, and look how it turned out? My dad died, and my mom wasn't the same person and basically forgot about Quentin and me. Even my brother and I were growing apart.

"I could picture you there. Some cool, artsy lamps hanging down. Some cool ivy or something. Yeah. That tracks with you. Some fancy bookshelves for all your studies. I can see it, Auds."

My face warmed at his additions, which was silly. He was being kind. That was who Theo was.

"That's the dream," I muttered, setting the tire down. "Do

you need me to grab the spare, or is it sturdy enough that you can finish?"

"I'll take it from here. You're one of a kind, girl."

I ignored the swoop of my stomach from his words. He didn't mean them to be anything special. Plenty of people knew all these things. "I'll check on Em."

She stopped crying and watched us, her rosy cheeks still red from the tears. "Can you show me how to do that? With Theo moving north next year, who will I call?"

"It's not too hard." I pulled out my phone. "There are videos online that explain all the steps in a super easy manner. I try to watch a few a month to prepare myself."

"Yeah. I should do that. Thank you."

"Sure." I shrugged, tensing when she put her arm around me and hugged. She squeezed me hard, and my eyes closed. She smelled like a spicy perfume, and her clothes were soft. Theo had hugged me recently, and besides him, it had been years. And two Sanders children hugged me, and I liked it.

"Okay, it's on, Emily. It'll be good." He stood with his hands on his trim hips, his face set in worry as he addressed us. "Audrey offered to either drive with you or drive you home. What would you prefer?"

"She can drive, please."

"And you're good to drive still?" Theo asked me, his lips pressing together.

I nodded. "I'll get her home. Go pick up your siblings. I'll just Uber home."

"No," he barked out before shaking his head. "I'm sorry, I meant, please don't. I'll drive you once I get them all fed. Don't take a rideshare."

"It's no big deal. It'll be like ten dollars."

"Audrey, I'm begging you, let me take you to your car. Don't leave. Promise?"

How could I not agree when Emily leaned into me and Theo stared at me with wide eyes? "Okay, I'll wait for you."

He sighed in relief and took off, leaving me with his sister. I wasn't sure why Theo wanted me to wait, but I would.

Even though it blurred the lines between us, I was having a hard time staying away from him.

12

Theo

I'd give Audrey a million dollars, and it still wouldn't be enough to thank her. I'd upset her earlier and yet she continued to help and stay at my childhood home for hours. Em—my angsty teenage sister—had hugged her. Daniel had a crush on her, and Penny loved anyone who gave her attention.

She fit in here, and the realization made my chest feel heavy. I had no friends willing to stick this out with me. It was hard being friends with someone who always bailed, and most dudes my age? They weren't worried about their families or home life. They were partying and living the dream.

Audrey understood. She'd lived it herself. I wanted to shower her with gifts, hugs, squeezes. There wasn't anything I could do to thank her, and it caused an unreachable itch deep in my core. She sat at our counter, laughing as Daniel told her a story about their school gopher wreaking havoc on class. He was serious too. The school had a gopher problem, and it was hilarious.

"Have you named him yet?" Audrey asked, crossing one leg over the other. Her whole demeanor changed when she laughed, and I froze in my spot. Audrey's smile lit up the whole fucking room. Pure joy.

My heart fluttered like a damn hummingbird.

"We named him Manders. Our teacher is named Amanda, so we named him after her because she's scared of him."

"I can't tell if that's cute or scary." She snorted. "Have you seen the gopher?"

"Oh yeah, we watch for him all recess. We sit there and wait. Some kids try to touch the holes."

"Wild. Your school mascot should be a gopher." Audrey yawned, and it shook me out of my trance.

She was tired. It was late. She'd changed her plans for me, and I'd begged her to stay. She was still in her damn scrubs.

"Auds, let me take you home."

"Oh." She blinked as a blush covered her cheeks. "Yeah. I'm sorry. I stayed too long."

"What? No, you didn't." Was she fucking serious? "You're tired. We still gotta drive to your car."

She licked the side of her lip before hopping off the stool and straightening her scrubs. "Thank you for letting me hang out with you. Glad you're okay, Em, and I can't wait to hear more about Manders!"

"You have to leave?" Daniel asked, his sad, pathetic voice echoing in the kitchen. "Are you sure?"

"She probably has other plans. Come on, don't guilt her."

"I don't, but yeah, I should head back."

"What if we do a movie and popcorn night?" Daniel begged. It was a Thursday night, a school night, and I wanted to say no.

"That sounds awesome," Em said.

Em never wanted to hang with us. Ever.

"Yes!" Daniel jumped off the stool. "You have to stay now, Audrey. We make the best popcorn ever."

"Oh, uh." She glanced at me. "I'm not...sure?"

"Do you want to stay?" Something like hope bloomed in my chest. If she wanted to stay and hang with my siblings, fuck. There was no saying what I was gonna do. No one did this. No one was that kind.

She pressed her lips together and played with her fingers. "If you don't want me to go, yeah."

"Do you think I want you to leave?" I asked, laughing at the end. She was brilliant. Why would she possibly think that? "I begged you to come here, Auds."

Her eyes widened before the blush returned. Then she gazed at me, her expression softening. "You did. Yeah."

"Come on. I'll grab you a sweatshirt so you don't have to stay in your scrubs."

She slid off the stool and followed me up the stairs. She walked quietly, and I waited for her at the top. She wouldn't look at me and kept cracking her knuckles like she was nervous.

"Are you alright? Are you uncomfortable here?"

She shook her head. "I'm okay, really."

"Audrey." I waited for her to get into my room and then I shut the door. She leaned against it, and I had the strongest urge to toss her on my bed and kiss the hell out of her. I wanted to suck the attitude out of her mouth and bite her lips until she panted. I did none of those things, but I wanted to. Badly.

"I need you to talk to me. You keep saying you're *fine* and *okay*, but you're keeping something from me. You know all my shit. You're in my childhood bedroom, for fuck's sake. You know my secrets. I want to know yours."

She swallowed loudly, the click of her throat like a gunshot in my room. "They're stupid."

"Your feelings?" I huffed. "Your feelings matter, and I care about them."

She closed her eyes as she took a shaky breath, and when she met my gaze, there was a new glint to her eyes. One I sure as hell couldn't figure out. "I'm not used to being put first or included or hugged. I'm struggling with how to feel right now."

"Put first? Hugged?"

"It doesn't—"

"If you say it doesn't matter, I will be fucking angry, Audrey." Did this beautiful, kind woman not get hugged? Why did that make me want to cry?

"I'm sure that kiss didn't mean anything to you. I know I'm one of many and that I'm not unique or special, but for a moment, I might've thought I was. And that's foolish and on me. So, when you didn't show up for the break, it solidified I was right in not being at the top of your mind. I'm not mad at you or upset, so please don't take it that way. We're still friends, Theo. I promise. I love your siblings."

I paced my room as she leaned against the door.

One of many.

Not unique.

Not being at the top of my mind.

"I upset you. I'm sorry. I knew I shouldn't have said anything. I'll leave."

"If you open that door, I will wrestle you to the ground. Stay. Give me a goddamn second to respond."

She paled, and I instantly regretted my tone. "Auds, honey, I shouldn't have yelled. I'm not upset with you at all. I'm upset with *me*. My mind isn't as brilliant as yours, so I need a second to formulate my response. Can you wait for me?"

She nodded.

"Here." I went to my dresser and pulled out an old crewneck sweatshirt that had faded hockey sticks on it. My mom found it thrifting for me years ago, and it was my favorite piece of clothing I owned. "You can put this on."

I also tossed her an old pair of gray shorts.

I meant to offer her to go to the bathroom to change, but

Audrey immediately whipped off her scrubs and stood there in a sports bra. She slid on my sweatshirt, which reached her thighs. Then she stripped out of her pants so fast I didn't notice anything and put on my shorts.

Words escaped me. Thoughts did too. The ability to breathe was shortly behind.

"Fuck, Audrey." My voice was raspy as hell. She looked sexy.

"What?"

She had no idea. I laughed and ran a hand over my face. My thoughts were a damn mess and probably out of line. I knew, deep down, that lusting over a teammates sister was against the rules, but she was in my room, in my clothes, and I didn't care.

"You look fucking good."

Her eyes widened. "But you say that to everyone."

I smiled and shook my head, taking a step closer to her. "No, I don't. I also don't have *everyone* come to my house, my child-hood bedroom, or wear my clothes either. I certainly don't let *everyone* meet my siblings."

Her pulse raced at the base of her neck as her eyes darted from my face to my mouth. "Oh."

"You are special to me. And unique. And I've thought about that kiss every single second since it happened."

She sucked in a breath. "*Oh.*"

I approached her slowly, pushing her stray hairs behind her ears and cupping her face. My heart pounded against my ribcage, and I was desperate to be nearer to her. She was intoxicating. Her skin was so warm and soft, and I trailed my thumbs over her cheeks, loving how she leaned into me. Like she, too, wanted me closer.

"*Theo!*"

I jumped. Penny's voice intruded on the moment, causing my pulse to spike in worry. She had nightmares and sometimes wandered out of bed five, six, seven times. "Fuck, I'm sorry. I want—"

"I know." She cupped my hands and smiled at me. It was pure understanding and a hint of flirty, and she could've asked me for anything, and I'd agree. I loved this smile. It was my favorite one I'd ever seen.

"Take care of your sister."

I kissed her forehead, lingering a beat before leaving her in my room. Maybe things happened for a reason. There was no time to explore this *whatever* between us. Throw in the Quentin angle, and it'd sober me up fast. Yet she wore my clothes, made my siblings laugh, and that shit mattered.

"Should I just go downstairs?"

"Yeah. Penny could be a while." I intertwined our fingers, wishing like hell my life wasn't what it was, and shoved it all down. Penny needed me. "Em can get the movie started. I'll join you when I can."

She nodded. "You are an *amazing* brother."

Her compliment ballooned inside me, filling me with pride and validation that yeah, I was doing the right thing. No one thanked me. My dad didn't even thank me for taking on the role of parent. He expected it because we put family first and made me feel like shit if I didn't.

My mom was the gentle parent, with words of affirmations for all of us all the time. When we lost that, my dad became a ghost, and we wandered around without someone fulfilling our innate need. I tried for my siblings.

And Audrey had just done that for me.

I added it to my mental list of all the reasons I needed to thank her. Maybe a nice dinner would work? It could be a date, but that meant I had to find time. As I grabbed Penny and cradled her to my chest, I made the plan.

Maybe my dad could stay the hell home and be a father.

That meant—I'd have a whole night to myself. A whole night with Audrey.

Excitement buzzed through me. I usually only felt that zapping sensation before a game, right as the puck dropped onto the ice. Yeah. I'd take her somewhere nice to eat. Maybe get dessert after.

It'd totally be a date. But if she didn't want to call it that, then it could just be dinner? Fuck. I hadn't thought about this shit in years. I hummed Pen's favorite nursery rhyme until she settled down and tucked her back in bed. In these moments, with my sister drooling and feeling so safe with me, I knew I'd made the right choice to be here this year. It was hard as fuck, but I'd remember these moments the rest of my life.

I grew up with mom and dad as their best selves. My siblings wouldn't. So, it was only right that I could help provide them with what I had while I was still here. Damn, the thought about leaving next year for Minnesota felt like a knife in the chest. Of course I had to go. This wasn't up for debate. My dad needed the financial help for my mom, and I'd do anything to ease her comfort. But leaving my siblings? Would my dad take care of them? I wasn't sure, and it killed me.

My phone buzzed with a message from an unknown number, and I checked it.

Unknown: The whole team is hanging minus you. Tell me again how they're gonna choose you over me? Fuck that, Sanders. You're over.

Ah. Lovely. Quentin. The thorn in my side who continued to ruin every pleasant moment. Of course I'd been invited to the hangout tonight. I was actually fun and cool.

But my responsibilities held me back, not that Quentin understood what that meant. I stood at the base of the stairs, not quite entering the living room and instead watching. Em and Daniel had pulled out all the stops for Audrey. Em made her our mom's old stove popcorn recipe. Daniel showed her how our Apple TV worked, which, come on. She already knew that.

Audrey gave nothing away. She thanked them and had the best poker face of surprise when they went through ten options for movies. Em sat right by her, Daniel on the other side as they put on Toy Story 4. It was a family fav and would make us all cry. Cool.

Just what I wanted. To cry in front of the girl I had very deep and complicated feelings for. Neat. As my brother rested his head on Audrey's arm, Quentin's text left my mind.

This mattered *more*.

"You two trying to embarrass me in front of a girl?" I said, jumping over the back of the couch so I was in between Em and Audrey. "You know I cry in this one!"

"We didn't do it on purpose, Theo!" Daniel yelled as I tickled his side. That meant putting my arm around Audrey, and yeah, I liked it.

"Yes, you did, you rascal!" I leaned closer onto Audrey to tickle him more, making him howl with laughter. Audrey giggled before intervening.

"Boys, boys, settle down. I'm not a part of this war."

"You are now." I put my other arm around her waist, holding her against me as I messed with my brother. It was honestly fucking perfect. This moment. It hit me hard, like a check to the chest. I wanted more of this.

"I'm a sneaky tickler though. I always win," she challenged. Without warning, she pinched my side, and I yelped, a high-pitched sound that rivaled a chihuahua.

"Oh my God, Theo, that was embarrassing." Em chose to look up from her phone then. Of course.

Audrey snorted and leaned onto me, her deep laughter vibrating against my chest, and the urge to kiss her overwhelmed me. How could this girl think no one would choose her? She was incredible.

"Enough, enough you animals. Daniel needs sleep so we gotta start the movie." It was already eight, so we were pushing it, but I wasn't the parent. My dad could leave his *work* and come home to do something any time he wanted.

Daniel was happy and Em was here, so yeah, this was a fucking win. The movie started, and Daniel settled down. Audrey snuggled next to me, and I about gasped when she rested her head on my shoulder.

I cuddled against her, breathing in her shampoo, and tried not to overthink anything. She wore my clothes, was at my house, and had the softest lips ever. Once the movie was over, I'd ask her out properly.

Only thing—we all fell asleep on the couch.

13

Audrey

I tended to dream in vibrant colors, often waking with my heart racing. Half the time, my dreams were of my dad before he died, chasing me on the beach. We went once when I was twelve, and it was a favorite memory of mine. The other times, it was of a patient I couldn't save.

This morning though... I woke up without a single racing thought or pounding heart. Sheets were cool and pressing against my face. It smelled like fresh linens and musk. A familiar, spicy tingle floated to my nose, and I opened my eyes to be met with an unfamiliar room.

"Where the hell am I?" I bolted up, my pulse speeding now. This wasn't my dorm, and I didn't remember going home with—

"Morning, Auds."

Shit.

Theo.

Theo Sanders.

Theo Sanders in the morning with a raspy, sleepy voice that hit me right in my core with lust. I squeezed my eyes shut, replaying the night before as fast as I could. I couldn't recall anything happening, but why was I in his bed?

At least I wore clothes.

"You sleep okay?"

The voice was distant, like he was on the other side of the room. Peeking one eye open, I found him standing with a pile of blankets and pillows on the floor. "What? Did you... did you sleep on the floor?"

"Yes." He flashed a grin. "You passed out, and I wasn't about to stay in bed with you without your consent." He tossed the blankets and pillows onto his comforter before scratching the back of his neck. "Before you get all riled up, I didn't mind. I'm glad you were relaxed enough to stay here. It means a lot."

"I don't remember going to bed."

"You fell asleep during Toy Story 4, thankfully before the part I cried." He winked and jutted his chin toward a side door. "The bathroom is in there if you need to use it. I don't have an extra toothbrush, but I find using my finger works just fine."

My brain woke up with a jolt, and I played with the hem of his sweatshirt. He gave me his bed while he took the floor. He was a professional hockey player. "Theo, why did you give me your damn bed?"

"Because?" He chuckled. "I feel fine, so don't worry about me."

"Did you carry me up here?"

He nodded, and the tips of his ears reddened. "You drooled a little on me too."

"Shut up." I tossed a pillow at him and wiped the side of my face, feeling for any evidence. "I didn't."

"You're so easy to tease." His grin widened. "You're fucking cute in the morning."

My stomach swooped from his words, and I wanted to bury myself in his comforter forever. I couldn't believe I'd slept in his bed. I hadn't had a sleepover in a decade. Never with a guy. He stared at me with an expectant look, like he was waiting for an answer, and my skin heated with his attention. "Uh, thanks for... the sleep. And the carrying. I can't believe I passed out."

"You were tired." He yawned, then walked toward his bedroom door. "Do you have classes today? I only have one on Friday, but it's in a few hours. I'm happy to drive you to your car whenever you're ready."

His words hit me. *I needed to leave.* "Oh. I'll change into my scrubs now. We can go in five minutes."

The smile fell from his face. "Audrey, you need to stop assuming things when I speak. I'm not rushing you out. Daniel and I agreed to make pancakes for you today when I took him to bed. My intention was that I don't want you missing class or plans because of me."

I chewed my lip. "You don't want me leaving?"

He shook his head and walked toward his bed, his gaze moving along my hairline to my mouth. "Seeing you in my bed, wearing my clothes, is doing something to me, Audrey." He dipped his head and kissed below my ear, then along my jaw to my mouth. "We have a lot to talk about, but I have never watched Toy Story with my family with any girl before. Ever. It's important you know that."

He then kissed a soft, barely there peck against my lips before leaning back. It was a tease, a total way to torture me, and I held my breath as he left the room. His lips were warm and full and perfect, and my insides were a hot mess. A heat spread through me, hot and aggressive and overwhelming. I shifted my weight because the pressure was growing so much it was almost unpleasant. My skin buzzed, and I needed to release this pressure. I had no idea how. But I whimpered, the heat expanding into a desperation.

I'd been horny before. I'd tried masturbating before, but

nothing came of it. I almost had an orgasm once, years ago, but it wasn't fulfilling, and I assumed orgasming just wasn't meant for me. It didn't bother me because I wasn't in a relationship. I figured I'd cross that bridge when I got there, but right now, I couldn't breathe with the heat spreading through me, lighting my veins on fire.

Theo had kissed me.

Twice.

Shit.

I leaned back onto the bed and slid my hands down his shorts. Moisture pooled between my thighs, and I shuddered at the feeling when I touched myself. It had never been like this. This desperate, fiery feeling.

"Hey, Auds." Theo returned, opening the door just as I bit down on my lip.

My world shattered.

His bed needed to sink into the floor and consume me. I removed my hand, my fingers wet from touching myself, and he picked up on what I was doing immediately.

His nostrils flared as he shut his door and leaned against it, wearing the most serious expression I had ever seen.

Time stopped. The creaking floor and the chirping birds faded into the distance as the only sound was my rapid heartbeat.

"Do you need help?"

Holy shit. My eyes almost rolled to the back of my head at his question. A growl escaped from my chest as the pounding need consumed me again. I squirmed on his bed, my brain battling this heat. This was a terrible idea, yet I needed it.

"I don't know. I've never really..." I trailed off, sucking in a breath when he bit his bottom lip and groaned.

"You've never what?"

"Orgasmed." Shame consumed me, a dull prickle attacking

my skin as I had to look away from him. It was embarrassing. It wasn't that I hadn't tried, but it just didn't work. He had to think I was pathetic.

"Oh, Audrey." He chuckled and walked toward the end of the bed, his eyes darkening with lust. His voice dropped an octave, all gravely and sexy. His gaze trailed from my face to my neck, then landed between my thighs. "I'd like to help you if you let me."

"I'm a virgin!" I blurted out, laying it all on the table. If he didn't think I was so out of his league, he would now. Maybe this was good. We could end this before it became anything because our relationship was complicated as hell.

But instead of recoiling or laughing or leaving, he shrugged. "That's fine, but honey, I meant talking you through one."

"T-talking?"

He nodded, and a pleased glint crossed his eyes. "I've barely kissed you and have yet to take you on a date. Even though I'm dying to touch you, I haven't earned the right yet."

I swallowed. He was being a gentleman, yet I wanted him to grab my legs and touch me. Help me out of my head. "So you're gonna stand there and..."

"Coach you. Tell you what to do." He licked the side of his lip again. "Fuck, this is a fantasy right now, Auds. I hope you know that."

"This? Helping me orgasm because I never have?"

He nodded. "You're in my bed, in my clothes, and you touched yourself. So yes. Now, are you comfortable taking off your shorts, or do you want to leave them on?"

"Uh." My face flamed. The doubts swirled. "I'm not... I don't know if I can do this."

"Do you trust me?"

Wasn't that a loaded question. I nodded, instantly. I totally trusted Theo, for better or worse, and that caused a weird pang deep in my chest. I didn't trust many people. It was too hard and painful, but with him, it was easy.

"Good girl." He flashed a grin and reached out to caress my calf. It was a featherlight touch, and I shuddered. "Reach between your thighs for me."

The absolute intensity of his face had me forgetting that I was embarrassed, that Theo Sanders watched me slide my fingers into the waistband and over my swollen pussy. My clit throbbed, and my core tensed from the proximity of pleasure. Already, this experience felt different than any other time before.

Hope burst through me. Would this be my first orgasm?

Theo took a shaky breath as he kneaded both calf muscles. "Mm, this is so fucking hot I can't even focus. Are you wet?"

I nodded.

He closed his eyes and groaned. "Have you fingered yourself before?"

"I've tried."

"Do it again. Insert one finger, nice and slow, then another. Find a pattern and then curl the ends of your fingers."

I did as he said, the warm walls of my vagina convulsing as I panted. Every sensation was in overdrive. The feel of his clothes and sheets against my skin was soft, a gentle caress. The smell of his sheets. The way his chest moved up and down as he too breathed heavily. The way his finger pads had little callouses on them, teasing the skin behind my knee as he watched me.

"Oh, shit." I arched off the bed a little bit.

"What are you feeling?"

"Heat. Just, everywhere." My voice was a whisper. "Theo—"

"Fuck, you saying my name..." He swallowed. "I'm as hard as a rock."

A thrill went through me. I turned him on. The heat

increased as I thrust my fingers into myself, and a rumble left Theo's chest.

"Touch your clit for me. Swirl it, then pinch it. Repeat it over and over." He stopped caressing my legs and gripped the bed, almost like he was barely holding on.

"It feels so good, Theo." I closed my eyes as sensations overwhelmed me. The pressure of my swollen nerve sent blasts of pleasure through me. "I'm c-close."

"Can I see you, please, baby?" His face contorted, like he was in pain. "I won't touch, I promise."

How could I say no? Maybe it was the hormones or endorphins, but I nodded.

He gripped the sides of the shorts and tugged them down, then did the same with my underwear. "Fuuuuck me."

His mouth hung open as the pupils dilated, and I lost it. I massaged my clit as a fire flooded my veins. First, my thighs clenched, and my lower back arched off the bed. I kept my rhythm as I forgot how to breathe. It was unlike anything I'd ever experienced. Colors burst from my eyes as I moaned so loud it hurt my throat. My fingers tingled with pleasure, my toes curling as I experienced my first orgasm.

I didn't know if it lasted a few seconds or a day, but when the pleasure left, I remained there, hands between my thighs as my pulse pounded in my ears. I was a noodle. Limp. Useless.

Something soft touched my calf, and Theo's thick hair was there. *He kissed my leg.* That was so intimate, so precious, my eyes prickled. *Theo watched me orgasm.* Holy shit.

"You are so fucking beautiful." He met my gaze, his still brimming with lust. "That was incredible. Thank you for letting me watch."

I nodded, my face flushing with awareness. My legs were wide open, naked, and Theo still stood there, studying me. I closed them, still in disbelief that that just happened.

"Do you need anything? Another one?" He winked.

Damn. Theo winking was dangerous. I giggled, and his smile only grew. "Another? No way."

"Hm, I beg to differ, but that can be another night." He adjusted himself in his sweatpants, and I gasped at his hard length. He cleared his throat and pointed to the shower. "I'm gonna take an ice-cold shower and get rid of this. You want to head downstairs?"

"Are you gonna jack off?"

His eyebrows disappeared into his hairline as he pursed his lips. "You know, Audrey, I just might."

The heat returned, the engulfing, pounding itch that started this whole thing. My core clenched, and I swallowed, seeing if it would go away. It didn't. Theo must've sensed it because he licked the side of his lip. This gesture would kill me. It was just so hot and simple it turned me on. "Uh, can you do it... out here?"

"You want to watch me?"

I nodded. "If that's okay?"

"Definitely okay." He moved toward a chair in the corner, a good ten feet away from me. He adjusted it closer to the bed as he breathed hard. "What do you want to see?"

"You."

His eyes flashed with pleasure as he let out a contented hum. He liked my answer. "I can't wait to take you on a date and do this the right way."

"There's no right way," I corrected. "Nothing about us makes sense."

"I'll argue about that comment later, but right now I need to stroke myself. You're still sitting in my bed with your pretty pussy wet." He took out his cock and stroked, and I froze.

Theo's forearm was thick with muscles, the cords rippling as he pumped his large and erect penis. I'd seen them for medical reasons but never like this. Holy shit. I moaned as I had to touch my clit again. It throbbed. It burned. I overheated as Theo spat into his hand and continued stroking.

"Oh my," I moaned.

"You like watching me?'"

I nodded as I swirled my clit again. "I can't breathe. It's so hot. You're so sexy, Theo. I can't even think."

"Mm, open your legs my way, baby. I want to see you while I come."

I shuddered. The full-body trembles had me thrashing on the bed as my second orgasm hit me hard. "Theo!" I forgot I was at his house, in his bed, and I just floated. The ecstasy exploded at the base of my spine, shooting in every direction as tears entered my eyes. It felt so good. Amazing.

"Yes, baby, god, you're so hot."

I opened my eyes at Theo's deep, commanding voice. He stroked faster, harder as he stared at me. He was mesmerizing. He stroked once more, tugged on his balls, and let out the sexiest, growly moan as he came into his hand. "Fuck, yes, Audrey," he whispered, his gaze never leaving mine.

When he finished, his eyes were lighter and filled with joy. "Damn. That was incredible. How are you feeling?"

He took off his shirt and wiped himself up before standing in front of me shirtless. I wanted to drag my fingers over his chest and abdomen, study every crevice of his body. I could write a thesis on how perfect his body was. "Uh..." I trailed off as he neared me.

He smiled as he bent down and kissed the side of my mouth. "A couple of things before I go shower. First, you are so fucking sexy it's distracting. Second, I don't do this with anyone. Just you. Don't let any other thought cross your mind about that. Third, we'll do this again, and I'll work my way up to touching you. Fourth—"

"This is a long list," I blurted out.

He snorted. "Lastly, can I please take you on a date this Saturday night? I want to treat you for being so fucking helpful with my family, but also, I want to spend time with you."

"Oh."

I experienced my first orgasm with him, two of them actually, yet the thought of being asked out on a date had me blushing. I had plans to study Saturday, but a date with Theo? The guy who reassured my worries before I could even state them? "Yeah, that sounds nice."

"I'm gonna kiss the hell out of you then. Prepare yourself." He kissed my jaw before heading toward his bathroom. "I'll drop you off after we eat, and I'm really sorry about this, but I have plans all afternoon with the team, so we can't hang out."

"That's okay."

"I know it is." He paused at the door, his face serious. "But I'd rather spend every free moment I have with you."

My stomach fluttered and swooped from his statement. Goose bumps spread on my arms from how much that comment meant to me. He wanted to spend all that time with *me*, the girl who was never chosen first. Holy shit.

He shut the door, leaving me with a thousand thoughts. Most pleasant, some not. Was there a rule book about going on a date with the guy your brother hated more than life? What about the fact we'd just watched each other do dirty things? I didn't know what was right, but the full-fledged excitement that hit me when he asked for a date was a sign.

We'd go on the date and figure out what we meant later.

14

Theo

What annoyed me was the fact that things went super well with the team yesterday, and it made me feel like something bad was gonna happen. My life proved the pattern of *oh things are going well* would immediately be followed with *let's fuck up his life.*

The team worked out yesterday, and five of the guys and I headed out after to talk shit. There wasn't any weirdness at all. They wanted to hear about the draft experience, what playing at Indiana was like, and then we ate pizza and watched Friday night football. Easy. Simple. Even one of Quentin's sidekicks showed up and wasn't a dick.

Reiner wanted an update on Quentin the following week, and while I didn't have one, I chose to focus on the other Hawthorne consuming my life. Audrey fucking Hawthorne. The most brilliant, wonderful, and sexy woman ever. I planned our whole date after working out the stuff at home, and Em even commented on my outfit saying I dripped of rizz.

My siblings loved her, and that solidified that all my feelings were right. I wore black slacks and a dark gray shirt buttoned up and put on my favorite watch. It belonged to my grandpa and made me feel like a million bucks. I wanted to look good for Audrey. I knew my looks, and I was thankful for genes, but a compliment from her meant so much more. It was wild how much I valued her opinion and thoughts. Like, this woman had hated me a few weeks ago.

I chuckled, pulling up to park outside her dorm when the thought hit me. Her and I were probably a not great idea. *Should we even do this?* I didn't have a lot of time, and there was the complicated matter of her brother always lingering over us.

Before my mom's stroke, I used to do pro and con lists with her, but now I stopped focusing on the cons all together. Life was too short. I could be injured tomorrow and never play hockey again, and the first thing I'd do? Beg Audrey to date me. So yeah. If hockey and Quentin were the only reasons holding me back, that was fucking stupid.

I parked and hopped out of truck just as Audrey waltzed from the dorm doors like she'd been waiting for me.

Any doubt vanished. Audrey gave me a shy, half-smile that hit me right in the chest as I admired every part of her. She wore her auburn hair down in waves, and her hair landed just above her breasts. Some dangly earrings shined in the light, and her lips were redder than normal. Damn. Those lips looked kissable as hell.

Her dress was a deep red, almost like blood, and it clung to her body, and *fuck*. The deep v in the front showed her ample cleavage. Flashes of her lacy bra entered my mind, along with the way her pussy had looked all spread on my bed. Shit. I didn't want to lead with my dick tonight. I planned to gain her trust. She was a virgin, and while a part of me, annoyingly, liked the thought of being the first one to show her how to fuck, she deserved more. I wanted her comfortable and safe.

"It's too much, isn't it?" She winced, and I felt like an idiot.

"No Auds, you look *stunning*."

A pretty pink blush danced on her face as I finally woke from my trance and ran up to her. I took her hand and kissed the back of it. Her pulse raced at her wrist. "Are you nervous?"

"Very."

She smelled delicious, and now that I stood closer to her, there was a mole right on her left breast that I desperately needed to touch. But that would come later. I had to hold it together until then. "What are you nervous about?"

I guided her toward my truck and helped her in, about groaning into my fist at the back of the dress. News flash. There was no back. Her entire back was exposed, and the dress hung just above her butt. It was so fucking sexy and so unlike anything I had seen Audrey in that it made me wonder if she'd bought it just for me.

Fuck, I wanted that.

So, was she wearing a bra? She couldn't be? *Not the time.*

"This seems so surreal with you. I like you, Theo, but I don't go on dates. I haven't... ever, really. One year, I went to a school dance with my friends and their dates, but never... me."

Again. Her comments punched me in the chest, and I wanted to give her the best date of all time. "Well, it's an honor I get to take you on your first one."

"You're getting lots of my firsts, Sanders."

"Oh, I'm aware and fucking love it." I winked as I started the car, and she blushed like I wanted her to. "Nervous because you don't know what to expect?"

"I've seen movies, so I know we're gonna eat dinner and talk."

"Sure, but you said you trust me." I put on the radio to some classic rock station and pulled onto the road. She crossed one leg over the other, and the slit showed her entire leg. "That's it, I

have to ask. Did you own this dress before, or did you buy it
for me?"

"I bought it for you."

A deep, satisfied rumble left my chest. "I fucking love it."

"I don't wear things like this usually, but I wanted to look
nice tonight."

"You buy sexy bras, Hawthorne, so you do like buying
naughty things sometimes. And this dress? Naughty. I want to be
kind and a gentleman, I really fucking do, but I can't stop staring
at all your skin."

"That was the point, Sanders."

Oh. I liked that snappy little comeback. Reaching over, I
gripped her knee and squeezed for a few seconds. "I really like
you too, Auds. This is gonna be a great night."

AUDREY WORE a half smile the entire dinner. It was so different
than her serious, no-nonsense expression I was used to. Her eyes
sparkled as she glanced around the restaurant, her glee evident.
She kept twisting a lock of her hair before meeting my eyes,
blushing, then repeating the process.

If I wasn't charmed before, I would be now.

"Tell me what you're thinking." I nudged her knee with mine
under the table. We both ate our side salads, and our main
entrees were on the way. She'd ordered a white wine, and I'd
opted for water. I was driving, plus, I tended not to drink much
to prepare for the season.

"This is wonderful." She scrunched her nose, and a giggle
escaped her mouth. "Everything smells so good, and the people-
watching! I've heard others talk about how they love watching
others and guessing their story, but I never understood it until
now. Like, the couple in the back who can't keep their hands off

each other. Or the family a few tables to the left. Are they celebrating?"

"What do you think they'll say about us then?" I reached across the table and ran my fingers over her palm. "That we're on our first date and that I'm counting down the seconds until I can kiss you afterwards?"

She pressed her lips together and rubbed them before her eyes lit up. "No. That we're estranged lovers who spent a year apart. We're different people, so we're deciding if we want to date again."

I shook my head. "Of course we do."

"Okay, hm, what if we're stepsiblings who fell in love? That's taboo."

"Audrey Hawthorne." I grinned. "Scandalous."

She laughed, the sound becoming familiar to me, and relaxed more into her seat. "I *am* funny sometimes. No one knows that about me though."

"Mm, what else don't people know about you?" I wanted all her secrets to myself. Call it irrational or weird or protective or obsessed, but after hearing her orgasm for the first time, I wanted to know everything. Even if it was a tiny, silly confession.

"This might not surprise you, but I'm a homebody and shy. I don't do things like this." She waved her hand around the restaurant. "My ideal Saturday night is a book and watching a show in my bed."

"I know you mentioned you haven't dated before. Did you ever see anyone in high school?"

She shook her head. "I kissed someone sophomore year, but he was popular, and I wasn't. I'm quiet, introverted. I don't need to be at parties or have everyone stare at me. Attention from others isn't what I crave. Then, well, someone was always sick in our family."

"What do you mean?" She'd mentioned her dad passing, but

this sounded serious. I continued running circles on her palm with my finger. Whenever I stopped, even for a second, her eyebrows pinched together. She might not tell me she liked it, but her body reacted like she did.

"My dad battled his sickness for a decade, and most of my childhood was going to visit him in the hospital or watching my brother. My mom dedicated her life to helping him, but then she lost her parents and her sister all within five years. Grief and illness follow our family. So, it never made sense to grow attached to anything because well..." She shrugged, and a dark, grief-filled look crossed her face.

Because well what?

"Anytime I found a groove and tried something, someone would get sick. Nursing and helping others are the only things that've been a constant with in my life." She swallowed and glanced around the room, her gaze hesitant and her posture rigid.

An aggressive, overwhelming urge to protect her grew in my gut. I didn't have the time or the energy to add Audrey into my circle of people who I cared for and would do anything for, but she was there, wedged next to my siblings. Her attention landed back on me, and one side of her mouth curved up.

That gesture had my throat tightening with emotion. "Thank you for sharing all that."

"You're so easy to talk to." She chewed her lip, red painting her cheeks, when her eyes widened at something over my shoulder.

"No." She gasped and ripped her hand away from mine. "Who is...what...I can't..." She pushed from the chair before I had a chance to stop her.

"Audrey, what's happening?" I craned my neck to search behind me, but no bad guy or person stood out. The momentary bliss of her opening up was shattered as I snapped my attention back to her, but she was gone. What the fuck?

My pulse raced as my gut churned. Who had spooked her this much? Who or what caused her to leave mid-sentence, without a word? It wasn't me. I was confident about that, but where had she gone?

She left her damn phone on the table, so if she was making a run for it, it wasn't great she forgot this. I pocketed hers, annoyed now I couldn't call or text her to see where she went. The entrance was the opposite way, so maybe she was in the restroom? Back hallway?

Would she leave the restaurant entirely?

Fuck.

My jaw tensed as annoyance worked its way to my muscles. She needed to be safe, and leaving in that fucking dress, without her phone, wasn't the best decision. My senses went into hyper-drive as I checked the two restrooms. Nothing in there.

Nothing in the back hallway.

All there was left to check was the patio which—shit. She totally went through there. I swore I could smell her lingering perfume as I pushed the door open and spied the side gate still open. We were miles away from her dorm. The gate creaked with a high-pitched squeak as the humid air filled my lungs, and there she was.

Audrey sat on the ground, her back to the restaurant brick wall, with her arms wrapped around her knees. Her hair hung around her, hiding her face, but she shook. Almost like she was...

A sob escaped, and my heart shattered.

"Audrey, honey." I crouched and placed a hand on her shoulder. Her skin was sweaty and cold, despite the heat. "What do you need?"

"Can we leave?"

"Of course." I slid my hand down her back, her smooth skin covered in specks of gravel. "Can I help you up?"

"This is so embarrassing, Theo. I'm not sure I can look at you." She sniffed and faced the other way when she stood without my assistance. "Can I just call an Uber or something and we pretend this didn't happen?"

"Not a chance." I brushed the rest of the rocks off her back and butt, the little pieces clinging to the silky material. A rush of heat hit me as I stared at her very curvy, very perfect ass, but that didn't matter at all. "Let me walk you to my car and then I'll settle the bill."

"God, our dinner! I ruined it. I ruined my first date." She sniffed again, and I said to hell with this.

I placed my hands on her shoulders, spinning her around so she faced me. Her scrunched nose and red cheeks were so damn cute. Even as her mascara formed dark circles around each eye, she was so pretty. "Audrey, the date isn't over. You haven't ruined anything."

Her bottom lip trembled as she took a shaky breath. "I'm sorry, Theo. Maybe this isn't—"

"If you say we shouldn't do this, I'm going to hard disagree. You're upset. Something happened, and when you're ready to tell me, I'll listen, but you and me? We fit."

"My brother is in there." She closed her eyes and hung her head. "With a girl I've never seen and... my m-mom. I haven't seen my mom in months, and she's here? She doesn't have money! And she's with Quentin? Without... telling me? I can't..." Another sob escaped, and I yanked her to my chest.

I wrapped her arms around me before squeezing her. I read once that when we hug, we receive endorphins that help our immune system, but you needed to feel the other person's heartbeat. So that was what I planned to do. I wanted to give Audrey all my heartbeats, to help give her strength when she needed it. Her head rested against my chest, and I rested my chin on top of her head, cocooning her for a few moments of peace.

It was easier focusing on her rather than Quentin. I hated that dude. And her mom not telling her she was in town? Something about money? A family dinner without inviting the one who'd held the whole family together for years? It wasn't fucking right, and I was furious. It was bullshit. How dare they do that to her? The sweetest, most selfless woman I had ever met? Yeah. I'd do whatever I could to cheer her up and help her forget what she saw.

And, hopefully not run into the Hawthornes on my way out. There was no way to know what I'd say to them, but it wouldn't be good for any of us.

"You're okay, honey, I got you." I rubbed my hands up and down her spine, breathing her in. She smelled delicious and felt so good in my arms. So soft and sexy and strong. "You're amazing, okay? Fuck your family. Fuck them for not telling you about this."

She snorted, which was a great sign. "I'm getting mascara on your shirt."

"Fuck my shirt."

"Is that gonna be your response to everything?"

"Probably." I fought a smile and squeezed her extra tight for a beat. Then, I cupped her face and stared at her, hoping she understood how serious I was. "I'm going to grab our food to go, then we're going to find the best place on campus to eat it, and we're gonna have the best night."

"Even if I cry?"

"Even if you cry." I wiped her tears with my thumbs, doing my damndest to not kiss her. Her lips were so full and wet from her tears, and I wanted to taste them. Kiss the sadness straight out of her. "Now, let me get you into my car. Then we can go."

She nodded and leaned into my hands. "Thank you. I don't deserve this from you, but it's really appreciated."

"Don't deserve this?" I ran a finger over her lip, giving in to my wild urge to kiss her. It was a form of torture. "Audrey, you have helped me out numerous times when I desperately needed it. You helped me with my sister after she freaked out. You're so fucking kind and thoughtful, so yeah, this is the least I can do. Be there for you when you're sad and upset. This isn't a burden on me at all. I'm glad you feel safe enough to tell me what's going on."

Her eyes welled up, and she sighed, her breath tickling my face. "You make it hard to not fall for you when you say things like that."

"Stop trying not to. I'm very fall-able."

Her famous snort returned, and I grinned. "There's my favorite girl."

She blushed and stood on her tiptoes, her hands reaching out to cup my face. We looked ridiculous, each cupping each other's faces, but I about gasped when she leaned up and pressed her perfect lips against mine in a quick peck. It lit me up and made me feel like I could fly. Her touching me first was a huge win and show of trust. "Thank you, Theo. You are one of a kind."

She released her grip, and we walked toward my truck, but my lips still tingled. Her act of kissing me might've been innocent, but it was huge that she took that first step. I felt like I could walk on water.

Earning affection was Audrey was becoming an addiction, and I'd spend the rest of the night earning it. Because any doubts I had earlier disappeared. I wanted this woman and would prove to her we could work.

15

Audrey

The embarrassment lingered, even if Theo had said all the right things to appease me. Sniffles kept returning if I let myself think about the fact Quentin, some girl, and my mom had made plans to have dinner and never once thought to tell me or ask me. She asked for money yesterday. Was the money I worked my butt off for used for dinner with Quentin and some girl? Hell, if my mom said she wanted to take us out to dinner as a family, I would've gladly paid for it.

I would've loved that. I missed our family dinners so much. We used to have them every Sunday before our dad got sick, and we hadn't had one since he died.

The absolute betrayal felt like a knife to the stomach. I did so much for both of them all the time. Bills, using my own money, my time getting Quentin to places so my mom could rest... all of it for what? My family to forget me? To use me like a bank?

I rested my head against the window just as Theo opened his door holding to-go boxes. This man...he was too good to be true, and I knew it. This wouldn't last, but to have his attention and care on me was unlike anything I had ever experienced. The dinner smelled amazing, and I didn't have to pretend to smile. "Thank you for doing this. Seriously."

"Of course." He set the boxes down by my feet and started the truck. "You'll be proud to know that I did not, in fact, punch your brother or say anything to your mom. I walked by them, ignored Quentin's jab, and walked straight to you."

"Quentin's jab?"

"Auds, do not ask me to talk about your brother." He pulled onto the main street and shot me a look. "So, where do you want to go?"

"Is it bad I just want to go to my dorm?"

"Not at all. To your dorm, it is."

It wasn't a far drive, and Theo spoke about nonsense but was still entertaining. He moved the conversation away from heavy things like my family or hockey or his mom, so the drive felt like two minutes before we were walking toward my dorm with carryout boxes.

"Have you ever had a date like this before? Dressed like a model but about to eat on a ten-dollar carpet from Walmart?"

"I can't say I have, but that doesn't mean this isn't awesome." He held the door for me as I opened the main doors and led us to my room. I got my key and let us in, suddenly aware how small my dorm was.

Last time he was here, he saw me in my bra.

Last time I was near a bed, he watched me experience my first orgasm.

My skin prickled with heat and excitement as Theo took off his jacket, undid the top button of his shirt, and rolled up his sleeves. The movement was hot. Distracting. My thighs rubbed together, and my lips parted as his thick forearm muscles bulged with every movement. Everything about Theo was so sexy to me, which was dangerous.

Nothing in my life lasted, so I knew this wouldn't, but that harsh reality didn't prevent me from enjoying him, from dreaming about another life with him.

"You okay?" he asked, his brows furrowed.

"Oh. Yeah. You're just... hot."

He grinned wide. "Oh. I mistook your face for worry, but you were checking me out?"

I nodded, and he swiped his tongue over the side of his mouth. His gaze moved from face to my collarbone, over my chest and down to the slit of my leg. "You're fucking stunning. Doesn't matter if we're in a dorm, outside, or in a fancy restaurant, you look perfect."

My breathing grew heavier as I fought a blush. The same overwhelming and distracting heat rattled through my core. It was almost uncomfortable how hot and tight my body was, desperate for a release now that it knew the feeling. I swallowed and stared at Theo's chest, the small portion that was exposed.

"You hungry? Want to eat?" Theo asked, his voice huskier than normal.

"I'm not hungry for our food." I didn't mean to say that. It was so forward of me, and I wasn't forward. I had no experience to practice. But I wasn't lying. The thought of eating food was the furthest from my mind. I wanted to ease this heat, to forget about the restaurant, and enjoy the limited time I had with Theo. Because it was temporary. I was fully, totally aware of that.

"Do you mean dessert? Cause, Auds, the way you're looking at me right now... I want to be a gentleman with you." He moved the boxes of food to my desk and faced me, his hands in his pockets and one leg crossed over the other.

This man was dangerously attractive.

"I want to feel you." My voice came out just above a whisper.

"Fuck." He ran a hand over his face. "I had this whole plan with you, you know? I was gonna take you for a walk after dinner, look at stars, then ask to kiss you slowly. It was gonna be romantic as hell."

"Sounds like it would've been, yeah. Well done." I stepped toward him, and he did the same. My room was too small for the both of us, and I was thankful when Theo's one step brought him to me.

"All I've thought about is kissing you, but I really would be a dick if I didn't offer to talk. Do you want to talk about what happened tonight, why it hurt? It would feel good to get it off your chest, and I'm a great listener. I'll keep my hands to myself the entire time. I'll offer my shoulder to cry on."

I shook my head, letting my gaze take all of Theo Sanders in. He was better to look at, to think about than what happened. I knew why tonight transpired as it did, even though the reality of it killed me. It was like a breakup with people who I loved. That tether snapped. I'd worry about it tomorrow, preferred that actually. I had this gorgeous man standing in my dorm room, looking like sin and orgasms, and I was the new Audrey. This Audrey asked for wild things. She voiced what she wanted instead of being in the background. The new Audrey would've confronted her only two living family members and demanded an explanation instead of hiding out back in pure agony.

I liked this newer version of myself.

It was thrilling.

"Kiss me, Theo, please."

"Mm." He smiled and ran his fingers over the slit of my dress, teasing the fabric and causing goose bumps to explode all over my body. He ran one finger up my side, teasing the side of my breast, before grabbing my chin and tilting my face up. "Be more specific, baby, because there's a lot of places I want to kiss right now."

"Oh my." I panted as Theo gently grabbed my hip and walked us back to my bed. He nudged me onto my back, his face right over mine, before he kissed my jawline. My eyes about fluttered to the back of my head. "Oh, wow."

"I'm just kissing your neck right now. Is this what you meant?"

I clutched at his sides, needing to grab something to prevent myself from thrashing around. My nipples were so tight from the fabric continually brushing over them. Theo's thick torso felt like a brick, all toned muscles, and I wanted to bite into him. "More," I begged, not quite sure for what.

He sucked one earlobe into his mouth, and my hips arched off the bed. The wetness from his tongue, the slight sting from his teeth, holy shit. Moisture pooled between my legs, and I needed him to touch me there, or I'd burst into flames. It was just true facts.

"Or did you mean right there?" He kissed my collarbone, sucking the skin a beat before dropping lower to the center of my chest. "You have this mole right here." He licked the upper part of my left breast. "I'm obsessed with it. I've stared at it every time you weren't looking. Fuck, baby, your tits are driving me wild. Can I feel or kiss them?"

"Kiss?" I foolishly said, my mind not quite working right. The feel of his hard body on top of mine combined with his cologne and kissing my neck, and I was overheated. A mere whisper of his lips on me sent me into hyperdrive.

He lowered onto his knees and cupped my breasts with both hands. "Fuuuuck, baby." He pushed them together before dropping his head and licking between them. "You're a dream. I'm such a tit man, Audrey, and yours are... fuck... I'm gonna be obsessed with them. They feel amazing. Can I see them before I taste?"

"See?" Okay, I had to stop repeating his words like a question, but did he want me to take off my whole dress? I wasn't... "See them?"

His blue eyes were simmering with lust, and he audibly swallowed before asking, "Do I have your permission?"

Did he? Of course, he did. He made me feel like nothing else mattered, and it was addicting. "Yes, Theo."

He growled in approval. Without undoing any part of my dress, he took my breasts out of the dress so they were right there, in his face. My hard nipples were an inch from his mouth as Theo stared with a slack jaw.

His pupils were dilated, his lips wet as he met my gaze for a beat. "Fucking perfect. Tell me what feels good, okay? Do you like this?"

He pinched each nipple lightly, and I let out a very unattractive groan. Chuckling, he did it again. "As I learn your body, I want concrete answers, alright? Your body might react to my touch, but that doesn't mean you like it. So please be direct."

"I like it." I clutched the sheets this time, his hair and chest too far away. He kept pinching and tickling my nipples, and the heat worsened. "I'm... it's..."

Then he placed his warm mouth over the bud and sucked and *holy shit*. I bucked off the bed. "Theo!"

"Mm, yeah, you like this." He switched between both, sucking lightly, then hard as he continually kneaded the other. Every touch sent a hurricane of sensations to my core, and it wasn't humanly possible to experience pleasure this fast.

"I'm... I'm..."

"What about this?" He released a nipple and blew his breath over the tip, the contrasting cold to the warmth of his mouth causing trembles throughout my body. "Or this?"

He swirled his tongue around my areola and flicked the beaded point, and heat exploded like a bolt of lightning from my nipples to my pussy. It was like there was an electric current threading between them, and my breath caught in my throat.

"Mm, are you close to coming?" He stared at me with a hint

of a smile, his eyes wild and a few shades darker than I was used to. "I really want to watch you fall apart again."

"I think so," I whined, grinding my hips against the air in a desperate attempt to feel something. "I just need..." I begged, gripping the sheets so hard they came off the bed.

He hummed against my breasts before leaning back to a crouch. His hands landed on the tops of my thighs. "Do you need me to help you?"

"Y-yes." The fire was roaring, but the anticipation of orgasming again was painful. It was close, yet not there. The few times I had tried in the past ended like this. "Touch me, Theo. I beg you."

A low, satisfied rumble escaped his chest as he slid my dress up to my hips. He breathed in deep before grazing his thumb over my panties. The slight pressure was enough for me to arch up again, my pussy a magnet pulled in by him. "Audrey Hawthorne begging me. Never thought I'd see this, but damn, I am a huge fan."

"Shut up," I said, snorting before it turned into a moan. He moved the fabric to the side so my pussy was bare to him. Nothing between us now. He slid his fingers through my wet lips, lingering on my clit as I slammed my head onto the bed. "No one... no one has ever touched me there before."

"Fuck, Audrey." He rested his forehead on my thigh and groaned. "You have no idea what those words do to me. That I'm the only one who gets to see your pretty pussy like this, dripping and waiting for me."

I shuddered. "Oh my god."

"Do you like this?" He swirled his thumb on my clit in a pattern, slow and consistent as the pressure built. Sweat beaded all along my body, and when Theo bit into my thigh, I came apart.

"*Theo! Yes, oh my god!*" Words flew out of my mouth, none of them making sense as I had the most explosive orgasm of my life. Heat blasted from my pussy to every limb, a magical prickle of pleasure hitting every nerve ending in my body. I forgot to breathe the pleasure was so strong, so after thirty seconds of bliss, I gasped for air.

"Breathe, baby. Breathe for me."

His breath hit my face, and amusement laced his tone as I panted like I'd run a mile. The first few breaths helped me settle and gave me enough strength to open my eyes. Theo sat next to me on the bed, wearing a huge grin as he stared at me.

"You are exquisite."

"Stop." My face flooded with heat. "No, I'm not."

"You are. You thrashed around the bed like a beautiful maniac. Your hair is everywhere, and I swear I can smell your arousal."

"Theo, Jesus." I snorted.

"No, it's insanely hot. I'm debating if I should I lick my fingers right now or not."

"Oh my god." I covered my face with my hands. "You're so *crass.*"

"Nah, horny as hell around you." Using his other hand, he brushed my hair off my face and removed my fingers covering my eyes. "I seemed to have messed up yet again."

"What?" I frowned. He had to leave. He had to go. He realized I was a dead end. I knew it would happen, but I didn't think it would happen right now. "You have to go. I get it."

He recoiled like I slapped him. "What? No. *No.* Why would you... Audrey." He chuckled, but there was a little annoyance to it. "I love being around you. I don't want to leave."

"Oh." My throat tightened with emotion. I felt silly for thinking he had to leave. Well, silly for voicing it. The thought wasn't out of line. "I don't want you to leave either."

"Good, cause I'm not." He grinned, this time kindness radiating from him. "I meant I messed up because I never got to kiss you how I planned."

My nostrils flared as he cupped my face and stared at me like... like I mattered. He cared for me, sure, but the intensity of his eyes had no business giving me asinine thoughts like this.

He licked his lips and closed the distance between our mouths and then Theo kissed me. It was soft at first, his lips soft and wet and warm against mine. He tasted like mint, and it made my mouth tingle.

"Mm," he groaned, cupping the back of my head as he moved to straddle me. I'd never, ever in my life, had someone straddle me with their body before, and oh shit.

I liked it. I liked his weight on me, the heat and hardness of his body. "Can, can I touch you too?" I asked between kisses.

"Baby, you can do whatever you want to me." He played with my hair and tilted my neck back, deepening our kiss as he slid his tongue into my mouth. The minty tingles exploded around my tongue, and the taste, the smell, and the feel of him were too much.

He was *perfect.*

I never wanted to forget this moment, being the subject of his attention as he kissed me hard, then soft. Delicate, then firm. My vision danced with black spots when he pulled back and frowned. "Auds, breathe, baby."

I gasped a second time that night. His eyes were heated but also worried as I took a few more breaths. "This is embarrassing."

"Do you struggle with breathing? Is there something I should know, so I don't... cause it?" An adorable wrinkle formed between his strong brows.

"No." I fanned my face, refusing to look at him. "That kiss... it was nice. Made me forget to breathe."

"Nice? Nah." He pulled me up, so we were chest to chest, and he forced me to look at him. "It was fucking amazing. I need more."

He kissed me again, nipping at my lip before he sucked the bottom one into his mouth. I had no idea how sensual a kiss could be, but after a few minutes of making out, I was on fire again. My lips hurt and stung from all the attention, but I didn't care. I'd missed so many moments like this because of life, so I was gonna soak this all up while I could.

"I love kissing you," I whispered, hating that I admitted something so dorky. "You probably kissed so many people but this—"

"Never you though." He kissed me again and hoisted me up onto his lap. "It feels different when you're kissing someone who knows the real you."

"And I... know the real you?" I asked, tense and aware that his hard erection dug into my ass as I sat on him.

He nodded and smiled; this time it was a gentle one. One that spoke of inside jokes. "You've met my family. You know my secrets. You've seen me freak out and knew how to help. So yes, honey, you know the real me. Don't think for one second that you aren't special to me, okay?"

I nodded but couldn't respond. With us intertwined like this, with the look in his eyes and the way he took care of me, it gave me a glimmer of hope that we could do this. In the short time we'd known each other, he'd changed my life, and I wanted to selfishly hold onto this feeling of bliss. Even if I knew it was temporary, I'd take whatever Theo could give me. I sure as hell knew I'd never meet anyone like him again.

16

Theo

Audrey looked at me like I had one foot out of the door already. She said the right things, but it was her damn eyes. They gave her away. She might not know, but she had the most beautiful, large expressive green eyes I had ever seen. They lit up when she was excited, widened when she was learning, and avoided anyone else's gaze if she was embarrassed or lying.

I hated that she assumed I wanted to leave. The woman didn't understand my obsession with her, but I could work on that slowly. Her lips were still red from kissing, and it took a lot of effort to pull back and not devour her whole. She had one orgasm, which had taken her mind off dinner and put her more at ease.

I wasn't gonna push her past her comfort zone, no matter how hard my dick was. "Want to heat up the food?"

"You don't want to..." She eyed my crotch. "Aren't you... shouldn't' I?"

"I'm just fine, okay? This is about *you,* and I'm not rushing you. We have plenty of time to learn other things about each other."

"Do you not want to?"

This damn girl. "Audrey. Please hear me. Of course I fucking want to, but your feelings and needs matter more than mine tonight. Never doubt that I want to experience everything with you."

"Oh." She did her cute little gasp again, but her smile didn't take as long to sneak out. "That's really thoughtful of you. I want to experience a lot with you too, but it's very overwhelming."

"We'll take our time. I like talking to you, hanging out. It doesn't matter. Yeah, I'm gonna think about you when I jerk off later, but for now, let's eat our leftovers."

"Do you care if I change out of my dress?"

"Not at all. Get comfy. I want to see lounging Audrey, please."

She blushed, and I helped her up from her bed. The dress was walking sin, and knowing she wore no bra the whole night messed with me in a major, fucked-up way. She hadn't had anyone worship her tits before me. Like... I couldn't comprehend that. At all. She was a queen.

"I might have a sweatshirt in here."

"From *who*?"

"Theo." She snorted and tossed me a large sweatshirt. "My brother."

I grunted. "Mm, I'll just take off the dress shirt. I'll be okay." While Audrey slipped into her bathroom, I removed the dress shirt, watch, and belt, which was at least more comfortable than nothing. But I would not wear Quentin's sweatshirt. Plus, he was two times smaller than me. Wouldn't fit.

I folded my shirt just as she came out of the bathroom in a hoodie and plaid pajama shorts. But she also wore hot pink fuzzy socks. I grinned hard. "You're fucking adorable."

"These are my clothes, usually." She tugged at the hem of the Central State hoodie. "I like to put them on the second I'm in for the night."

"I love it." I really, really did. It showed a more playful side of her. One that no one else got to see. I was becoming addicted to being the *only one* to do everything with her. She was my own oasis at this point. "So what else would you do if you were in for the night? What's your schedule?"

"Ah. I read books. Watch a few shows." She chewed the side of her lip, a sign she was nervous.

Why in the hell would she be nervous?

"What shows?"

"You'll probably think they're silly." She waved her hand in the air, brushing my question off. "I have a few plastic forks we can use but not any napkins. I can run to the kitchen to grab some, but it would take a few minutes to get there."

"Auds, sit your cute ass down."

She froze and lowered herself onto the ground, where I set our to-go boxes. "Do you not like to answer questions about yourself?"

She shrugged. "I'm not used to being asked them."

My heart fucking broke for her. I made a mental note to ask about her day and her classes and her homework, daily. My entire life was question after question, all about hockey, but with her, she just let me be. She gave me the space I needed to be myself, and the more I was around it, the more I craved it.

"Get used to it then." I winked and passed her a few rolls. "I want to know everything."

"But I'm boring." She took a bite of the roll without butter, and I filed that away. Did she not like butter, or was she nervous and needed to put something in her mouth?

"Who told you you're boring? I think you're fascinating." I

dug into my chicken and mushrooms. They were lukewarm, but I was starving.

"I'm not, Theo." She played with one end of her hair before meeting my eyes. "I don't want you to think I'm playing you or anything. I'm not cool at all."

"Do you think I care about *cool*?"

I didn't get where this was coming from. It was like once she put on her comfy clothes, her attitude changed.

She shrugged. "You probably do. Probably should."

"Audrey Hawthorne." My tone caused her to stare at me with wide eyes. "What just happened? I thought we were on the same page with us, but you're...fuck." I pinched my nose, annoyed that I didn't pick up on her mood faster.

She shoved away thoughts at dinner with our attraction, but now that was over, so her emotions returned, and she was prickly. I knew she would push away instead of opening up about their hurt.

"What do you need right now, honey? Do you want to talk about what happened?"

"No. I'd like to be alone when I think about... what we saw."

"Well, that's not happening." I took another bite of my food. "You've been there for me in so many ways, so I'm not leaving this dorm until you talk to me about what you're feeling."

"I didn't invite you to spend the night."

"Okay, I'll sleep on the floor."

"You can't. It'd injure you. I won't do that."

"Then we share your bed." I went for another roll and met her eyes. "I can do this all night. Banter with you, hold your hand, push you. But I'm not leaving."

"Theo." She stood and paced the small area near her door. "My family doesn't even care about me. I have two people left, and they don't even want to see me despite everything I do for them. I can't be with *you*. You have the best siblings, and what am I? Alone. I'm not enough for my own mom and brother to invite me to a simple dinner. They use me for cash. That's it. I'm a bank."

"Get it out, baby. Be mad. What they did fucking sucked."

"I don't understand. I try calling my mom, but she never answers. Doesn't want to talk because I remind her of him, yet she'll text or call me and demand more money. Just a hundred bucks for food here and there. I'd tutor like crazy just to send her money because I promised my dad I would help her, even though she's cruel to me. And my brother," she trailed off, and emotion clogged her voice. "He bails on me all the time. He doesn't value me, and I'm so mad about it. I love him. I love him so much, and I'm just nothing to him. Nothing to my mom."

My heart raced as anger flooded my veins. "You're not nothing."

"No one stays in my life, Theo. No one." Her voice returned with a force. "Tonight proved it."

I set my plate down and walked up to her, placing my hands on her shoulders. "Tonight proved that your brother and mom are selfish. Unkind. People have a way of showing their true colors, hon, and yours are just the best. Their actions aren't a reflection of you at all. They're a mirror of who *they* are as people."

She sniffed, and the sound tugged at my heart so damn bad.

"You don't need them, but they sure need you."

"Clearly not for anything besides money." She hung her head, and I said fuck it. I picked her up and cradled her to my body. I moved the blankets back and slid in, cuddling her against me. "What are we doing?"

"When I was ten, I was upset about some dumb thing at school. My mom's best friend had a kid who was like a brother to me, but he made me mad. So, it felt weird to be so upset at someone who was like a brother at the time. My mom brought us to my room, shut off the lights, and said we could say whatever we wanted in the dark. I could be mad at her, at Curtis, and it was okay. I didn't have to hold back because the lights weren't on. So that's what we're gonna do. Now where is your light switch?"

"By the door."

I quickly shut it off and was back in bed with Audrey. "I'll start. I'm fucking angry that your family makes you think less of yourself and asks you for money. It's so selfish and unnecessary. Now yours."

"I'm angry because I do so much for Quentin, and it's all for nothing. He lies to me, avoids me, and all I wanted was a best friend. We've been through so much, and I thought he'd be my forever friend, but he's not, and it hurts so badly."

"I'm angry because he doesn't deserve you as a sister."

She sniffed, and I held her tighter against me. Her head rested on my shoulder, and she fit there perfectly. "I'm angry because even though I have all these feelings, I know if he calls me, I'm gonna answer. I wish I could just cut him out of my life because he only hurts me, but I can't. I even picked up tutoring slots this week so I could send him money for fun."

I didn't like that, but this was her time. "Because you care so much about him. You have the biggest fucking heart, Audrey. It's incredible."

"It feels broken sometimes."

"Nah, it's not. I know it." I kissed the top of her head as she snuggled deeper. "I'm so sorry you went through this."

"It's not your fault."

"Sure, but I'm fucking sorry you're sad. It's killing me to see you sad."

"I'm sorry I turned inward earlier. You were right to call me out on it. I'm not used to someone else caring, and it's out of routine for me."

"I'm angry that your life has you feeling this way, but I care so much. Too much. And I won't stop, okay? Tell me you need space, but don't shut me out. Please?"

It was the please that got her. She was tense as a board until I added the last word, and she relaxed against me. Almost like she gave up fighting me. "I'll try to get used to it, but like I said, having you care about me is so strange I might forget."

"Then I guess I better do a good job at reminding you then."

We lay there for ten, twenty minutes before her breathing slowed. Her hand moved toward my chest where she dug her nails into me, like she was afraid I'd leave. I was already hooked on her, but after hearing her open up tonight? There was no way she'd get rid of me. Zero.

Even when doubts intruded, I shoved them away. Who the fuck cared about Quentin and his three friends? They were dicks, and the team knew it. Instead of trying to repair anything, I should blow the team dynamics up. Show Audrey who he really was.

But no. I couldn't do that. Not when she admitted she'd forgive him no matter what. Fuck. I wanted her to punch him in the face.

She sighed in her sleep, just as my stomach growled like a whale. Damn. I forgot I was still hungry. I never got to finish.

"S'that you?"

"It's fine, baby, go back to sleep."

"You're hungry." She pushed up to her side and a part of wanted to yank her back against me. I liked her there. Wanted to keep her there with her little hand clinging to me.

"I like cuddling with you."

"But I'm the reason you didn't eat twice." She scoffed, her annoyance evident. "You need to eat. Come on."

She climbed over me and switched on the light. With a shy smile, she put my leftovers onto a plate and popped it in her microwave. Her bare legs were distracting as hell while she had her back to me. She had a mole behind her right knee and another one on her calf. I smiled, once again pleased I knew these secrets about her.

"I like your moles."

"My what?" She faced me. "Moles?"

"Back of your legs." I pushed up and lowered myself to draw a line between the two of them. "It's sexy knowing you have these cute birthmarks back here."

"I never realized I did." She gave me a bashful smile and shoved her hair behind her ears. "Thanks, I think."

"I'm gonna keep reminding you until you believe it, but I love learning all these things about you." I bent down and kissed her on the mouth softly. She let out a hum of contentment before I pulled back. "Yeah, really like kissing you."

She blushed as the timer dinged. She removed my plate and scanned the room before pulling out her desk chair with her leg. "Here, you can sit there so it's more comfortable for you."

"Where will you sit?"

"The floor?"

"Then we both sit there. I'm sitting by you." I sat criss-cross as Audrey slowly lowered herself next to me. Everything felt right here. We spoke about my mom and her dad, what they meant to us and how the remaining parent sort of died when they lost their spouse. We talked about our clinicals and how badass Marcy was. We also joked about the grossest things we had to do.

It was so fucking easy being with her. I wasn't stressed about my family or my siblings or the NHL. I was happy. The future had a million possibilities that could happen, but they didn't freak me out as much. This bond, this connection with Audrey surpassed all the doubt. I just had to make sure it didn't destroy her relationship with Quentin.

That was the only seed of worry I had because if she had to choose between him and me, he'd come first every time.

17

Audrey

It had been two days since Theo spent the night, and my stomach still fluttered thinking about it. We'd spooned. The entire night. I'd never slept next to another human like that nor had I felt so safe. Theo made me feel... normal, secure, and protected. I didn't realize one could feel this way, and I couldn't keep a dreamy smile off my face.

I walked in a semi-trance to my classes that Monday, lost in thoughts, and that was why I didn't see my brother until we were ten feet apart. It wasn't often we crossed paths on the quad, but seeing him in person caused a horrible pang in my chest. All the horrible feelings from Saturday came back, clouding every good thought I had, reminding me I knew better than to be happy.

That didn't happen to me. Good things never did.

"Auds, what up, sis?" Quentin flashed a smile as he clutched his bag to his shoulder. Two other guys on the team stood next to him, all of them wearing Wolves shirts with the hockey logo, but I couldn't even speak.

My words were stuck between the anger and hurt. My text to my mom last week was still unanswered, yet she'd accepted the cash I sent her with *that's all you have?* Quentin never reached out to me first. My pulse raced, and my head spun. *Breathe.* Theo's kind yet firm voice from Saturday repeated in my head, and I sucked in oxygen.

"You good?" Liam or Lenny or Landon asked. He was tall and played defense, I was pretty sure. He seemed to pick up on my spiraling, but I nodded and avoided their gazes.

I kept walking. My legs took charge to get me away from him. If I could just walk faster, I could take the first left, and sure, it'd be longer to the lab, but it'd be easier.

"Audrey, what the hell?" Quentin's voice was laced with annoyance. "Is there a reason you're not stopping?"

"Class," I whispered, still not slowing or looking at him. There was too much hurt in me, too many feelings.

His fingers wrapped around my forearm, gently, and he stilled me. "Are you okay? You're acting weird."

"I'm fine." I stared at the sidewalk, where three ants went after a chip. They had to have friends on the way soon. "I need to go, Quentin."

"How are clinicals going? You started, right?"

Oh. He wanted to talk about this *right now?* No. I jerked my arm out of his reach and mumbled, "I'll talk to you later."

He let me leave, thankfully. But my heart raced. My pulse was elevated, and it made me dizzy, but I couldn't stop. I didn't want to talk to him or see him. I needed more time. I heaved for breath as I pushed into the building with our labs.

I leaned against the wall and let the cool tile sooth me for a few minutes. My phone buzzed, Quentin probably, but I didn't glance at it. I wasn't ready.

For someone who avoided confrontation at all costs, this was overstimulating. Too much. I wasn't equipped to handle these feelings.

"Auds?"

A familiar, safe voice neared me, and I sought comfort in it. I found Theo's kind eyes and ran toward him. He wore a sweatshirt and shorts with a backward hat, and he opened his arms wide for me, and I slammed into him. He surrounded me in a huge hug, his cologne and the fresh scent of laundry filling my nose. His heartbeat was strong and consistent, and I matched my breathing to his.

There.

Calm.

"Honey, what happened? I'm glad to see you, and I was worried how you'd greet me, but I was not expecting a bear hug." He chuckled and tried to end the hug, but I clung harder. "Are you okay?"

I nodded. "Just need to breathe for a second."

"Ah, yes. Good ole breathing."

He held me for a minute in the middle of the hallway as students walked by. I didn't care. They could judge me if they wanted. Theo was safe for me. I took one last inhale and glanced up at him. He smiled at me, his gaze warm and gorgeous, and I blushed.

"This is embarrassing."

"You hugging me? Nope. Not at all. I love it." He placed his hands on my hips and dug his fingers into the skin exposed between my shirt and jeans. "I do need you to tell me what brought you to this rescue hug though."

Guilt stabbed me in the gut. The one regret in all this was the fact I hated complaining about Quentin to Theo. Theo had to deal with so much shit on the team because of Quentin's injury, and the fact my brother hurt me meant Theo would never bond with him.

"I can see the indecision on your face, your debate if you should tell me. I'm asking you to tell me. Please." He rubbed his lips together, and my own tingled.

I wanted to kiss him, but I wasn't sure I could. We weren't there.

"I ran into my brother, and I couldn't talk to him. I freaked out mentally." I exhaled, telling him the truth. "He tried talking to me, even grabbed me—"

"He *grabbed* you?"

"Not, not anything bad. Just, stopped me when I walked by." My voice shook. "I can't avoid him forever, but I can't even look at him without my chest aching. What should I do, Theo? Avoid him until I feel better, which might not ever happen? Confront him? God, the thought of doing that gives me hives."

"Ah, I'm so sorry, Auds." He moved one hand from my hip to my collarbone, his thumb gently massaging my shoulder. "I don't know what to tell you because we're so different. But you do need to do what feels right. Maybe you tell him you need space and ask him to respect it."

I swallowed. "Yeah, maybe I'll do that."

"What class are you heading to now?" He stared right at me. He never once let his attention shift to anyone moving around us, and it was an intoxicating feeling.

"Lab simulation with Professor Grundy."

"Ah, nice. Just left hers. Do you have plans after?"

"Library," I said out of habit. "But its changeable! I'm free if you're asking to hang out. I can. Do you want to hang out with me?"

He grinned. "You're the cutest, but I have to get my siblings in about thirty minutes today."

"Oh. Yeah." I swallowed down the disappointment. I didn't realize how much I wanted to spend time with him. We'd texted a few times since he left my dorm Sunday morning, but I didn't know what to expect. Maybe that was a one-time thing? Yeah, that made sense. I didn't want to get my hopes up and be hurt.

A line formed between his brows as he exhaled. His minty

breath hit my face as he rested his forehead against mine for a second. "Auds, your sad face kills me every time. I'm sorry."

"It's okay." My stomach was in knots, and I was too hot. It was forward of me to assume he wanted to hang out. "I should head to my labs now."

"Baby, no, please. I can't let you go when you're upset." He cupped my face now, his eyes searching mine. "Do you want to come over? I didn't mean to upset you. I wanted to know what your plans were, if you had something fun to take your mind off your brother. You could join us for dinner at the house."

"Oh, no, that's a family thing." I forced a smile, hating this so much. I didn't know the rules. I didn't know how to date. I didn't know how to handle all these feelings, when I'd been numb most of my life. I stepped back. "I'll see you tomorrow morning at the hospital."

"Why are you pulling away?" He frowned, his shoulders sagging. "I want to hang out with you. I always want to see you. You know that, right?"

I nodded, just needing this conversation to be done. Between Quentin and Theo, I wanted a good cry. Which, that wasn't me! I didn't cry. I carried on. Distracted. All these feelings were gonna make my body shut down.

"I fucked this up." He ran a hand through his hair, and regret lined his face. "Fuck. What can I do Audrey?"

"You didn't fuck up." I swallowed the ball of emotion, counting the seconds until we walked away. "We're okay."

I had no idea what *okay* meant, but it seemed like the right thing to say.

"I wish I didn't have to be a parent right now. I wish so badly." He frowned again and gently grabbed my hand and intertwined our fingers. "If my life wasn't what it was, I'd wait for you after class. I'd go buy you flowers, and we'd walk back to your place. Or we'd get ice cream."

I gave a half smile. "It's a nice idea."

"Why do I feel like I'm losing a part of you?" He shook his head, his jaw flexing. "Can you please join us for dinner? Daniel and Penny would be so happy. Em might even stay home if she knew you were coming. I know it's not fun or exciting, but it's the only thing I can offer, and I feel like we need to talk."

"Need to talk?"

I blinked. That sounded like a breakup. But we weren't together-together, right?

"Oh shit. Shit. No! Not..." He laughed and yanked me against his chest. "I need to leave before I ruin everything. Your sad face is brutal, and it's making me ramble like an idiot. I meant I want to hang out with you. Talk. See you. Kiss you. Will you please come over for dinner?"

This time, he hugged me like he needed me. I enjoyed his siblings a lot, and the other choice was to be in my room alone. My phone buzzed in my pocket again, and even though I knew it was unlikely, Quentin could try and stop by. I wasn't ready for that, so yeah, going to Theo's family's house was the better option.

"Okay, I'll come over."

His relief was instant. His muscles relaxed, and the pang in my chest loosened. Maybe I wasn't the only one unsure of what we were. "Thank you. Thank *you*."

"Can we maybe talk about what we even are? I'm struggling with it," I whispered into his chest. "I don't know the rules, and because I don't have guidelines, I'm nervous and unsure."

"Baby, yes." He chuckled softly, the rumble of his chest vibrating my face. "Happy to talk this through with you. Whatever you need to feel better."

Every time he said baby, my insides did a flip-flop.

"Do you want to spend the night tonight?" He cupped my

chin, and his blue eyes sparkled down at me. "We could drive to clinicals together."

A bolt of heat went through me. I wanted more cuddles, more exploding of our bodies. Even the thought of it had me clearing my throat. His grin widened, like he knew where my thoughts were going. I nodded. "Yeah, that sounds good."

"Wear the sexy bra, *please*."

I snorted at his haggard voice, and his eyes softened. "There she is. My Auds is back. I love that fucking snort."

The endless swooping feeling returned, and instead of being self-conscious, I liked his attention. "I'll think about it."

"Please." He pressed his lips to mine once, then twice. "Mm, I want to kiss you more, but you'll be late. I can swing by your dorm after I pick up my siblings?"

"Yeah. That sounds... great." I smiled and tried not to think about the tingling sensation all over my body. All from a promise, from a kiss. "Thank you."

"For what?"

"Just being you."

"Might be the nicest thing anyone's said to me." He winked and slowly stepped back. "See you later, baby."

This would be the third time we spent the night together, and an explosion of nerves blasted through me, causing my stomach to flutter. This was big. Good. Amazing.

I just couldn't let anything get in the way.

That meant continuing to ignore my brother and mom, push the hurt away and enjoy my time with Theo...while it lasted.

18

Theo

Reiner: Let's check in tomorrow morning after your 9am class. I'll have coffee.

Theo: You got it, Coach.

I pocketed my phone and ignored the growing tension in my gut. I hadn't made progress with Quentin at all. If anything, I despised the kid. Pretty much thought him hopeless.

Anyone can change given the right motivation. That was a momism that hit me out of nowhere. She'd know what to do about this punk ass. She'd have ideas and would brainstorm with me to help him out. She believed in people, where I did not.

"Why are raccoons the way they are?" Daniel asked Audrey as we sat around the kitchen table. Irritation gripped me as I realized yet again our dad wasn't home. This shit was getting old. This was beyond me *helping out* and instead was *me doing everything*. Dinner ended an hour ago, and both Penny and Daniel kept asking Audrey a million and one questions. None that were relevant to a) their life, b) their homework, or c) the conversation.

Yet, Audrey giggled and had the patience of a saint. She'd

google on her phone if she didn't know the correct response, which would only lead to weirder questions. Raccoon research turned into beavers, which turned into bears, then circuses, then lion tamers. There was a real animal-like theme.

"I want to play with lions. They don't scare me."

"You're so brave. Can you roar like a lion?" Audrey asked.

That turned into a whole production. Daniel and Penny roared as loud as they could just as the front door opened.

The keys jingled, and the conversation stopped dead. Our dad walked in and paused at the entrance to the kitchen. *Are you fucking kidding me?*

"Hi, Daddy." Penny smiled at him and slid off her chair, hugging his legs. "Watch me roar like a lion!"

He picked her up and complimented her fierceness, but it was lacking luster. He seemed tired, but he was always tired. Bags hung under his eyes, his shirt was untucked, and he reeked of guilt.

He should. I sacrificed a night on my own again to watch *his children,* and he was home?

"Where's Emily?"

"With Jace." I fought the urge to bark at him. It never ended well. I loved my dad. I fucking loved this family, but when he waltzed in any time he wanted, just assuming I'd take care of everything, annoyance grew and grew under my skin like a weed. What the fuck was he gonna do next year when I was gone? Daniel stared at me, like he was watching my reaction to form his own. I forced a smile. "We've just been hanging out with my friend Audrey."

"Oh." My dad wiped his hands on a towel and forced a grin. "Hi, Audrey, I'm Dave."

"Hi, Dave." She shook his hand, but he received no smile of hers. She stared at him with the same impenetrable gaze I used to see. A part of me was glad to see her almost seem mad at him, like she was on my team. "You have the most wonderful children."

The compliment caught him off guard. He blinked before running a hand through his graying hair, a slight blush covering his cheeks. "Thank you. Yeah, Mona and I got lucky."

"You did. All of them are amazing." Audrey met my gaze, and her face softened. "Theo is taking good care of them."

Her words were meant for praise, but it was a reminder of how much my dad missed, how much he chose not to be a part of our lives as he dealt with his grief. My posture stiffened but then Audrey grabbed my hand under the table. Her warm fingers curled around mine, like she was protecting me, and it made me want to keep her forever and say fuck it to the avalanche of consequences that came with us being together.

"Yeah. Theo has been a huge help the last year. I'm sure he told you what happened to Mona." He swallowed and poured a glass of water, his movements rigid and awkward. Almost like he wasn't comfortable in his own home.

He avoided us as much as he could, so it made sense.

"He did share what happened. I'm so, so sorry."

"Yeah. Me too."

My dad rocked on his heels, eyeing Daniel. "Want to play a game before bedtime?"

"Dad, I don't go to bed for another hour."

"We can still play a game. We haven't played Uno in a long time." He pulled out a deck from the junk drawer and held it up. "Winner gets bragging rights?"

"I don't know." Daniel slumped his shoulders and stared at Audrey. "We were going to play—"

"I'll play with you, daddy!" Penny jumped up and down, right before she yawned. "I'm so sleepy."

"Let's get you to bed, pumpkin."

"Theo usually takes me," she said, yawning again. "But you can tonight."

My dad swallowed, clearly uncomfortable, but I didn't care. He wasn't around. What did he think was gonna happen?

Audrey squeezed my fingers before letting go. "Daniel, how about we play a quick game while your dad puts Penny down, then you and him can play Uno?"

"Okay. Sure."

Audrey commanded the room with poise as my dad and Penny left us, and Daniel went straight into Guess Who. He liked being around Audrey, and I couldn't blame him.

They went through two games before my dad returned, offering me a polite smile as his son barely wanted to go with him. I wasn't sure why my dad was home, and I didn't care. But some damn communication would've been nice. It'd be one thing if it felt like we were doing this together instead of me just saving the family at the risk of sacrificing my entire senior year.

"Let's go to my room." I held out a hand, and she took it, the lines around her mouth tight. "What is it?"

"Should we hang with your dad when he comes back? Should I go?"

"Baby, you are not leaving." I tugged her until our chests were flush together. Her addictive scent of vanilla filled my lungs, and the urge to devour her returned. I ran my nose along her jaw and nipped her ear. "I'm so fucking glad you're here."

"Theo." She pushed my chest, and I released her instantly. I didn't want to, but she held all the power. It was important she knew that.

"Whoa, don't... I liked your embrace. I'm just worried about your dad knowing I'm here. Is that weird?"

"He doesn't care. Truly. He hardly pays attention to us as is, so me having a girl here isn't a big deal."

She chewed the side of her lips and frowned. "Because it happens all the time?"

"No." I grinned. "But you being even slightly jealous is adorable." I kissed her again, but she jumped back. "Why are you moving away from me, woman?"

"Your *dad!*"

"Ah." It hit me then. She was nervous. This was new for her. "Come on, then."

I led her upstairs to my room and shut and locked the door. It was just us. Finally. "You're not nervous now, are you?"

She nodded. "Not because of your dad though."

"Me?" I played with the ends of her long hair. Her eyes fluttered shut, and I leaned forward to kiss her. It had been too long since I'd tasted her mouth, and I was desperate. Her lips tasted like cherries, and I groaned. "You taste *so good.*"

"You're always minty." She wrapped her arms around my shoulders as I deepened the kiss. She kissed like her personality. She was shy at first. Timid. Unsure. But with a little patience, she opened up, and the real her came out.

The warmth of her mouth and the way her hands grazed my pecs, then my sides, had me hot as hell. She'd never touched anyone else like this, and I wanted more of her firsts. "I want you to touch me. I need you to." I broke apart the kiss and whipped my shirt off. "Please, baby."

"You're upset." She licked the side of her mouth as her eyes heated into a deep, dark brown. She swallowed, loudly, as she dragged her fingers over my shoulders, over my pecs and down my abdomen. My muscles clenched for her, and she dug her nails into me. "You are divine, Theo. You're beautiful."

"That's *my* line, honey."

She shook her head and grabbed my hips, pushing me backward. I let her lead me, and when my knees hit the back of the bed, she pushed me down. "You distracted me when I was upset.

I can tell your dad coming home messed with you, so can I distract you?"

Images of her thighs spread, her pussy dripping, and her cries muffled from coming filled me, and I nodded. Hard as a rock. "Please. Do whatever you're comfortable with."

She shuddered and gripped the hem of her shirt. She hesitated, her eyes unsure, and I touched her wrist, understanding she needed a little guidance. "Did you wear something for me?"

She nodded as heat flooded her face.

"Show me then, baby."

With one breath, she removed her shirt and tossed it next to mine on the floor. She stood between my thighs; her perfect, massive tits barely constrained in a black lacy bra. Her dark pink nipples were pointed, pushing through the fabric, and my mouth fucking watered.

"Goddamn, Audrey." My tongue legit swelled in my mouth. "Do I get to taste them again?"

"This is about you, Theo." She chewed her lip as she ran her fingers over my neck and to my pec.

"Sucking your tits *is* for me. Please. Lean forward, straddle my lap."

She obeyed and then her tits were in my face. They were so heavy and full I could die and go to heaven right then. Through the fabric, I nibbled on her beaded tips until she squirmed on top of me. I loved her heat, the weight of her on me. Her bare skin touching mine. "Mm, this is perfect."

She ran her fingers through my hair, pulling the ends, and I groaned.

"Did that hurt?"

"Uh huh, I love it." I couldn't stop licking her tits. They were the sexiest, best tits I had ever seen and would live rent free in my mind for the rest of my life. "Pull my hair more."

"Oh." She giggled but then I bit down on her tit, and she jumped. "Theo!"

"Do you like the sting?" I dug my hands into her jean-covered ass, wishing she was naked. We needed to go her pace, but fuck me, she was a walking dream. "Or do you like the gentle caresses?"

"All of it with you."

"God, that's a sexy answer."

"Theo." She sat back, forcing me to let go of her nipple. "You make me feel... I love all of this. Everything."

"Mm, baby, I like hearing you say that." My cock was rock hard and grinding against her. She was so tight and warm, even with clothes on.

"What do you want to do? What do you need?"

"You naked," I barked out. She ran her fingers through my hair and kissed my jaw. It was so sweet and spicy at the same time I groaned. "I want to see all of you and taste between your thighs. Let me taste you, baby."

"Oh." She sucked in a breath, and a familiar sexy as hell blush covered her cheeks. "Are you sure?"

"The most sure." My eyes flashed as I sat up and set her on the bed next to me. "The thought of tonguing you—being the first one to bring you pleasure down there has me hard as a rock. I want to taste your pleasure, Audrey. I need it."

"Well, if you *need* it then why would I stop you?"

"Exactly." I chuckled as I leaned over her body and kissed between her tits. They were divine. I slid one strap down of her bra, then the other, and unhooked it so her tits hung free. They were massive. My hands couldn't contain them, and I buried my face between them as I licked everywhere. Her skin was smooth and salty, and she let out the sexiest little mews.

"Theo, oh my," she moaned.

I fucking loved those sounds.

I undid her pants and slid them down her legs, leaving her in thin translucent panties. She'd shaved, which was unexpected for me. A bolt of lust went through me, making my brain stop functioning at the moisture evident between her thighs. I ran my nose along the fabric and tongued her over it. She smelled *perfect.* "Oh, honey, yes."

"Theo, I'm so hot. I'm burning up right now. I need... are you going to touch me?"

"Everywhere." I slid the fabric to the side, repeating the process as I gripped her thighs. She was so fucking wet for me. I flicked my tongue around her clit, going slow as I spelled out my name over and over. Her back arched off the bed with each movement.

"How does it feel, Auds? Is my tongue on your pussy okay?"

"Theo, oh my god." She gripped the sheets so hard her knuckles were white. "This is insane. This is... oh yes. Right there."

I took her swollen nerve in my mouth and gently bit it. I sucked it, hard, and flicked it in a continue rhythm as her orgasm hit her. Her thighs clenched around my head, and her throaty cries went straight to my cock.

"Yes, oh fuck. Theo!"

I drank her up, absolutely transfixed with her body. She came for a minute, her orgasm the best thing I'd ever tasted. I couldn't stop myself from lowering my waistband and fisting myself. I was so fucking turned on from this perfect woman. She owned me, and fuck, I needed to release this tension.

"You are fucking perfect," I said, flattening my tongue along her pussy as she caught her breath. "You get a minute before you come again."

"Again?" She pushed onto her elbows and stared at me. Her wide green eyes were gorgeous and hooded.

"Yes." I sucked the skin of her inner thigh, then bit it to the point it left a mark. I stroked myself hard, but I needed it wetter. I ran my fingers over her juices, then slipped inside. "Fuck, you're so tight and wet. Goddamn, baby. You're my obsession."

She gasped when I took out my fingers, licked them, and spat onto my hand to continue stroking myself. "Theo. Are you..."

"Yes, baby. The taste of you alone is making me come."

Her eyes flared as I winked. "Timer's up."

I flattened my tongue and went back to eating her. She almost flew off the bed when I stuck my tongue inside her. The act was so fun and filthy, but I didn't care. She was everything. Giving her pleasure was everything.

My cock swelled, and I pumped harder and harder, my own orgasm nearing as her second one did. She screamed my name as I sucked her clit harder than I had before, and she came gloriously. Watching her fall apart was a gift from above. No other way to describe the way she cried out, how her hair fell all over my bed, how her smell and taste were addictive. It overwhelmed me, and I came in my hand, unable to stop myself.

"Fuuuuuck, *Audrey, yes.*" Fucking stars blurred in my vision as the most pleasurable orgasm rocked through me. It was all her. Her body, sounds, and taste fueled me in a way I had never experienced before, and fuck, I wanted it again.

"Theo, did you just come?" She sat up, a wrinkle between her brows. "Are you—I wanted to—"

"Oh. I'll be ready again." I quickly cleaned up the mess with my shirt and tossed it into a basket. Then, I dove back onto the bed and crawled over her. "Taste yourself on me, baby. Taste how good you are."

I kissed her and sucked her tongue, enjoying the hell out of her gasps and cries. "The next time I come, it's gonna be from your mouth," I whispered.

"I've never..."

"I know, honey. I'll walk you through it. The thought of teaching you how to suck *my cock* is already getting me hard." I kissed her mouth again, groaning into her because she was a living dream.

I was obsessed with her. Audrey was... damn. We still had to talk about us and our future, but tonight, I was gonna show her how good things could feel.

19

Audrey

I woke up warm and content, a feeling I hadn't experienced in a long time. It was the moment between dreaming and being aware of surroundings where my heart beat faster and the urge to want more hit me. Staying behind the scenes was easier, focusing on others' wants and needs was easier than concentrating on my own. Way less pain, way fewer opportunities to get hurt. But after falling asleep wrapped in Theo's arms and hearing him murmur such kind things... I wanted it. Plus, holy shit. Experiencing him going down on me? Unreal.

Un freaking real.

So, the continual buzzing of my phone intruded on the thought, and my gut tightened like it knew who was calling me. *My brother.*

"Do you need to answer it?" Theo's morning voice grumbled. His breath hit the spot behind my ears, and it sent a flurry of goose bumps over me.

"I don't want to."

"Then don't." He kissed the center of my neck. "You don't owe anyone anything. Remember that, okay?"

My screen lit up the room, and Quentin's name flashed. The urge to ignore him forever was there, but I switched the situation around in my mind. If *he* didn't answer me for a whole night, I'd lose my mind. He could be freaking out, but it wasn't likely.

Yet, the guilt of hurting him *hurt* me. Would this ever go away? Probably not. It came with the baggage of borderline raising him.

"You'll feel better if you answer him." Theo reached over me and grabbed my phone to hand to me. "I can leave the room for a minute if you'd like."

"What? No. It's your room. I just... I can text him." I sighed, and Theo put a reassuring hand on my hip. I wore one of his extra-large shirts, and I loved how the material bunched up on my thighs. I felt safe around him, in his clothes and surrounded by his smell.

"Do you want to talk it out first with me?"

Another stab of guilt hit me. "Theo," my voice cracked. "How can you be so nice about this? You should hate me, my brother. I was so mean to you and—"

"Stop." He caged my face with his hands, one strong forearm on either side of my head. He kissed me softly, and his eyes softened. "Families are complicated. Look at mine."

"Sure, but—"

"That's it. I'm into you. We're dating."

I gulped. My face prickled with heat. We'd never talked last night, not like I needed. We were too caught up in the moment, but despite the connection we had, it still worried me to explicitly ask what that meant. Self-doubt intruded as my thoughts clouded. I didn't have my shit together at all with my brother or mom, and I didn't even know what *dating* meant. Why would he be into me at all?

"I can read your face so well now." He smiled and kissed my forehead. "You want to know what dating means, yeah?"

I nodded. "Please."

"Well." He pursed his lips, his eyes twinkling. "It can mean different things to different people and couples, so it's important were on the same page. I can tell you that the way I feel about you is different from anyone else I've dated, but I want to make sure you're there too."

My jaw tightened as my stomach swooped. Different was good. Yeah. "I'm there, I think."

"You think?" He grinned and tickled my side. "Auds, I'm not beneath playing dirty for you."

I snorted. "Okay so we're dating..."

"Exclusively." He held my gaze and did the intense stare again, where his gaze moved from my left eye, then right, then my mouth, and repeat. It was quite intoxicating.

"Yeah?" he added, a slight line between his brows.

I was silent for too long. "Yes. Definitely yes."

"You're so fucking cute. Okay, we date exclusively."

"Do we... tell people? Not that I have anyone to tell, but if you want to keep it secret, that's... I get it." I gulped. There. That was my darkest insecurity. He wanted to hide it because he'd get shit for it. *But I hugged him in public, and he didn't seem to care.*

He rubbed his lips together as he studied me. Something flashed across his face, doubt or worry or something horrible, and I tensed, waiting for his words to crush me. But then one side of his lips curved, and he nodded. "I will follow your lead on this."

"Are... are you sure?"

"Yes, Audrey." He kissed my cheek and pushed up from the bed. "Call your brother back."

"Wait." That couldn't be it. We needed to discuss more. Right?

"Hm?" He rubbed his face and yawned and looked so vulnerable and adorable that my chest ached. I'd never get tired of seeing him stretch or sleep or yawn or breathe.

"Is that it?"

"I thought so. Is anything unclear? We can keep talking all you want. I want you sure on us." He threw his scrubs onto the floor from his third drawer. "What's going through that brilliant mind of yours?"

"I thought it would be more difficult. Like, arguing or something."

"What would we argue about?" He chuckled and cupped my face, his blue eyes sparkling. "You're my girl. I'm proud of you, us, all of it. Nothing to argue about. If you want to hide it because of your brother, that's okay with me for now. Someday, I might want more, but I'll follow your lead."

"Oh."

"Yeah." He rubbed his thumb over my bottom lip. "Now, we need to get moving, or we're gonna be late, and Marcy terrifies me. You call your brother while I get ready."

He left me in his room while he disappeared into the bathroom, and I faced my phone. Ten missed calls. Ten texts.

All from Quentin.

Where are you?

Are you alive?

AUDREY WTF IS GOING ON

WHY WON'T YOU ANSWER ME?

I'm going to your dorm.

Where the fuck are you???

Okay, I'm freaking the fuck out. You're not at the library.

My gut churned worse than the one summer I threw up on a roller coaster. I hated making him worry, but he rarely considered my feelings. My fingers trembled with unease as I hit dial. It was six am, but he always got up early, ever since he was a kid.

"Audrey? Are you okay?" his voice sounded ragged, like he'd been screaming.

"Hey," I said, squishing the blanket in my hands to rid myself of this horrible worry. "I'm fine."

"Why the hell didn't you answer me? I've been fucking looking for you everywhere. Where are you? Did you check your phone, or was this fun for you? Did you think about how worried I'd be?"

Of course, he turned this back on me, and my eyes watered. *You owe him nothing.*

"Enough." I stood and paced Theo's room. "Did you ever think I didn't want to talk to you?"

"Audrey. What... what's going on?" His voice took on a tone I had never heard before. He seemed upset.

"Did you ever think about that? That my world doesn't revolve around you and your feelings? I know it seems like I do revolve around your feelings since you discard me whenever you feel like it." My voice cracked, and I didn't care if he heard my hurt. "You don't care about me or what I'm going through, so please just... leave me alone."

"Audrey, no, where are you? Can we talk? This... are you drunk?"

"No. I'm not drunk. I'm with someone who actually makes me feel good about myself, okay?" My hands shook so hard I dropped the phone, just as Theo came out of the bathroom with a towel wrapped around his waist. Water dripped down his chest, and he was a damn smoke show. It wasn't his look though that hooked into me like a fishing wire. It was the look his eyes and the way he mouthed *I got you.*

He held out his arms, and I walked into them.

Quentin's voice grew hoarse. "With *who?* Are you seeing someone? I should know about that, Audrey."

"So should I, but you and mom had a great dinner without me. Now I have to go."

I hung up as Theo squeezed me against his chest. "I didn't handle that well."

"There is no right or wrong way to handle family shit. Hell, I'm probably fucking that up every day,"

"Maybe we are a decent pair then. You and your dad, and me and my brother." I sniffed, and he chuckled, the deep rumbles in his chest vibrating against my face. "I hate that I care so much."

"It means you have a big heart. A good one. Now, let's go let Marcy boss us around for a few hours for fun. Nothing like needles and blood to take the mind off family drama."

"So romantic."

He laughed, and it was so easy how seamlessly we fit together. I still had my doubts that crept in every few minutes, but being with him made me dream about a future of us together. One that seemed magical and filled with joy. I could imagine the two of us living together and hanging out with his siblings, but that wouldn't be reality. He'd travel all the time for hockey, and hell, he was leaving after this year. I had no idea what we'd be then.

Even as Theo made me laugh as we got ready and drove to clinicals, a part of me knew this would come to an end at some point. I'd just soak up every minute of it while I could.

THEO DROPPED me off at my dorm after a long twelve-hour shift. Marcy wanted us to experience one full-length one so we knew what we were up for, and my feet ached. I wanted to sleep for a week, but there wasn't time. She gave us two more studies to read and then our group project had to present our status PSA, and of course no one had done their part. It was like the bubble with Theo popped just like that, and my real life came flying back.

It also didn't help that Quentin leaned outside my dorm with his arms crossed. "Stop the car," I demanded, my throat tightening. "My brother is up there."

"Mm," Theo pulled off to the side and put his truck in Park. "You do know he's aware we're partners?"

"Is he?" I didn't tell him. "You told him?"

He nodded. "Do you want me walking in with you, Auds?"

"No, just." I huffed and swallowed the ball of emotion growing by the minute. "You are such a trigger for him. If he sees me with you, he could—"

"Could he *hurt you*?"

"No! No. Never." I pushed my hair behind my ears, nervous as hell. Theo was too still, too expressionless. "I don't know why he's here."

"He probably wants to talk to you after your phone call." His voice was natural, calm. I hated it.

"Are you mad at me?" I hated that I had to ask, but I felt his disappointment deep in my pores, and it made me feel like shit. "I'm sorry. Please... I don't..."

"I'm not upset with you." Theo stared at my brother and sighed. "I get it. You don't want to anger him more."

"Yes. Exactly."

"Okay." He tapped the wheel and glanced at me, a sad smile on his lips. "I'd love to walk you to your dorm, hang out a little, but another time then."

I nodded. "Thank you. I'm...I'm sorry."

"Hey." He took my hand and kissed the back of it. "I'm into you, okay? I'm patient. Someday, we can tell him."

"How are you not worried about hockey with us?"

"What's there to worry about?" He gripped the wheel and wouldn't glance at me. "Quentin isn't going to be on the ice a lot, and even if he were, he's not... it doesn't matter. I'm not worried about the team at all."

"What do you mean *he's not?*"

"Baby, please don't do this, not now." His face was pained. "Go talk to your brother, but I'm gonna wait here for ten minutes. Call me if you need me, okay?"

"Okay." I gripped the door handle but then leaned over and kissed him. "I'm, uh, into you too."

"Don't make me blush," he teased, and that joke made everything all better. My time with him wasn't coming to an end yet.

I waved before jumping out of the truck, still far enough that Quentin didn't see how I would've arrived. I had no idea how long he'd stood out there, but when he saw me, he pushed off the wall and hobbled toward me. "What are you—"

"Can we talk?" he interrupted me, his gaze frantically moving over my face. "I can take your bag. Here."

He yanked it from my shoulder, almost too hard, because it hurt my skin, and he cussed. "I'm sorry. Shit."

"It's fine." I took my keycard out and opened the door to my building. He followed, not saying a word. Usually, he chatted nonstop. Mainly about himself. Or hockey. Or his friends.

Now, it was silence.

God, when was the last time things were actually good between us? Four years ago? I didn't know, but I was so tired of the façade. Being with Theo retaught me how to have fun and find joy. Quentin hadn't been someone who brought me joy, not in a while.

"Can I come in?"

"You're asking?" I fired back. He'd usually barge in without pausing. Like his presence was a gift to me. Unlocking the door, I pushed it open, and he followed.

"Do I, uh, not normally ask you?"

I shook my head and crossed my arms. "Why are you here? I asked you to leave me alone."

His face twisted in pain as he ran a hand over it. "You saw me and mom."

Fuck. The way my stomach caved had me grip the side of my chair, and I sat. I nodded. Despite there being a few days of distance, the image still hurt so badly. I lost *my parent,* and Quentin still had his.

"That wasn't supposed to happen."

"Clearly."

"No, it's not like that, Audrey." He sat on the edge of my bed, gripping his head in his hands.

"What is it like then? I'd love to know. Mom only talks to me when she needs money. Did you know that? Every week she texts or calls me and demands money and tells me I'm self-ish. I sent her the money that probably paid for your stupid dinner."

His eyes widened and he gasped. "What?"

I wasn't done. "You act like I have no life and will just cater my schedule to yours. I don't want to be in a family where no one loves me anymore."

"That's...dramatic and not fucking true."

"Yes, it is." I swallowed and held my own. "When was the last time you asked me to do something *I wanted* to do? Do you even know what I like? Do you ever ask about how I am or what I'm doing? Never. Not once. I tell you I don't want to talk, and you bombard my phone, disrespecting what I asked. Even now, I said I wanted distance, and you show up at my place. This isn't what family does. It's not even what friends do. I think... I think you need to leave. I don't want to see you."

"But you're my sister."

"Yeah, but being related doesn't mean shit." I held it together.

I didn't cry. No tears. "I'm done with a one-sided relationship. I deserve *more*."

"Audrey. Audrey." He kept blinking as he paled. His hand was on his chest, and his eyes lost that normal mischief. A part of me felt bad for hurting him, but he was a grown man. He could handle his own emotions and needs. Not me anymore.

God, my palms sweated, and my pulse was dangerously high. I'd said my part. I did it without falling apart. My adrenaline was crazy high, but that was a problem for later, not now. "Why are you still here?"

"This is crazy."

"No, it's not."

"Can we... talk about this? I can explain Mom. But the money... I don't..."

"I honestly don't care. I'm an afterthought for you both, and I'm sick of it." I went to the door and opened it. "Time to go."

"Please... please don't." His face looked pained, like this actually hurt him, but that was absurd.

He would miss my money. That was it.

"You have your girl-whatever, mom, the team. You have enough people in your life who can be there for you. You don't need me." The first urge to cry hit me, thinking about the fact that I didn't have many other people. Really just Theo, but that was temporary.

I'd be alone, but at least I wouldn't be disappointed.

"I'll give you time, but we're still friends, Auds. It was you and me for so long." He reached out like he was gonna hug me, but I backed out of it. "I don't know what happened for you to turn against me, but I'll figure it out."

"Start in the mirror. Now, goodbye." I shut the door and leaned against it, the sobs hitting me the second he was out of view. The adrenaline had to escape now. It was overwhelming. I had never been so cruel in my entire life, and I wanted to throw up. I'd hurt my brother. The person who I used to love more than anything.

Fuck.

I was gonna be sick. I ran toward the bathroom and barely made it before throwing up. I hadn't eaten all day, so it wasn't much, but the shakes started, and I wet a washcloth just as someone knocked on the door. *How dare he...* "I told you to—"

It was Theo.

"I couldn't leave without making sure you were okay. Oh, honey." His face twisted with concern as he walked in and pulled me into a hug. "I got you. It'll be okay."

That's when I knew I was in trouble with Theo. He held me as I cried, and I fell completely, foolishly in love with him. The one guy I should never fall for, I did, and he owned my heart now.

20

Theo

There was an extra pep in my step as I walked toward Coach Reiner's office the next morning. I was so damn proud of Audrey for sticking up for herself against her brother. She finally saw that he wasn't an angel, and while I hated how much he hurt her, it was the right move.

It's the same thing I need to do with my dad.

I didn't mind confrontation because I didn't have an ego, but challenging my father wouldn't end well for me. He'd yell back that I hadn't gone to see my mom, which was true. He'd say this was harder on him, and I had to take care of the family. He was never home, and it was rarely just the two of us, and this was something I didn't want my siblings around for. So, instead of worrying that Coach Reiner was gonna rip into me for not mentoring Quentin enough, I thought about seeing Audrey later.

With a big sigh, I pushed into the stadium and almost ran into Cal Holt. "Holt," I said, holding up a fist with a smile. "You're a legend."

He nodded and fist-bumped me back. "Sanders. Heard you signed to the Acorns. Their defense sucks."

"Ah, your people skills haven't improved since joining the NHL then, huh?"

He snorted and glanced down the hall. "Reiner wanted us to talk if we had time. Said you had questions about next year and how to work with difficult players."

"Huh, I definitely don't recall asking either of those questions, but he's a schemer."

"Yeah. He is." He ran a hand through his hair before almost-smiling. "He's a pain in the ass but a good fucking coach."

"Want to meet at the rink later, see if you can keep up with us younger players?"

"Oh, you're on."

He walked away, and my grin increased. I'd heard about Cal Holt the last few years. Who hadn't? He'd been aggressive and a total headcase when he started out. He'd turned it around, recently got married, and made life in the NHL seem possible. It wasn't some far-out, unknown future. He played hard, had a life.

Maybe I did have some questions. Like, how often did he go home? Was he able to afford supporting someone else? What was different from college hockey to the NHL? What was harder?

Damn. Reiner was right.

I knocked on his door, a small blip of nerves overtaking me as I walked in. He stared at a whiteboard with a play scribbled on it, and the second I neared him, he pointed his pen at me.

"What do you think our biggest weakness is?"

The answer came to me immediately. "Power plays and defensive zone coverage."

"Why?"

"Are these trick questions? Do you want me to answer honestly?"

"Yes."

"To which one, sir?"

His lips twitched. "Smart-ass. What's your take? You've only scrimmaged with us and seen tapes."

"Correct—I've also played *against* you." I went to the board and pointed at one of the symbols. "The team has no chemistry or coordination together. If they played as a team and not as individuals, it'd be different."

Jonah Daniels stood at the doorway, one eyebrow lifted. "Do you not know how to do your job anymore? You had two beers last night. That's it."

"If you took *your* job as team unity better, I wouldn't have to ask Theo here."

"Lies." JD snorted. "That's not my role, and you know it. What everyone needs is to get lost in the woods and bond and shit."

"We're gonna scrimmage, and every single person is gonna play a different position. Losing team cleans the other teams' lockers." Reiner pinched his nose. "You make any progress with Hawthorne yet?"

My face heated. "No, sir."

"Why not? I asked you to, didn't I?"

"You did, Coach, but—"

"I don't care." Reiner's eyes narrowed. "You're the missing piece this year. We all know it. I need you to get him on board. It's either that, or his future in hockey might end sooner than he thinks."

The small, ever-present knot in my stomach doubled. I really didn't like Quentin, but if he got kicked off the hockey team, that would devastate Audrey. She said his scholarship was key for them, and she carried the financial burden, so if he lost that... it'd fall on her. I shook my head, a new motivation hooking itself in me. I couldn't do that to her. I refused. "Okay, Coach."

"What position would you put everyone into switch it up, shake things around?"

We spent the next hour going over possibilities, and two of the other guys on the team joined us. Liam was the goalie, and Hannigan was the junior forward who was faster than me. They were chill as fuck, and when they asked me to head to the party that night, I couldn't say no. Not after Reiner wanted me to focus on the team.

I just had to call my dad.

～

"What do you mean you won't be home?" he asked, an hour later. "I wanted to run into town—"

"Dad. I have team stuff. I can't get out of it." My patience zapped immediately. "I'm home every night."

"As you should be. Your family needs you, and now I'll have to rearrange my entire schedule for this." He sighed, and I gritted my teeth together. "You need to be better at communicating this stuff with me."

"You realize I can't do this when the season starts? Or when I move to Minnesota next year? Who will help you then?"

"I know you think the NHL is the path for you, but I'm not sure anymore. You'll be far away from us. Plus, being in health-care is more respectable and would let you be near us more." His voice grew hard. "Your mother wanted you to do this. She wants you close. You can't do this to her."

My throat clogged as I fought with myself. There were a million things I wanted to say, all pointing out he was fucking wrong and selfish. My mom always told me to fly, to be myself, to get the hell out of this town. She'd be cheering me on the loudest. My dad was using her to keep me here to help *him*.

"I won't be home tonight. Take care of your children. See you tomorrow."

"Theo!"

I hung up. I called Em immediately, and she understood, offering to help with Daniel and Penny since I wouldn't be home. Having her there was a relief, because yeah, she was a teenage girl more worried about Jace, but she loved our family and would help. Sighing, I ran a hand over my face. I needed to hash this out with my dad soon. I couldn't be his emotional punching bag forever. My thoughts raced with the best way to do this, and that was when Audrey texted me. My perfect distraction.

Audrey: Hi. Do you want to hang out tonight?

Fuck. Of course I wanted to. But the hockey guys... well... she could come to the party house? Nah. She wouldn't. Not with her brother. This sucked. I needed to do this with the guys, but if I turned her down, she'd stop asking. She was flighty as hell, and the second she found a hint of rejection, she'd be out. And I craved being around her too much to not see her. Hell, being with her made me forget everything else.

Then what do I do?

Theo: Any chance I could convince you to come to a party at the hockey house?

Audrey: You're partying?

Theo: I'll have to update you. Reiner ripped into me about bonding with the guys more... so I have to. Can you sneak in? That could be fun.

Audrey: Would my brother be there?

Theo: Eh. Maybe, but... I need to see you tonight. So either you sneak in with me and we have fun hiding, or I stop by your place for a booty call.

Audrey: What if I don't want to hide?

Was she joking? I'd fucking love that. My relationship with

her didn't affect my game on the ice at all. And the guys wouldn't give a shit either. But Quentin... I'd deal with him then. But us going public? Hell yes.

Theo: Then you go as my girl. I need to get you my jersey to wear anyway.

Audrey: Your girl. I really, really like that.

Theo: Me too, Auds. Want me to come get you?

Audrey: Yea. But, um, hey. What should I wear? I've never been to a party.

This girl. My chest ached for her, and god, I wanted to protect her and show her everything she missed being the damn parent for her family. The only difference between her and I was that I had three years of fun before responsibility got in the way. She said it had been this way since she was seventeen? That... no. She needed the whole experience. I'd make sure of it.

I couldn't tell her just to wear anything. She truly didn't know.

Theo: your crop top and black jeans look amazing on you.

Audrey: Thanks, yeah, okay. I'll see you soon.

So proper. So nervous. I could almost feel her nerves about this and the fact she trusted me? Yes. It felt good. I already wore a black shirt and jeans, perfect for a house party. And with that, I picked up some flowers for her and went to her dorm.

I'd had pre-game jitters before, where your body fluttered and the feeling felt surreal. Your heart beat a little faster, you sweated more, and every sense was heightened. This was like that but more. Us going public? Us... doing this thing, knowing who her brother was?

Nerves. Big ones.

I held flowers and stood outside Audrey's dorm, a nervous smile on my face as Audrey opened the door. Her vanilla scent hit me first, then I drank her in. Her hair was down and curled,

194   JAQUELINE SNOWE

her lush waves falling over her shoulder. Her green eyes popped in color, like she'd put more makeup on than normal.

"Is this okay for a party?" she asked, her voice missing her usual snark. "I wasn't sure."

"You look perfect." I leaned forward and kissed her softly, trying not to obsessively inhale the smell of her skin. People had smells, and she smelled divine. End of story. "Baby, you look gorgeous."

"Thanks." Pink tinged her cheeks, which brought out her green eyes, and I loved all her expressions. She twisted the end of her hair as her eyes widened at the flowers in my left hand. "Did you bring *me* flowers?"

I nodded and shoved them at her like a tool. Those nerves doubled in size, and I worried she wouldn't like them. My high school girlfriend only wanted roses, but red tulips fit Audrey.

"They were mom's favorite, and they reminded me of your hair."

She grinned so hard and brought them to her chest. "I love them! Thank you, thank you so much. I've never... no one's brought me flowers since my dad did when I turned sixteen."

I entered her dorm and studied her as she stared at the red petals, her eyes a little glossy. Before my mom had her stroke, my dad would bring her flowers once a month. They made my mom so happy every single time. She acted surprised and thankful, and my dad would blush and hug her. Things were different now, but those gestures every single month always stuck with me.

Audrey chewed her lip, but her eyes lit up with joy as she put the flowers in an old plastic cup she had. "It's not the nicest option, but I don't have a vase. I want to put them right by my bed!"

God, my mom would love Audrey. Shit. I could totally bring Audrey to see her at the long-term care facility. I hadn't gone to her in months...not because I didn't love my mom but because it was too hard. The guilt that was always there flared. Maybe Audrey was the answer. The way to get over my fear of seeing her.

What the fuck.... I usually could push these feelings away and focus on the now, but with the red tulips and thoughts of my parents and Audrey's happiness, the emotions were pushing out of the box.

"Hey, you've been quiet." Her smile fell, and she walked toward me. She lifted her hand, dropped it, then put her hand on my forearm. "Are you okay? You usually talk way more than this."

I cleared my throat and focused on the windowsill instead of her face. The concern and sympathy sitting there ruined the whole moment. She was so happy, and I'd ruined it. "I'll be okay, just in my head."

"Look at me." She cupped *my face* this time, gently guiding my face toward hers. "Can you tell me what's going on, so I can help? I know all your facial expressions, so something is bothering you."

"Stare at me a lot?" I arched a brow, my emotions regulating faster around her.

"Yes, Theo. You're kind of hot."

"Kind of?"

She snorted and swatted my arm. "Okay, there you are. You're back. What happened?"

I ran a hand down her side and gripped her waist, letting myself enjoy the heat of her exposed skin and the bravery of her going to the hockey house with me. It couldn't be easy. "I haven't visited my mom in two months. When you smiled at the flowers, it reminded me of her and how much she'd love you."

Audrey nodded, like that explanation made perfect sense

despite me holding out on all the guilt I had about it. "Do you want to visit her?"

My throat clogged as I nodded. "I haven't been able to. I'd say I was busy, but I was avoiding it because she's different now. She's not... my mom."

"Do you want me to come with you?" She slid her hand into mine, intertwining our fingers. "Because I will. I'll be there for you. You're the backbone for so many people, Theo, and I'll be yours."

"Fuck, I love—this." I yanked her toward me and buried my face in her neck. "You are incredible, just... wanna stay here instead?"

She tickled my side. "No! It's my first college party."

"Why didn't your brother ever take you to one?" I asked the question that annoyed me. The guys always had siblings tag along for a beer pong day or just to chill. It was normal as hell.

"He liked to keep his worlds separate."

"Well, I don't." I tilted up her chin and kissed her slowly. She tasted like mint and cherry, and I groaned when she slid her tongue into my mouth. Every single time Audrey initiated something with me, it felt like a gift. Her touch showed me how much she trusted me to give me this.

Her heart beat hard against my chest, and I slowed the kiss, not wanting to go too far before we left. I rested my forehead against hers, my breath coming out in heavy pants. "If you keep kissing me like that, we'll never leave."

She giggled and wiped the side of my mouth. "My lipstick got on you."

"Good. Everyone knows I belong to you then."

Her eyes widened. "It still feels surreal that we're doing this, that you feel this way about me." She trailed off, like I was supposed to finish the end of her ridiculous sentence.

When she didn't finish, I pushed her hair behind her ear, my chest aching with how much I cared for her. "Because of my height? Or my sense of humor is too crude for you? That's what you meant, right?"

She clicked her tongue. "You are witty, Sanders. I'll give you that."

"It's *amazing* we found each other. Remember that. The fact you want to come with me tonight means so much, Audrey. Now, prepare for it to be a shitshow."

We left the flowers in the dorm, and we made our way to the hockey house. I hoped Quentin wouldn't show up or that Audrey would be okay if he did. Given the choice between her brother or me, there was no way she'd ever side with me. Not yet at least. I planned to show her and continue earning her trust, but we weren't close yet. So, Quentin could derail it all.

Suddenly, I regretted asking the girl I was falling in fucking love with to come to the party. We were too new and fragile to survive an altercation, but the glow on her face, the way she kept smiling... I couldn't deny her the chance of her first party. "Ready, baby?"

"I'm so nervous I could throw up. Yes! Let's do it!"

I kissed the back of her hand and led us up the porch, where I vowed to give her the best party experience of her life.

21

Audrey

Music blasted around me, the loud bass and fast-paced tunes filling every part of the large house. There was so much to look at, at any point, and my senses were in overdrive. There were couples making out on the couch, a bunch of drinking games going on in various rooms, and lots of laughter.

My idea of a party came from movies or TV shows, where people would do keg stands and chants. This was more chill. Some parts were crazy, but I found myself relaxing after scanning around the room and not seeing Quentin or his friends. Other guys on the team were there, most of them super kind.

Theo introduced me as his girl to five of them. I was just Audrey. His girlfriend. And it was so easy.

I smiled into my cup as someone approached me.

"Why are you smiling like that?" A dark-haired, young guy grinned at me. "Seems unfair that you're not sharing good news."

The first drink loosened me up, so my usual nerves and social awkwardness went away. This guy was on the team, I was sure. Maybe a sophomore? "This is my first party, and it's better than I thought."

"Oh, first hockey house party? This is pretty tame." He downed his cup and jutted his chin toward mine. "Need another?"

I stared at the empty vodka soda. I rarely drank, but it felt fitting to do it at my first party. Plus, Theo was here. It was about damn time I did things that weren't following every rule. I didn't have clinicals tomorrow, so screw it. "Sure."

"Come on then, girl." The guy took my hand and led us from the spot in the hallway toward the kitchen where all the drinks were kept. His hand was smaller than Theo's, and it felt weird holding it. The kitchen smelled clean. I expected trash or beer, but no, lemon something.

"You sniffing the air?"

"It smells good in here." I chuckled. "So yeah. I am."

"You're fucking cute." The guy nudged his elbow into my side. "I love it."

"Oh." I blushed, hard. No one but Theo had ever complimented me in my life, and my skin felt too tight. "I'm uh, with someone."

"I'm sure you are, look at you." The guy winked. "What were you drinking?"

"Vodka sprite."

"Sit. Come on." He hit the counter before he poured a shot into my cup. "Need me to lift you?"

"Audrey."

Theo stood at the entrance to the kitchen, his eyes zeroing on the guy next to me. A muscle in his jaw flexed as he took two large strides toward me. Without a warning, he cupped my face and kissed me *hard.*

Holy shit.

This wasn't a kind kiss. He nipped my lips, sucking my

bottom one before moving his knee between my legs. Heat exploded all over me.

"Christ, Sanders. Take it fucking down. Point made."

Theo cupped my throat, his large hand almost covering the entirety of it, where his thumb rested on my pulse point. His eyes darkened, and he licked the side of his lip with a slight smile.

"I see you've met my girlfriend."

"Yeah, fucker. I got it. Damn." The guy shoved Theo's side with a laugh. "Audrey is a hot name."

"No." Theo glanced at the dude. "Move on, Hannigan."

"Audrey, right? You're stunning. When this old fuck leaves next year, let me know." He winked. "Your drink is ready."

"Th-thanks." Jesus. My skin flushed, but tingles continued all over my body. Theo stared at me, his nostrils flaring like he was mad. Oh no. He thought... "No, he wasn't... I didn't..."

"I know you didn't." He smirked before picking me up and setting me on the counter, pushing my legs apart so he could stand right against me. Heat radiated off him, and he smelled so good. My favorite scent.

"Mm." I closed my eyes and breathed him in. "I love how you smell."

"Good." He ran fingers up my leg and thigh, over my stomach and between my breasts. "You want to know what I don't like?"

I opened my eyes. "Don't like?"

"Finding you in the kitchen with some guy standing too close to you, complimenting *my fucking girl* when it should be me." He dragged his fingers over my bottom lip. "I haven't experienced jealousy before, but holy fuck. He touched you."

"I'm sorry." My mouth trembled. "I didn't... I don't even know. I'm so sorry."

"Baby, don't apologize. This is just making me feel things that are too forward, too much for you."

"Too much for me?" I reared back. "What does that mean?"

"I'm trying to go slow, to respect you." He closed his eyes and stepped back. "Yes, I need to go slow with you."

Anger flared. "Why? Are you holding back?"

His eyes flared. "Yes. I am. Because you're inexperienced."

His words felt like a slap, even though I knew deep down they was true. My body recoiled on its own, and Theo saw. His eyes widened. "Fuck, Audrey, no that came out wrong. I didn't mean it in a bad way."

"Okay." I swallowed down the hurt feelings and confusion. The second drink didn't sound as fun anymore, but we'd only been there an hour.

"You're not okay." He placed a hand on either of my thighs. "Why aren't you fighting back? Fight me. I was just a jealous asshole. Call me on it."

It was so hard to do it. But he was right. "I want to know what you're holding back. I really don't like it when you hide things from me."

"Baby." His face softened. "I don't want you to feel pressured. That's what I meant about inexperienced."

"Okay, but I want to make that call myself." I gulped. "You said you were jealous. What does that make you want to do? Do I need to go find that guy again?"

"You little devil." He laughed, but his eyes swirled with lust.

He liked it.

"Hannigan, yeah?"

"Last warning, Audrey."

"Is Hannigan single?" I smiled and ran my tongue over my bottom lip, Theo trailing the movement with heated eyes. "He told me I was fucking cute."

"Fuck." Theo ran a hand over his face before picking me up

off the counter. He hoisted me over his shoulder and weaved us through the crowd and into a back room before shutting the door. "Need to taste you now."

He slammed me against the door and kissed me so hard it almost hurt. It was possessive and hot and holy shit. I had never been kissed like this in my entire life, like he was marking me for the rest of my life. I'd never be able to forget this moment, the way he groaned into my mouth and dug his fingers into my ass like he would die if he didn't touch me.

The room was pitch black, the music from the party blasting, but it was just us in this room. My body hummed with want and need, and I met his fervor with my own. I kissed him back just as hard, and he growled. "Yes. Kiss *me,* Audrey."

I dug my nails into his back, wrapping my legs around his waist so his erection dug into me. He shuddered when I pulled his hair, and I'd never felt more powerful. "Don't keep anything from me, Theo."

"Fuck, baby." Using his hips, he held me up against the door as he lifted my crop top up and took a nipple in his mouth with one breath. He bit each one hard, sucking and teasing them before he lowered himself onto the floor. "Scream my name when I make you come, baby. I need everyone hearing you say it."

"Wh-what are you doing?" I gasped. He removed my jeans and panties, guiding them down my legs with shaky hands. It was almost like he couldn't control himself, and somehow, that got me hotter. This beautiful, perfect man was like this for me. Unreal.

"I'm claiming this pussy as my own." He put each of my legs around his shoulders and growled against my thigh. "You smell so good, like you're mine."

"Theo." I arched into the door as he spread my lips apart and flattened his tongue against my clit. Holy shit balls. He sucked the swollen nerve hard, then nipped it, which caused me to buck against the door and caused a huge boom. Everything was on fire, and his tongue could put it out. Was the only way. But heat gripped me, and I squirmed against his mouth, grabbing his hair to grind myself against him. This was the hottest moment of my life.

"Fuck my fingers while I lick up your cum."

Holy. God.

"Lick them first." He held two fingers outside my mouth, nudged inside, and I sucked them. He shuddered as I screamed in pleasure, before he slid them back between my legs. My head knocked on the door. "Scream, baby. Louder."

"Yes, Theo." The orgasm was growing closer by the second, and he curled his fingers as he sucked my pussy, and I lost it.

"Louder," he commanded. "Scream for me."

"*Theo! Yes!*" I cried out as I saw literal stars. Theo was on his knees, his fingers thrusting inside me as his tongue worked magic on me. I clenched his head between my thighs, never wanting this moment or orgasm to end. "*God, yes.*"

"You are exquisite." He bit my inner thigh. "Extraordinary."

I blushed even though he couldn't see me and then his lips were on me. "Taste your pleasure, baby. Taste how good your pussy is."

I kissed him back, and he groaned so hard I shivered. "Did I scream your name loud enough?"

"No, you little minx." He kissed my neck. "You'll come more. I want everyone knowing exactly what we did up here. I want everyone seeing this hickey on your neck." He sucked the skin hard, his chest rumbling with pleasure. "God, your skin. Mm."

"What else do you need to know I'm yours?"

He sucked in a breath. "This is perfect."

"Theo." I swallowed. "I want to feel all of you."

"It's too soon." He stilled, his erection jerking against me. "I'm getting off from your pleasure, baby, I promise."

I shook my head, but he couldn't see it. I felt around the wall for the light and turned it on. We were in a study of sorts. "Theo, I want to feel all of you. No holding back."

"I'm not fucking you for the first time in a random room at a house party." His nostrils flared. "You deserve more than this."

"But I want it." I dragged my nails over his chest. "Please."

His jaw flexed. "Don't beg me. I can't say no to you." He ran a hand over his face. "Audrey, baby, I want your first time to be special. Perfect."

"Being with you *is* perfect."

"Fuck," he groaned and took a deep breath. "Fuck, baby."

I removed the rest of my clothes and closed the distance between us. He let me remove his shirt and undo his belt. He was massive and could stop me at any point but let me take lead. "I wanted the full experience, yeah? Losing my virginity at a college party is pretty spot on."

Plus, I was growing more desperate to connect with him. We'd done everything else but *this,* and taking all of him was what I wanted. We were really together, and I wanted it all.

"You're more than that." He stilled me as we were both naked, and he stared at me. "This is more. What we have is fucking special. You know that, right?"

I nodded as my eyes watered. I wanted to tell him that I loved him, but that was too soon. It might freak him out. Even though he was jealous as hell and clearly had feelings for me, love was too fast. He'd crashed into my world and brought life to everything, and I'd remember and love him forever. Sleeping with him just solidified how much he'd changed my life. Plus, the logical side of me knew this wouldn't last forever. He had a whole future ahead of him, but I was done being responsible all the damn time. I wanted to enjoy Theo Sanders while I had him.

"Please, Theo," I whispered against his lips. "Be with me."

His hands shook as he dug into his discarded pants pocket and pulled out a condom. A zing went through me that he had it there, that he wanted to sleep with me. "Put it on me."

I ripped it open and slid the condom on him. He moaned and kissed my forehead as I pumped him. This man was perfection, and he wanted me. It still blew my mind. "Theo—"

"You tell me to stop at any point, okay? Promise me." He swallowed hard and held my gaze. "If it's too much or—"

"I promise." I didn't say I had no intention of doing that whatsoever, but it appeased him as he lowered us to the floor.

It wasn't the most romantic setting with the music and party-goers raging around us, but that all faded into the background as Theo kissed my neck and tugged my earlobe. "You are the sexiest thing, Auds. I'm obsessed with you."

He kissed down my chest, swirling his tongue around my nipple before coming up and sliding his tongue into my mouth. Kissing him never got old. The same heat and pressure from my earlier orgasm returned, and I grew heated. Ready. Primed. "I want this," I moaned, and that did it.

He guided himself inside me, his deep, contented sigh vibrating against my chest. "Fuck, baby. You feel so good."

His cock entering me stung a little. He was massive, and for the first few seconds, I tensed. But he slid out and in, kissing and touching every part of me, and that sting disappeared really fast. A wonderful sensation grew in my core, and I dug my nails into his back. "Oh, this feels... yes."

"Am I hurting you?" He lifted his head, and concern swirled in his eyes.

"No." I gripped the back of his head and pulled him down to kiss me. "Not at all, you feel amazing. I love this." *You.* That was what I wanted to say.

"God, you're amazing." He moaned against my mouth as he

thrust into me slightly harder. It took him deeper, and a burst of pleasure hit me. Yes. *My G-spot.* I'd heard about this but holy shit. He hit it over and over, whispering how amazing this was in my ear as he held onto me tightly.

I loved the heavy weight of him, all his muscles constricting and tensing as he fucked me. He was all strength and stamina. He continued at a slow pace, deepening his thrusts so my clit was stimulated, but I could tell he was being gentle. Too gentle.

"Theo," I arched my back, the heat intense as the need to release gripped me. "Stop going slow. I want the real you. All of you."

"Not our first time, baby." He sucked my neck. "This is about you, not me." He gripped my ass and lifted so the angle shifted, and whoa. I was gonna orgasm.

He never changed his pace, and the continual rhythmic thrusts combined with the angle and Theo's lips on my skin. I held onto him as the orgasm overtook me. There was something so insanely hot about feeling his cock inside me while I came. I clenched around him, crying out his name as I rode it out.

"God, you're beautiful." He licked my neck and face, his voice husky and hoarse. He was on the edge. "Perfect. Your pussy is perfect and made for me, Audrey."

"Yes, Theo." I clenched around him, wanting to hold onto the orgasm as long as possible because the way I felt with him staring at me with lust in his eyes? Invincible. "Holy shit, that was..."

"Fuck." He buried his face in my shoulder. "I'm gonna come, baby. You're... yes. Audrey, *you're fucking sexy.*"

I'd seen Theo come before, but feeling his body tremble and his cock twitching inside me? My eyes fluttered with pleasure. I loved seeing this side of him, knowing I could make him feel good, and I held onto him as he orgasmed.

When he stilled, he pushed up and grinned down at me. His

dimple popped out, and the same familiar and loving expression swirled in his eyes. "Damn. That was... are you okay?"

He pulled out of me and quickly tossed the condom into the trash can near us. Then he helped me sit up with a line between his brows. "Audrey, are you alright?"

I nodded, but he pulled me onto his lap and squished me against his chest. He smelled like musk and sweat, and I breathed him in, pushing away the thoughts that I could be with him forever. "Thank you," I whispered, kissing his jaw.

"Thank you? Why are you thanking me?" He ran his hands down my bare back, over my shoulders and sides. It was like he couldn't stop touching me, and I was here for it.

"Because I got to experience this with you."

He sucked in a breath and somehow hugged me even harder. "You own my heart, Audrey Hawthorne. You truly do. Be careful with it, yeah?"

My eyes prickled, and I tightened my grip on him. "I will."

It wasn't a declaration of love, but I'd take it. Theo and I were going into dangerous territory. I was already in love with him, and he might be close. As he held me and made me laugh the rest of the night, a horrible, unwelcome thought lingered at the back of my mind.

He had to worry about his family and go play hockey miles away. Would hanging out and falling more in love make it that much harder to leave? He'd asked me to be careful with his heart. He took care of everyone else all the time, so it was my duty to take care of him... even if that meant hurting myself in the process.

22

Theo

Quentin seemed off today.

I couldn't pinpoint *what,* but the asshole seemed upset. More than usual and not at me. It had been a few days since the party, and while I would've preferred to spend every waking second with Audrey, naked, I couldn't. She knew I had to focus on the team, and plus, she was off her study routine because of me.

We agreed to do our own thing this afternoon, even though she was on my mind. Was she hungry? Had she packed a snack? I often found myself buying pretzels just to have on me around her. The straight kind, not the twisted. To her, they tasted different. I fought a smile. Just thinking about her put me in a better mood.

"You're so fucking annoying." Quentin played with a straw wrapper and tore it into ten pieces. "Sitting there with a stupid smile. Why are you even trying? I hate you. You hate me."

"You're spicier than normal. Want to talk about it?"

"No. Not with you." He ran a hand over his face, and that's when I noticed he had dark circles under his eyes. Like he hadn't been sleeping. He yawned and stared around the student union without his usual swagger. I chose this spot because it was public, so if he wanted to swing at me there'd be witnesses but also because I was hungry. I picked up a fry just as he asked, "Have you ever fucked up?"

Whoa. He'd asked me a question.

"Of course, I have. We all do."

"No, I meant with someone you care about."

Shit. Did he mean his sister? I wasn't sure I could handle talking about this knowing how upset Audrey was. I immediately tensed, but this was good he was opening up. Maybe he realized he was the problem. *Maybe Audrey can forgive him.*

That was ideal for me. I'd be a mess without my siblings' care, and even though she said she wanted him out of her life, I knew it was a lie. She loved him. She was just hurt.

"Messed up with someone I care about?" I thought about my dad and how he hadn't spoken to me since I'd snapped at him. Instead, he'd been having Em be the translator between us. A rock formed in my gut, and I put that shit in a box for another day. "Yes. I have."

There. That was the truth. I wish I would've handled my dad better, made us a team instead of enemies.

"Did you fix it?"

I shook my head. "Q, I know you hate me because you blame me for your injury. I kinda get it actually, but as your captain and someone who wants you to be good mentally and physically, you gotta give me more than this."

"I do hate you."

"Yes, that's been noted." I sighed.

"Has my...you see my sister at clinicals, right?"

I nodded, keeping my face neutral. I wasn't giving him any more about her.

"Audrey is the reason I'm here. At this school, playing hockey." He hung his head. "She wants me out of her life."

"How does that make you feel?"

"Like shit, what do you think?" he snapped. "She won't text me back, and I'm worried I can't fix it. This is stupid, talking to you about this because you don't want to help me in any way or could—"

"Quentin," I barked out, making him look at me. "Let me make this clear. I'm on team Audrey. When you work clinicals at the ICU with someone, you go through things and bond. I respect the hell out of her and want nothing more than for her to be happy. And for some reason, she loves your dumbass. So, I do care. I do want to help you because it'll help *her*."

His jaw ticked. "I'm glad she has a friend in her corner."

More than a friend. But I just nodded.

"When you hurt someone you love, how do you fix it? That's where I'm stuck. I don't know if you know this, but our dad died when we were in high school, and it was bad. Like, really bad. Audrey became the parent of the house. Our mom...she isn't who she used to be. She uses Audrey...Fuck. Telling you this sucks. I don't... I should go."

His voice shook, and it was so clearly a cry for help my heart squeezed in my chest. I thought about Audrey helping Em, holding her that day she got the flat. This was Audrey's Em, and all the hockey bullshit disappeared, and it was just me and Audrey's brother. Her only real family left.

"My mom had a stroke and is in a long-term facility. My dad stopped being a dad. It's been almost a year and a half now, and it's been *hell*. I'm too afraid to go see her, and my dad and I barely speak. I know what it's like, what you're going through. Only, I'm the Audrey in this situation. I'm the oldest. I'm the caretaker for my three siblings, and if I was fighting with one of them, it would kill me."

Quentin gulped and stared at me with wide eyes. "Wait, what?"

"That's the reason I asked to transfer here. My siblings live thirty minutes from campus, and I have to pick them up from school, make sure they have dinner. Because if I don't? I can't guarantee my dad would come home." I swallowed the bitter pill as I shared with Quentin. "Our relationship changed. I'm not the fun older brother anymore. I'm the one who feeds them, puts my five-year-old sister to bed. Instead of living up my senior year before the NHL, that's what I'm doing every night. All I do is give myself to them. I'm sacrificing a lot *for them*. But they're young. You're not. If Audrey had to do even a little bit of that with you... that girl sacrificed everything for you and your mom. Now, my siblings are grateful as fuck, and we've bonded together through this. Have you? Are you grateful?"

Fuck, what was I gonna do next year? I would *miss* them so much.

He stared across the cafeteria and shook his head. I didn't intend to knock the sails completely out of Quentin, but he looked defeated. "Audrey has always been the responsible one, the more mature and smarter and better one. My mom is ashamed of herself and can't be around Audrey out of embarrassment. And she's struggling financially when Audrey has been frugal. She failed as a parent, and her daughter is a better one."

"Have you talked to your sister about this?"

"No. I'm not sure I deserve to after hearing this from you. She's never... she yelled at me for the first time in our lives last week. I had no idea she was upset or hurt or anything. She's always been stable and consistent and there for me."

"But have you been there *for her?*"

He shook his head. "No."

My phone buzzed, and I fought the urge to look at it. It was probably Audrey, and this wasn't the time. I'd stop over there after this, but I hope, prayed, and wished that this chat with Quentin helped their relationship. She needed her brother.

"It's hard knowing you're a part of the problem, but owning your shit and apologizing is the only way forward. Your sister is stubborn as fuck, but her heart is huge. You should know this."

"Yeah." He cleared his throat and stared at me with watery eyes. "I'm sorry about your mom, Theo. I don't know if it's better or worse than losing a parent."

My throat clogged. "Thank you."

"I still hate you."

"Yes, I know."

"But I don't want to punch you in the face as much. A little still."

"Okay, good. I'd hate for our bonding sessions to work. It'd just go to my head too much."

Quentin's mouth twitched before he sighed. "Can I ask you a question?"

Don't ask if I'm dating your sister. Not now. Not after progress.

"Yes, I am good-looking and smart. I know it's hard to accept."

"Fuck off." He laughed and rolled his eyes. "It's about Audrey. Is she happy? I worry that she's too busy and regimented. I thought my intrusions on her life were spontaneous and a way for her to have fun. She's so focused. But she told me all the times I would drop in were just my way of showing her I didn't respect her life."

"Ah, yeah." I took a sip of water and carefully treaded through this question. "She is happy. Have you ever seen her face when she talks about nursing? She lights up, dude. She's meant to do this work. Her schedule calms her down, and like me, when she became the *parent*, routine is the only way to feel in control and safe. She needs it, and if she's said this to you, and you ignored it, that is disrespectful. She has fun. She does shit, but on her own time. Be a part of that."

"Okay, good. I'm glad she's happy." He smiled with a sad look in his eyes. "We used to be best friends in high school. Before my dad died, we'd do a lot of stuff together, and it was so easy. We got into some shit too." He laughed but then scowled at me. "Okay, this is enough."

"You're the one still yapping. I thought we said our goodbyes earlier." I held up my hands. "Walk away any time."

He stood and glared at me, but his expression lacked his usual wrath. Then, he frowned. "When do we meet again?"

I shrugged. "Reiner expects us to get matching tattoos and wear bracelets, Taylor Swift style soon."

"Could we, uh, next week? Here?" He stared at the ground and gripped the straps of his bag so tight his knuckles were white. Almost like he was *nervous*.

Damn. "Hell yeah. We can even hug if you want."

He flipped me off and turned to leave but paused. "Thank you, Sanders." Then he took off.

The Hawthorne family was wedging itself deeper and deeper into my heart. Quentin was struggling, and it was hard to picture him as Em. Just a kid who suffered loss and was trying to figure shit out. She made mistakes all the time. Sneaking out, smoking weed, trusting bad friends, but that didn't make me love her less.

Was Reiner right pairing us up? Seemed like it.

Hoping the text was from Audrey, I checked it, and my stomach dropped.

Dad: Come home. It's Mom.

Fuck. The momentary bliss evaporated.

My first urge was to ask Audrey to come with me. But she was doing her own thing. We agreed. Yet... fuck it. I needed her. I called her.

"Hi!" she answered, all cheery and sunshine. "I miss you."

"I'm sorry to bother you right now," I paused and cleared my throat. My voice was hoarse and filled with worry.

"You can always bother me! What's wrong?"

"It's my mom. I don't... my dad texted me to come home. Can you—"

"Do you want me to come with you?" she interrupted. "I can meet you in five minutes. I'll pack up now. Unless you don't want me too. I can also not."

I snorted. She was fucking cute. "No, baby, I really want you with me."

"Then I'll be there. Text me where you parked."

God, she was perfect.

The thought of facing my dad's news alone sent shivers down my spine. I wasn't over the first time he told me the news of her stroke. Having Audrey with me would make it all better. I knew it.

It didn't take long to meet at my truck, and she stood there like a breath of fresh air. Her hair was down and wavy, and her sundress was a light purple and fit her perfectly. She chewed her lip in concern, but her eyes lit up when she saw me coming.

"Do you want me to drive? I can, but maybe you want the distraction?"

"I want a kiss. That's what I want." I tossed my shit into the back and marched toward her. "Every second I'm not kissing you is a waste."

She giggled and jumped onto me. Fuck. I loved this wild side of her. The side no one else got to see. She wrapped her legs around my waist and threw her arms around my neck and kissed me. I could feel the heat of her pussy near my dick, and I loved how every time we were together, she got a little bolder. She nipped *my* lips this time, and I groaned into her. "You taste so good, Auds."

"I missed you." She kissed down my jawline. "Which is silly. I saw you yesterday."

"Nah, I missed you too." I missed her all the damn time. "You look beautiful. I love this dress."

"Oh, thank you."

I set her down, and she smoothed it out, her usual pretty blush covering her face. "Are you wearing your lingerie under it?"

She looked to the left, then to the right, a naughty expression on her face before she pulled the top of the dress down to show the very see-through, very sexy bra. Her nipple poked through the fabric, right in daylight, and a bolt of lust hit me. "Fuck, Auds. You're trying to kill me."

"You asked." She shrugged and adjusted herself. "I was hoping to see you tonight."

"Well, I have no idea what's gonna happen with my dad, but knowing you're wearing that will be a perfect distraction." I sighed and ran a hand through my hair. "This could be a rough night. Will you stay with me?"

"You don't even have to ask, Theo. Of course, I will. Whatever you need. If you want me to leave too, I will. Sometimes, dealing with shit alone is better."

"Nah, I'd always choose you with me."

She gave me a soft smile, one that met her eyes, and my heart skipped a beat. How the fuck was I gonna survive without seeing her every day next year? I was addicted to her now, and the season hadn't even started. Panic clawed at me. I couldn't lose her. She was the best thing that had happened to me.

"Then come on, Sanders. Let's go see what your dad has to say. I'll be with you the whole time." She took *my hand* and led me to the passenger seat of my own car. She helped me get in, which was so silly and sweet, and bent forward to kiss my cheek.

"You don't have to be strong for me, okay? Be that for everyone else, but be real with me."

"Fuck, you are... lovely." I swallowed down the urge to say more, but she was incredible. I wanted her to know I would legit die for her at this point.

"As are you." She cupped my face, and a shadow crossed her face. Before I could ask what she was thinking, she masked it and hopped into the driver's side. "To your house?"

"Yup."

She didn't ask any questions on the drive. Instead, she told me the wild story of her group for a class and the interesting people she'd chatted with. She talked about next year and the hospital she wanted to work at. She also spoke about going to our first home game and how excited she was to watch us play. And maybe, if Em, Daniel, and Penny were up for it, she'd like to go with them.

She distracted me from the shitshow waiting for us, and I couldn't ask for a better girlfriend. For real. The drive flew by, and the butterflies of dread filled me but not as badly as we walked toward the front door.

She gripped my hand. "Lean on me when you need to, okay? I got you."

"I don't deserve you, Hawthorne."

"Yes, you do. We deserve each other." She squeezed my palm. "You can handle this. You're so strong, Theo. You will get through this."

Suddenly, I didn't want to go inside. I wanted to run away with Audrey and live in the woods. What if my dad said Mom got worse? What if she'd died, and I'd never visited her out of fear? Fuck. Fuck!

"Deep breaths. Hey, look at me." She inhaled and exhaled, modeling deep breaths until I followed. "It could be good news.

You don't know until you know. Worrying won't change the outcome right now."

I nodded, but she stood on her tiptoes and pressed the lightest kiss on my mouth. It was too short, too sweet, but it was perfect. She was perfect.

She opened the front door, and we walked inside. I had no idea what to prepare for, but it wasn't my dad sitting at the kitchen table waiting for us.

23

A udrey
    I went into fight-or-flight mode. My job here was
    to support Theo, but every part of my body buzzed
with adrenaline. Was his dad going to leave them entirely,
making Theo the parent of three kids? I'd help him, if that
scenario was true.

Or had his mom passed? Or showed improvement?

Or were they going to fight it out?

I wasn't sure, but I'd be ready for every outcome. Theo shook
and was so fucking scared I wanted to crawl inside his body to
give him my strength.

Theo froze, right in the hallway, his eyes wide as his hand on
mine gripped so tight it hurt.

"Sit down." His dad gestured toward the table, his attention
landing on me. "You're welcome here too. Audrey, right?"

"She's not leaving," Theo barked out.

"Hey, let's sit, okay?" I tugged his arm and guided us toward
the kitchen chair. It was like moving a cement block, and I
pushed him into the chair before taking the spot right next to

him. "Mr. Sanders, could you please share your news? Do you not see Theo is freaking out?"

His dad studied his son, the trepidation present on his face minutes ago shifting into worry. "Theo, I'm sorry. This isn't— she's okay. She's doing well actually."

Theo swallowed, and I gripped his hand. I drew circles on the top of his wrist, hoping he would focus on the sensation. "Good. Good."

"She might be well enough to move home soon, where she won't need 24/7 care within the next year or so." His dad sighed, and the sound echoed in the kitchen, the stress radiating off him in waves. I felt bad for him.

"This is good news, but I rushed here. Why?"

"She wants to see you. I think... and well, there's something I need to admit to you. I-I—" He paused and hung his head. "Okay, maybe this would be better to discuss alone."

"No." Theo's voice left no room to argue. I even sat up straighter. This didn't feel good. The air changed from the initial good news, and I bit the inside of my cheek, trying to form a game plan for what Theo would need.

"Fuck, I should just... you were right the other night, okay?"

"About what?"

"I've been a terrible father and husband."

"What does that *mean?*" Theo's entire body turned to ice, and his voice dropped an octave. "I know you've been a terrible dad, but husband? What does that fucking mean?"

His dad sniffed and ran his hands over his face. "I had an affair." His dad stood up from the table, pacing the kitchen where Theo froze.

His skin grew cold. His face remained unmovable. He could've been carved into stone before he said, "You had an affair."

Oh god. His voice was dangerous, low, and lethal.

"Your mom knows. You couldn't make me feel worse than I do." His dad's voice cracked, and I wished to be anywhere but here.

This was personal. His family. I tried moving my hand, but Theo held it tighter. No. I could be here for him, like he was for me with my brother.

My heart pounded against my ribs, my stomach rolling with nausea. Theo had to be fucking destroyed.

"She refused a divorce. I offered her one—"

"So she'd lose her fucking insurance?" Theo yelled. "You'd do that to her, wouldn't you?"

"No. *No.*" His dad's face was red, and his eyes watered. "I fucked up. Badly. With you, with her. Probably Em. Daniel and Penny still hug me. I don't deserve their trust. I didn't handle the stroke well at all, and I was set on my life imploding. And you know what kept me going? You. You took charge and made sure our family was okay, and I'm indebted to you the rest of your life. But I'm ready to own my shit and be better. You can hate me. You should. I lied. All those nights working, I lied."

Theo breathed so fast, his chest moved up and down nonstop. A muscle in his jaw kept ticking, and when he spoke, his voice cracked. "I'm so fucking mad at you."

"I know you are." His dad shrugged and looked so pathetic and sad my own eyes watered. "Be mad at me. Be furious. But you calling me on my shit awoke something in me, and I'm sorry it took so long to wake up. You don't have to watch your siblings anymore. I'll take care of everything. You can enjoy *your* life as you should."

"Are you going to tell Em?"

"I'd rather not." His dad gulped. "But if you choose to, I'll deal with it. I'm not avoiding the truth, but I don't want her hating me when you leave next year. And she would. She follows your lead on everything, Theo."

"Why even tell me?" Theo's palm sweated so much it dripped between our hands, but I didn't dare move an inch.

"Because you deserve the truth from me." His dad moved his eyes to me, his red-rimmed and devastated. "Please, take care of him."

"I will." I nodded, hoping that gesture gave Mr. Sanders some reassurance. Theo would be so hurt by this, and I'd help him. I'd do whatever it took. "Come on, Theo. We should leave."

"One more thing, Theo." His dad's voice shook now. "I'm sorry I told you to not play hockey. That was selfish of me, and I regret that the most. Your mom is more pissed at me for saying that to you than the affair."

Theo's eyes fluttered, and I wrapped an arm around his waist, moving him out of the kitchen and onto the front porch. The fall air smelled like bonfires, and the sound of crickets and cicadas surrounded us. It would've been romantic if Theo wasn't about to break down.

He plopped down on the front step, a vacant look in his eyes as he stared off into the distance. I moved right in front of him, waiting for him to meet my eyes. "What do you need right now? A rage room? A drink? To run? I can't run fast or well, but I'll run with you. Or I'll drive next to you. Yeah, that's more likely. Do you want to be alone? I don't want to leave you, Theo, but I can like, take you to a field and stand at a distance."

"No, don't leave." He ran a hand up my thigh and closed his eyes, resting his forehead against my stomach. "I'm gonna fall apart. I can feel it."

"Stop fighting it then. I'll help you pick up the pieces when you're done, okay?" I ran my fingers through his hair and sniffed. "You don't have to be strong around me. Just be yourself. I'm not going anywhere."

It took a few seconds, then he released the most gut-wrenching sob. His shoulders trembled as he cried. It broke my soul apart. I held him, my own eyes watering as he lost it. "It's okay, Theo. Let it out, sweetheart."

It lasted maybe fifteen minutes, him resting his face against my stomach as I held onto him. Holding him, being the person to comfort him was the most influential moment of my life. I was put here to help him. To be there for him in whatever way he needed. "What do you want to do next?"

He wiped his face with the backs of his hands and gave me a sheepish smile. "I'm sorry I cried on you. Not my best moment."

"Theo Sanders." I cupped his wonderful face. "Don't you dare apologize. This what couples do for each other when the other isn't as strong."

He laid his hands over mine, and his sad blue eyes shifted. "You're amazing." He kissed me, his lips still salty from his tears. "Audrey, I—"

"Do you want to go see your mom?"

He blinked. "Will you come with me?"

I nodded and held out my hand. "I'll drive you. Just tell me where to go."

"I-I...Auds, baby, I haven't been in months. She might hate me." His jaw flexed, and his eyes lost the momentary warmth. "She's there but not herself. It's hard. I miss my mom, not...I sound so ungrateful."

"No, you don't." I rubbed his back and regrouped. "I'm not going to force you, but if I were you, that's who'd I'd go and see."

"Okay. Yeah. I should. I'm gonna be a mess after though."

"You're *my* mess." I winked, earning a laugh from him. The magical sound was all I wanted. I missed it. "I really want to meet this woman, Theo. She raised you, and you're the best person I know."

He pushed up and wrapped his arms around me, lifting me off the ground in a hug. "Thank you for being here with me."

"There's nowhere I'd rather be."

We drove in a comfortable silence to the care facility about twenty minutes from his house. It was only six at night, and they were still letting visitors in until seven. We signed in, and I took note of the decorations. This place seemed homey, comfortable. Music played from a speaker, and all the workers smiled.

"Is Mrs. Sanders still in the same room?" Theo asked, his voice barely a whisper.

The woman nodded with an understanding smile and pointed us down the northwest hallway. Theo's posture shifted as he stalled.

"Audrey," he begged, and I joined him and intertwined our fingers.

"It'll be okay." I swallowed my own grief, this reminding me of that final night I said goodbye to my dad. Tears prickled at my eyes as Theo led us to a slightly open door. A woman lay on the bed with a TV on next to her. She had the same light brown, blonde hair as Theo, and her gaze was the same dark blue. She was beautiful.

Her attention slowly moved toward Theo, and the way her face shifted to a smile broke my heart. She was happy.

"Theo."

He ran toward her and pulled her gently into a hug. They each closed their eyes, and I wished I could take a photo. It was precious. Special. She cupped his face and said something to make him laugh. Thank god.

"You seem well," he said, sitting on the edge of the bed. "I'm so fucking sorry I haven't visited."

"Nonsense. You're in your senior year!"

Theo had mentioned she showed remarkable progress from her aphasia. She couldn't speak the first year but could communicate. She did aggressive therapy and had been communicating well the last six months. A stab of heartache hit me, thinking about his dad and what he'd done.

People reacted to horrors differently. My mom cut me out of her life apart from demands for money. His dad fucked up, sure, but he was still there and wanting to be better. I understood it, even though Theo didn't.

"I love you, Mom. I won't go this long without visiting or calling."

"Don't apologize. Are you happy? How is your dad?"

Theo tensed and met my eyes. She followed her attention and smiled. "Are you a new nurse?"

"Ha, no, she is a nurse, Mom, but this is Audrey. My girlfriend."

"Theo!" His mom grinned, and she blushed. "I'm in my pajamas."

"Mrs. Sanders, it's okay. It's such an honor to meet you as-is. Your son... he is the best person I've ever met. Will ever meet. You should feel so proud." I swallowed and shook her hand. "You raised quite a man."

She nodded and smiled warmly at me. "I did, didn't I?" She beamed at her son. "Thank you for coming here."

"I actually really wanted to ask you something, Mom."

"I can step out for a second?" I pointed to the hall. "I'll give you a minute."

"No, please stay." His eyes pleaded with me, and I couldn't deny him. Not now. *Not ever, really.*

"If you're sure?" My gut clenched at the thought of hearing him and his mom talk about his dad. It was messy. Hard. Emotional. It made me think of Quentin and me and how difficult our next conversation would be. *If we ever talked again...*

I swallowed. I wanted him to apologize and make a move. I needed to know I mattered to him for real and not just as an obligation. I missed him, even if our relationship wasn't ideal.

Theo pointed to the chair next to the bed, and I sat there,

legs crossed. Once I was settled, he went back to his mom. "Dad told me about the affair. I'm so fucking mad I can't even..."

"I forgave him, Theo." Her voice was kind but firm. "I love your father, and I know he loves me. The last two years have been tough on him. He wasn't supposed to tell you."

"It's been hard on him, sure, but who's been picking up the slack, Mom? Me. He stepped out and left me to be in charge. I... I don't know if I can forgive him. He cheated on you. You. He lied. Numerous times. I can't... lying is a choice. One he made."

His mom slowly blinked and cupped his hand. "Theo Kingston Sanders. You are the best child any parent could dream of. I'm so mad at him for abandoning you. I'm so sorry you had to step up." She swallowed, and she pulled back, a vacant look in her eyes. She sucked in a breath and stared at me, then Theo. "Who...what was I saying?"

Theo blinked and leaned back, the light in his eyes dimming as he stared at his mom. Cognitive confusion, losing a thread of thought, all of that was normal from a recovering stroke victim. Seeing it real-time, in the middle of an intense conversation, was hard.

"Mom." Theo's voice cracked. "Hi, it's me. That's my girlfriend."

"Oh, she's lovely." She beamed at me, no trace of recognition on her face. "Why are you both here?"

"I missed you." He kissed the top of her head, lingering for a beat before he hugged her. "I won't stay away so long next time."

"Nonsense! You're playing hockey! Have fun." She yawned and waved at me. "Excuse me, I need to lay down. Will you both stay for lunch?"

"Oh, no thank you.' We're full." I smiled, avoiding Theo's knowing gaze. It was hours past lunch. "You rest, Mrs. Sanders."

"You seem wonderful. Would you visit again?"

"Absolutely." I squeezed her hand before holding it out for

Theo to take. He kissed his mom's forehead and let me lead him back outside. The air cooled slightly, and the sunset greeted us over the nice lake nearby. Theo inhaled a few times before letting go, wrapping his arms around my shoulders and tugging my back against his chest.

"I wouldn't have been able to do this without you. I hope you know that. You are... everything, Audrey." He kissed my temple. "You saw how she was... and my dad..."

"It's complicated." I closed my eyes and enjoyed how he felt around me. Large thick muscles, warmth and strength, soft clothes and gentle touches. For avoiding feelings most of my life, the loneliness was all worth it to wait for him. For us. "The love she has for you is real. It shines through."

"How can she say she forgives my dad when she can't remember things?"

"It's probably short-term memory loss. She'll remember the big stuff. She seemed healthy, happy even. Seeing you made her smile, and that's not a memory she'd lose."

He huffed and kissed my neck. "Can I stay with you tonight? I'm gonna be a mess, and I just want to lay naked with you."

"That we can do." I'd take care of him, like he had with me thousands of times. Because that was what a relationship should be like. You took turns leaning on each other. It wasn't one-sided. I vowed then and there, I'd rather be alone and friendless than to accept half-friendships. That meant no more trying with my mom or Quentin. Unless they reached out and wanted to repair our family, I'd focus on myself and being happy.

With Theo, I felt whole again. I missed this feeling. I just hoped we'd make it last when he left to play for the Acorns.

24

Theo

It was our first game for the season, my final college home opener. I deserved a goddamn Oscar for being able to focus on hockey at all with the rest of my whirlwind life. In the three weeks since my dad announced he was a fucking cheater, I'd made more of an effort to see my mom.

It hurt every single time, but Audrey went with me. Sometimes, she stayed in the hallway. Others, she came in and played Uno with us. Em, Daniel, Penny, and I still hung out three times a week, but my dad kept his word. Not sure his word was worth shit after twenty-one days, but he'd stepped up. He came home from work, picked up my siblings, and went back to being our dad.

He didn't seem like he lied. The two times he was late, he'd shared his location with me as he was at the store. He promised me he'd never lie to me again, and he said he wanted me to *live* my life.

How did I even do that?

Spending every second with Audrey, learning more about her, and getting to experience things with her. My life had been go-go-go all the time with fleeting relationships where there was no deep meaning. The fact I had someone like her? It made everything seem less intense.

I stood on the ice as someone sang the national anthem and stared into the crowd. Audrey was there. Her auburn hair was in a high pony, and she wore a navy and orange hoodie. It wasn't *my* number on the back, but she was here. For me.

My chest filled with pride.

She shared she wasn't sure about coming because of Quentin or her mom, but she wanted to see me play. She sat by Em, the two of them laughing at something on my sister's phone, but something ran into my arm and made me lose balance.

"What was that for?" I hissed, not drawing attention during the song. Fucking Quentin Hawthorne stood next to me. His injury had improved, and he could skate. Not play during the game, but he could gently practice. I was happy for him as a fellow athlete. Being injured was a special kind of hell.

"My sister is here," he said, his voice much less sarcastic than what I was used to. Things were less weird between us, but I wasn't about to hug him or be besties for life.

Even after our *chat,* he hadn't reached out to Audrey. I knew because I'd asked her. I hoped our talk would knock sense into him but nope. The kid was still an idiot.

"I texted her and asked her to come."

Oh. My stomach tightened. I thought she came for me. "Good, yeah?"

It didn't feel good. I wanted her for myself, regardless of how that sounded. I'd never voice that to her, but the blip of annoyance did intrude.

"I didn't think she would. She never came to my games before, ever. Maybe a few times in high school, but dude, I've been thinking about what you said. I need to do something for her."

Oh, she never came to games. That meant she came for me. Okay. Phew.

Get it together.

"What are you thinking?" I asked because he expected it. Well, that wasn't entirely true. I wanted to know. Seeing Audrey upset made me feel aggressive, protective, and feral things I wasn't accustomed to. So if he could make her less upset, that would be great for me.

"She loves reading, I think." He paused and glanced at me, like I was supposed to confirm for him or something.

I kept my face neutral. He cleared his throat and continued, "I'm gonna get her a few books and bring her favorite drink. Tea, if I remember."

"It's coffee." I fought the urge to roll my eyes. "I'm glad you want to do something nice." The intros ended, and I hit Quentin on the arm as a goodbye before skating over to Reiner. He held a fist, and I hit it.

Instead of running plays last week, we switched positions and ended up having a *fun* practice. I played goalie and fucking sucked. Hannigan played forward and scored twice on me. It went to his head, but by the end of the two hours, we felt like a team instead of separate individuals all playing hockey on the ice.

Right as I got into position and the puck dropped, my mind switched to *hockey.* My sole purpose was to play the game, and every other thought left my mind.

No more worries about my mom or dad. Nothing about Quentin. Audrey was a nice blip in the back, but I forgot about all of them. It was me and the ice and the guys.

Jefferson won the face-off, slapping the puck to me, and I flew into action. Skating was a part of my blood, who I was. With the smells of the gear and sounds of the metal on ice, I was home.

My pulse raced as I headed for the goal. Peters was open, so I passed it. He fired it back, and I slapshot the puck right past the goalie. *First goal of the season.*

Sirens blared, and the guys huddled around me, offering compliments that felt good as fuck. I couldn't wait to be in the NHL on the large scale. But as Hannigan and Liam congratulated me, my gaze went to the stands. Em and Audrey were on their feet, huge smiles on their faces, and it hit me.

I wanted Audrey to *be* in my family. I wanted her at all my fucking games, and yeah, the NHL was my future, but so was she. I nodded up at her but felt the back of my neck prickle. Quentin's attention went from me, to her, then back, and he narrowed his eyes.

This damn punk was a pain in the ass, for real.

The game continued, and I scored another goal and had two assists. We took our home opener for the year, and Reiner was giddy. Him and JD hooted and hollered in the locker room, talking about teamwork and how true collaboration was what the game was about. Not personal stats. They mattered, sure, but cohesiveness mattered more.

"What did the Acorns say to you before you signed, Sanders?" JD asked me, as we all sat around in our post-game celebration. "Any advice for the rest of the guys?"

The room quieted, and every guy faced me. It was a powerful feeling, knowing they looked up to me and respected me enough to listen. Even Quentin stared at me without the usual judgement. If anything, it seemed like he was in awe of me.

"We played like a team tonight. Like everyone's success mattered equally. That's the whole point of being on a team. It doesn't matter how many goals one of us scores. The assist matters, and the amount of blocks Hannigan had was insane."

"Fuck yeah, dude." One of the guys hit Hannigan on the back.

"Hannigan!"

Cheers followed but then everyone quieted and stared at me again. My face heated but not from embarrassment. It was pride. I was fucking proud that I was a leader on this team, that Reiner wanted me to help and I had. "No one has a role too big or too small here. Every fucking one of us matters. Even Quentin." I pointed to him, and his eyes widened. "He's been at every practice, taking notes, watching film, and giving input. He can't play, yet he's with us every single day."

"Yeah, Q. Yeah, Q!"

Reiner leaned against the wall with the goofiest smile on his face, and he nodded at me when I met his gaze. That little nod told me enough, and the same proud, happy feeling filled me up. He took a chance on me transferring here, and I didn't want to let him down.

"If we play like this every game, no one can beat us. So, let's keep playing like a pack. Let's go, Wolves!"

Howls and barks, claps and cheers echoed in the locker room. It'd be a long season, road trips and hard opponents, but instead of dreading it, I was excited. Maybe it was the fact I didn't have to rush home to babysit or the fact Audrey was waiting for me after the game, or maybe it was the win and two goals I had, but my life finally was looking up. I showered and packed my shit and was out the locker room door to find my girl.

I'd stay with her tonight. Most of the guys wanted to go party and celebrate the win, but I'd only do that if Audrey wanted to tag along too. It was weird to join a team my senior year. I didn't have the connections with any of them. I liked them. Trusted them on the ice. But the bonds the others had that formed three years ago? I didn't have that.

And I'd be out of here once I graduated.

Girlfriends and family members waited outside the locker room, and my gaze instantly sought Audrey and her auburn hair. I did one scan and didn't see her. Frowning, I did another, and Em waved me over.

"You did so great, bro." She hugged me. "I was texting Jace the whole time about you. He wants to come watch next time. Would that be okay?"

"Jace?" I cringed. I really didn't like him, but I couldn't tell her that. "Uh, maybe. Hey, where's Auds?"

"Oh, her brother wanted to talk to her. Why, should I have gone with them?"

"Nah." I sighed and tried to find her again. They wouldn't have walked far. "Do you need me to drop you off at home?"

"No. Jace is picking me up." She beamed. "I really like Audrey, Theo. Did you know she gave me her number to call her if I need anything? Like, she knows you're leaving next year but said she'd still be around and would always help. That's so nice."

Audrey would do that. Give herself to my family, even if I was gone. She'd do it even if we broke up or didn't work out. Even though breaking up wasn't an option. That wasn't my plan at all. I'd do anything to make sure we stayed together. Her offering that to my sister just proved how good of a fucking person she was. Damn, I loved her.

"Oh, there she is!" Em pulled my shirt and pointed toward the west hallway. Quentin and Audrey faced each other, and he hung his head.

My feet twitched with the urge to run to her. I remained here though, watching and waiting. She didn't seem upset. There were no tears on her face, no red cheeks from her anger either. If anything, *he* seemed more emotional than her.

Had he figured out we were together? Had she told him?

"She told me they had a fight, and she wasn't sure if she should forgive him. I told her if you and I ever fought, it would kill me. And that younger siblings aren't used to being the ones to take the first step in fixing something. So, if he wanted to say sorry, she should listen."

"When the fuck did you turn thirty years old with your advice? Who are you?" I chuckled and pulled her into a half hug. "What the hell, Em?"

"I've learned a bit the last two years," she said softly. "From you."

My heart twisted in my chest knowing I'd leave next year. We'd just have to FaceTime every day or something. I loved my family despite the dramatics. "Don't make me feel things. I can't handle it."

She laughed just as Quentin hugged Audrey. He wrapped his arms around her, and she squeezed him back, her gaze meeting mine over his shoulder. I loved how she sought me out, and in that one look, with her large green eyes and half-smile, I knew she was okay.

"They talked it out." Em sighed. "Good. I think she downplayed how much he upset her."

"She tends to do that."

"Don't let her do that to you. She's good for you, dude."

"Fully aware." I shoved Em away, teasing her. "Where is your ride?"

"Oh, he's here now."

"I'll walk you out." I quickly texted Audrey to meet me outside, that I was going to ensure Em got in Jace's car okay. "Need to make sure your *boyfriend* is safe."

"Ugh. Come on. He's fine. You've met him before."

"Yeah, but still."

I was ready for Em to go to college and forget that loser, but that wasn't until next year. Too much time for Em to make poor choices with him. Maybe our dad would step in and stop it.

We walked out, and Jace leaned against his car, his face

breaking into a huge smile when he saw my sister. "Hi, Em. Theo!"

"Hi, baby!" She ran to him and hugged him. It was a little too much of a hug for my taste, but I shooed them away and watched the car disappear down the road. She seemed happy, and that was honestly all I wanted for my siblings. To feel safe and happy.

"Good game, Sanders."

I spun around, a smile on my face as Audrey approached me. "Liked seeing you in the stands today." I pulled the string on her hoodie until her shoes touched mine. "Everything okay with you and your brother?"

She chewed her lip, her eyes sparkling as she gripped my waistband. "That's what you want to talk about? That was my first time really watching you play, and you are *incredible.* I'd much rather go to my dorm right now with you."

Oh. Yes. I liked this.

I grinned. "To do what?"

Her signature blush spread across her face, and she giggled. "Get naked."

"Mm, I knew you were perfect for me." I cupped her face and kissed her hard. "Fucking loved seeing you in the stands."

"Wondered if you were showing off or if you really were that good," she said, her lips brushing mine with each word. "Em seemed to think you were flaunting for me."

"Maybe I wanted to make my girlfriend proud."

"I always am, Theo. But you are exceptional on the ice." She held my gaze and said the words in a serious, deep tone. "You're incredible."

"Thank you." I cleared my throat. I wanted to yank her against me and declare my love and demand she never leave me. It so wasn't the time, plus I needed more details on her brother.

Instead, I kissed her again and held her tight. "And thank you for being so kind to Em."

"Don't thank me for that." Audrey sighed, and her minty breath hit my face. I loved her little sighs. "What are you grinning about?"

"You. Just you."

Her eyes warmed, and her cheeks pinkened as she intertwined our fingers. It felt so natural, and there was no hesitation on her. We were finally *together* without a doubt. "We can talk about your sister and my brother later. Right now, I just want to spend time with you."

God, I loved those words. My life was a dream right now, and instead of worrying when the other shoe would drop, I was gonna enjoy it. "Lead the way, baby."

25

Audrey

Quentin was *trying.*

It had been a few weeks since the home opener where we hugged, and he promised to be a better brother. A real friend to me. I wanted to trust him because I missed my brother. But time would tell the truth.

Today was the day we were meeting up at a diner to *hang.* He wanted to hear about my clinicals with Theo and my plans for next year. And he offered to pay and insisted I'd never pay for another one of our meals. My stomach still squirmed with anticipation, but us talking again was worth giving it a try. Em really hit me in my feels talking about how she felt about her brother. Her *older* brother. I never gave much thought to sibling dynamics, but hearing her, a wonderful upbeat innocent girl who went through a lot, talk about the hurt she'd feel if she and Theo fought, it woke me up.

Quentin wasn't innocent in this, but he didn't have to be guilty forever. I played with my straw wrapper when the door to the diner chimed. *Not Quentin.*

Theo: Let me know if you need me, okay? You got this, Auds.

Audrey: I can do this.

Theo: Call me after. I don't have to be at the rink for another few hours.

They had another home game tonight, and Theo's dad was joining. It felt big. Massive, even. They hadn't really spoken since that night at his house, and just like I was opening up with my brother, Theo was doing the same with his dad.

People were complicated. People weren't all good, nor all bad, but talking out feelings fucking sucked. No one wanted to do it, and the cycle of resentment grew. Some things were able to be repaired. Not everything.

Like the texts from my mom I never answered.

Mom: send me money or I'll starve

Mom: you think Dad would be proud of you? You were so selfish, Audrey

Mom: please, I'll miss my bills

Mom: honey, I was hungry. I'm okay now, please help me?

Mom: DID YOU TURN QUENTIN AGAINST ME? HOW DARE YOU?

Mom: I'm calling your BROTHER.

The last one was sent yesterday. It hurt, but I blocked her. She had Quentin's number and my email and address. If she wanted to make an effort, she could.

The remaining guilt stabbed me, picturing what my dad would say if he saw us now. He'd want me to try, but I had been. I could only take so much before I had to let her go.

Theo's struggles reminded me that it wasn't our job to emotionally babysit our parents. We could help, be supportive, but the relationship had to be reciprocal and genuine. Maybe I'd be ready to talk to my mom again, but I could decide that later. For now? I was better off without her.

My brother and I? Theo and his dad?

They were repairable if *both* parties were honest and willing. And they were.

I planned to meet his dad after the game, and the three of us would grab a drink somewhere. Em volunteered to watch her siblings so the two of them could make up. Again, I adored Em. She was so mature for her age.

The same bell chimed, and my brother walked in. He ran his hand through his hair, ruffling it before giving me a small smile. He held a green bag in one hand. His jaw flexed, and he waved, kinda awkwardly.

It was endearing.

"Hi, Auds." He slid into the booth across from me. "How are you? You look great. Happy!"

I rolled my eyes at his overeagerness. "Thanks, but no need to come on that strong."

He winced. "I'm-I didn't mean to. I brought you something."

"What? You didn't have to do that." Surprise colored my tone. He wasn't a gift giver, at all. "I'm happy to see you."

"I bought you books and coffee. I realize now you probably don't have a grinder in your dorm. I can buy you one though, to make freshly ground coffee." He ran a hand over his neck and glanced out the window. "I've been talking to Theo." He paused, stared at me, and cleared his throat.

My stomach swooped. They'd talked *about me*? Did my brother know? Did I want him to? Theo and I hadn't talked about this.

"I know you two are friends and have clinicals together. Anyway." He waved his hand in the air. "I realized that I've been a shit brother for a while. I took advantage of your kindness and heart, and I'm sorry. I'm so sorry. You held us together and shielded me from so much pain, I know that. I hate knowing I hurt you."

I blinked, completely unsure how to feel about his confession. The knots in my gut untwisted as he said the words I'd dreamed of hearing. He seemed different. He didn't carry the same egotistical aura I was accustomed to. There was no smug gleam in his eyes or bounce to his step. "Thanks for saying that."

"I didn't see it, and I think... this injury and our fight, it really taught me a lot. I'm nothing without hockey, and that's fucked. I lashed out at people who care about my well-being and you."

"What about your girlfriend or whatever?" I managed to ask without disdain. I was hiding Theo from him, so him keeping her secret wasn't that scandalous. It hurt less knowing he might have reasons for the secrecy.

He closed his eyes. "We're not really together. Mom... she sometimes comes to visit and always expects me to be dating. I don't know why. It's weird, but Kelly always pretends to be my date. I like her, but we've just been pals."

The mention of our mom hurt. It was foolish to think Quentin would cut her off just cause I did, but hearing him say it so casually caused pain in my chest. "Mom comes to visit you? When? How often?"

He swallowed, and his attention flicked away from me.

"Quentin, we agreed to be honest if we're going to try being friends instead of siblings." I took a sip of my iced tea. "Answer me, please."

He nodded, and a dark, sad look crossed his face. "I've seen her probably four times a year. At first, I asked if we should invite you, but she always said you were too busy and to leave you alone. I believed her."

I chewed my lip. I'd never had my mom visit for anything the last four years. It was always, *always* about money. I'd ask her to come see us on campus, and she'd ask me to pay for her trip or if I could go see her instead. Every conversation made me feel insignificant. It hurt, so badly, because I remembered who she used to be, but grief changed people. I sniffed, a prickle forming in my eyes. "So you two have a good relationship."

"I'm so fucking sorry, Auds. I don't know why she did this. She's made comments about not wanting to bother you, but she's also said she's ashamed that you're a better parent. I think with what happened to dad, she took on the role of a sister and you the parent. She's embarrassed."

"And using me for money every week, even though I'm in school? Making me feel like shit? Telling me I had to pay for her if I wanted to see her? Demanding I send her checks to pay for bills or Dad would hate me?" Damn. I didn't want to cry, but here I was, tears and all. I dabbed them with a napkin, and I thought about running. I could avoid this and run to Theo, who would hold me.

But I had to do this. I owed it to my brother. We'd hash this out and then, only then, I'd decide if it was worth it to work on our relationship.

"Don't cry, I hate this. I didn't know about the money. I had no idea. That is fucking horrible. I just... liked being her favorite, okay? You were Dad's. And then you held it all together and were so good during everything. I was jealous, and knowing Mom liked me more, even for stupid reasons, felt good. I regret it—"

"*Held it all together?*" I whispered. "Quentin, I've been a fucking mess. I don't have friends. I study all the time and work my ass off to earn every penny to support you and Mom. If I don't, then we don't have food. This is—"

"I fucking know." Quentin squeezed his eyes shut. "I'm sorry. I don't know how to fix this, but I want to. I'll do whatever you want. Please. I'll cut Mom out. I won't see her. I refuse to take a penny from you now, forever."

Hearing him say those words was enough for me. The last knot in my chest loosened, and I found myself smiling. I could feel my dad's approval as I said, "No, that's not what I'm asking, Q. Mom needs you. She loves you. Don't cut her off. She might lose her will to live."

"But she's been so horrible to you."

I shrugged. "Yeah, but not *to you*."

I rubbed my temples and noted my brother's misery. He really seemed sad, sadder than I had seen before. "Why do you even want to fix this? Seriously."

"Why?" He tilted his head.

"Yes." I thought of Em and all the things she said about Theo. My younger brother, who I supported, told me he was jealous. "Why do you even want to be friends?"

"Audrey." He laughed. "You're funny as hell, wicked smart, and creative. I remember all the games you'd invent when dad was dying or how you'd make recipes from nothing or how you found out Mom and Dad couldn't make it to my final home game, and you did everything to make sure my senior night was special. You've always been there for me. And now it's my turn to be there for you."

My stomach twisted with hope, and more tears fell. "That was nice."

"I love you, you buffoon." He kicked my knee under the table. "I'm sorry I was an ass. I've been learning from the guys on the team I was pretty unbearable. Them and you calling me out, it kinda woke me up."

Nodding, I took another drink just to have something to do with my hands. They trembled. "So you're gonna be less annoying now?"

"Eh, don't go that far." He handed me the bag. "This is a 'forgive me' gift but really because I know you love reading. You used to read fantasy before life got crazy, so I looked up the hottest ones right now with good reviews."

Oh. "That's thoughtful." I pulled out each book and smiled. "I've been wanting this author, thank you."

"And I think you should call out mom like you did with me. It'll be hard, but—"

I shook my head. "I don't think I will. I love her, and yeah, she's struggling, but she's not someone I want a relationship with anymore. Maybe she'll change one day, but it's not worth it right now."

"She always asks about you." He frowned. "Fuck, enough about her, tell me about your clinicals. What's the weirdest part?"

We talked. We talked for over an hour where he asked me more questions than I to him. First time ever. I learned about Theo mentoring him. That I had no idea. I also learned he respected Theo. The dude he swore revenge on and to hate forever. It was fascinating, but I understood it. Theo was a loveable, wonderful guy who won over his worst enemy.

Quentin had to leave for the game but left me more than enough money to cover the check. As I paid, someone familiar caught my eye. *Theo's father.*

My breath caught in my throat at the scene in front of me. He sat with another woman. Their heads were close together, and *oh no.* Theo literally told me yesterday how happy he was that his dad was a changed man.

And now he was here with another woman. Unacceptable. No. Anger gripped me, but Quentin popped the door open with a grin. "Come on, I'll drive you back, sis."

I didn't want to bring Theo's family drama to my brother, now that we'd just mended our conflict. I trusted him but not with Theo's secrets. I bit my tongue, my hands clenching into a fist at my sides as I stared at his dad. He never looked up from the woman, his gaze entirely on her, and I wanted to chuck a glass at him.

He lied. He fucking promised Theo that he wouldn't step out again.

I can't tell Theo.

That was clear. It would kill him. So as Quentin drove me back to campus, since Theo dropped me off, I vowed to keep it quiet. I'd confront Theo's dad at the game tonight to knock it off. That way, Theo would never find out.

I just had to keep it together enough for Theo to not find out.

MEET me outside the side door. I need to see your face.

Those were Theo's words in a text, an hour before the game. Butterflies exploded in my stomach at the urgency of the message. I'd never had the whole boyfriend experience, so flutters and swarms of nerves danced down my body as I stood outside the hockey rink side door.

He'd never sent anything like this, so a part of me wondered if he'd learned about his dad and wanted to talk. Or maybe something happened with his mom? I wasn't sure, but as the door creaked open, I held my breath.

"Hi, baby," he said, smiling. He wore his hockey uniform minus the skates. His hair was messy, like he'd run his hand through it a hundred times, but his eyes made me melt.

They were soft and warm. "Hi," I replied, unable to stop a smile myself. A part of me hated knowing I kept a secret from him, but what kind of person would I be to upset him? Right before a game?

"I missed you today, and Reiner said we had ten minutes before pre-game shit started. Figured I'd shoot my shot. How are you? God, I love your face." He cupped my collarbone, then neck and face, his gaze caressing me as his smile grew. "And you in this jersey? A dream."

I blushed and focused on the dent in the door. "I'm good, ready to see you play."

"My dad is meeting you right? You gonna sit together? He texted me he might be late because he was caught up at work."

At the mention of his dad, my body turned to ice. A rock. Frozen. My throat seized, and it took all my effort to remain neutral. Clearing my throat, I nodded and avoided his gaze. "We might, yeah."

"Whoa, what's wrong?" Theo frowned and grabbed my hands. "You're tense."

"No, I'm fine." I forced a smile as my heart raced. I wanted to confront his dad first, not tell Theo. The anger slithered like an angry snake, weaving its way through my chest. How *dare* his dad do this again?

Theo's frown deepened. "Fine isn't the most reassuring word. I can read you like my favorite book. Please, tell me what's wrong."

I shook my head before I could get any words out. "Nothing. I'm good. Ready to see you play."

Theo studied my face as his jaw tightened. "You promise? You'd tell me if something was wrong? It's not your mom or brother?"

I shook my head. "Not them, I swear." This was where I had to make the right call. He knew something was off, somehow, because he paid so much attention to me, and my poker face was trash. I had to distract because he had a game in an hour. I stood on my tiptoes and wrapped my arms around his shoulders. He melted against me as I kissed his jaw. "I promise. Now, I need my boyfriend ready to kick ass on the ice."

He let out a small laugh and kissed below my ear. His blue eyes warmed as he pushed a lock of hair behind my ear. "Love knowing you're here, Auds. Love it a fucking lot."

"Play hard, be safe." I kissed his mouth, ignoring the race of my heart at his use of the term *love*. I loved him with everything I had, and that meant making sacrifices sometimes.

"See you later, baby." He kissed me one more time before winking and heading back into the rink. I exhaled and rubbed my temples for a minute, hoping that'd ease the tension.

Maybe I'd tell him after the game. Yeah, I didn't want to keep anything from him this big, but at the same time, if I could speak to his dad, I could get him to stop. All I knew was I refused to let Theo get hurt, and I'd do anything to prevent it.

Two hours later, I sat in the seats Theo gave us, and his dad wasn't there. I stood with an empty seat next to me, and Theo was having a rough game. First period flew by without a single goal. There had only been a few shots attempted, and they weren't pretty. Hannigan, our goalie, blocked a ton, but it was already 0 and 3.

The opposition had possession most of the time, and their defense was strong. Better than ours. Theo was off. I could tell. He was playing with less attitude and slower. He didn't have his usual swagger, and I hoped with all my being it had nothing to do with our chat.

My chest ached with worry. Where was his damn father? He told Theo and me he'd be there to hang with me and see Theo play, yet as the second period finished, his seat was very empty. Fuck, the nerves and anxiety around this were paralyzing.

I wasn't sure if it was my imagination, but I swore Theo knew I sat here and hadn't once looked my way. I'd be hard to miss. It was front row.

At the start of the third period, it was 1-4. The other team kept slamming into Theo, roughing him up. The crowd roared at him, rallying behind him since he'd become a crowd favorite. It was so easy to root for him with his easy smiles and obvious teamwork. He received the loudest cheers the last month, scoring twice most games. He made the other guys look good while he played too. But tonight, he was off. *Still.*

"Let's go, Sanders! Score!"

"Come on, Theo!"

He was checked into the wall, his face a few feet from mine, and I held my breath until he pushed off and skated past the opponent. *Phew.* This game was rough, and while Theo was large and fast, he could still get hurt.

He passed to Liam and shot the puck right into the net.

The sirens blared. We were only down two now. Their coach yelled orders at them, and Theo nodded. The other team had minor penalties back-to-back, and the Wolves operated a power play with ease.

Liam to Peter, Peter to Theo, Theo to Blaze, back to Theo, then Peter and goal! I jumped up and down, screaming with the crowd next to me. It hit me how much I loved watching the game. I'd avoided it with Quentin, but with him and I working on us and Theo? I needed to watch more. It was fun.

The third period flew by. The Wolves were still down one with the last few minutes. The Wolves had been undefeated at home, but with the final seconds, Theo blitzed down the ice, his stick work unparalleled. He pulled back, shot the puck, and—

He missed. The game ended with a loud blast, and the Wolves lost.

The hushed silence of the crowd was so loud. A collective sigh overtook the rink as the guys left the ice. Theo hung his head as he disappeared into the locker room, and my stomach hurt for him.

He took every game seriously, and every win mattered. But the guys were human, and shit happened. I'd reassure him everything would be fine.

. . .

M<small>Y NERVES TWISTED</small> as I made my way toward the family area. I'd avoided thinking about his dad most of the game, but now that I saw him standing against the wall, the rush of anger returned full force. He'd ditched me at the game for *work* and made me lie to Theo. He smiled when he saw me approaching.

How dare he look happy when he was cheating on Theo's mom again? Confrontation was so hard for me. My body rebelled against it, but I'd do this for Theo.

"Audrey, hi." He waved and offered a small smile as I approached him. "Sorry I didn't make my way to your seats. I got here late and hung out in the standing room area with a buddy from work."

I nodded, words escaping me. How did I bring this up? What was the right protocol here? Theo hated liars. He made that clear, and keeping something from him felt like being choked. "You—"

"Next time, we should sit together, Audrey. I want to get to know my son's girlfriend. Is that... would you like to for next home game?" he asked, his expression tight, like he was nervous.

I nodded again, annoyed that I felt bad for him. No. He was lying. He could've sat with me today but chose not to. "Listen, Mr. Sanders."

Commotion started behind me, and I knew the players were exiting now. I had seconds. Theo never came out first, so I rushed. "You need to stop the affair. You promised Theo you wouldn't do that again. Yet you lied. After everything you did, your lies will crush him, Mr. Sanders. You need to end it now. He's been so happy. He deserves *better*," I said, my teeth gritted as my eyes watered.

My stomach twisted in knots, and I wanted to throw up, but I'd do this for Theo. He needed someone looking out for him, and I volunteered.

"Audrey." He frowned, his face paling. "I did. I-I stopped." He glanced around, his face red.

"No. I saw you with a someone." My throat felt like I swallowed an entire pillow. There was no saliva in my mouth, and I could barely get my words out. "You were huddled with some *woman* at the diner today. You held her hand. You told Theo you were *caught up at work!*" I whispered. "You weren't. You were caught up with her."

He blinked and held up his hands, shaking his head hard. "What? No, that... please, don't—."

"I won't tell him, if that's what you're worried about. I won't do that to him. Not your selfless, incredible son." I sniffed as angry tears welled up. "You can't do that to your wife or your son. Please. Stop the affair."

"It's not what you think—" He shook his head furiously. "No, Theo, it's not true! Audrey's misunderstanding, I promise. She doesn't know."

"What?" It took my brain a second to realize he wasn't speaking to me. Instead, his gaze was over my shoulder. *Theo.* No, I didn't want him finding out about this. A spike of panic clawed at my throat. It would kill him. I spun around, but Theo wasn't glaring at his dad. He stared at me with accusation all over his face.

My stomach heaved. Why would Theo be mad *at me*? I blinked, tears prickling at the angry gaze aimed at me. "Wh-what—what's wrong?"

"You weren't going to tell me?" He pressed his lips together as his jaw ticked. "That's what you just said. You had no plans to tell me my dad was cheating again? That's what you lied about earlier."

"I'm not cheating, Theo! I swear. She saw me with another woman today—"

"So when I asked you what was wrong before the game,

that's why you were acting weird? Because you knew this and didn't want to tell me?"

There was an icy coating to his words, and they felt like little icicles stabbing my chest. I'd never heard this directed at me before, and my knees shook. "I-I wanted—"

"No." He shook his head, his nostrils flaring. "You kept it from me. I asked you if something was wrong, and you *lied*. The one thing... so what? You were hoping to confront my dear old dad and keep it from me?"

I nodded as the ground swallowed me up. "I didn't want to upset you before—"

"There's nothing to be upset about," his dad butted in. "She misunderstood. The woman she saw me with wasn't—"

"So she did see you with someone?" Theo arched a brow. "Unbelievable. I have a shit game and then this... I need some space. I just... gotta go."

He marched by us without another word and disappeared through the exit. My chest ached as a horrible pang took hold. A part of me knew we wouldn't last, that this had an end date. We didn't make sense on paper, but my god, it hurt. The look on his face. The coldness to his words.

I was gonna lose it.

My chest heaved as a warm hand landed on my shoulder. *Theo's dad.*

"Audrey."

I flinched and jerked away from him. I didn't want him to yell at me too. "I'm s-sorry. I was trying to protect Theo because I love him, and he doesn't need any more pain. But I lied to him after he asked me not to." Fuck. My jaw trembled, and tears fell now.

"I know. I understand why you did what you did. Theo will too. Just give him some time. It's important for you to know that the woman was my new therapist."

"Therapist?"

He nodded as a sad look crossed his face. "She specializes in helping partners whose spouses go through life-changing injury. Today was our first meeting face-to-face. It wasn't an affair. I stopped that night I told Theo."

"You're seeing *a therapist*?" My stomach bottomed out. "Oh god. I was wrong. I'm so sorry. I messed this up. All of it."

"Hey, it's alright." He patted my shoulder again. "I'm glad Theo has someone looking out for him."

I had to get out of here. I assumed my plans with Theo were done. "I should go, yeah. Bye."

"Auds," a familiar voice said my name. "I'll walk you home."

My brother joined me as I left the stadium, and I didn't have the energy to worry over what he saw or heard. I was just glad to not be alone. We walked in silence back to my dorm, and once I was inside, alone, I broke down.

I'd remember my time with Theo in the future and smile, but right now? It felt like dying. Each breath hurt as I crawled into bed and cried.

26

Theo

I was fucking angry.

Anger and adrenaline went hand in hand, and the energy leftover from the game combined with the mad. Audrey lied to me. She had kept information about my dad from me and told me nothing was wrong. I knew something was off before the game, and it bothered me the whole time. I let her *lie* throw me off my game, and I'd played like shit.

I couldn't do that again, not in the NHL. I couldn't let Audrey affect my game, and I had. All because of my fucking father.

He was cheating again. She knew. She hadn't told me.

It hurt. I couldn't have a girlfriend who lied to me. And Audrey was just so damn genuine I hadn't expected it. It hurt. It fucking hurt to feel betrayed like that. And she knew how hard I was working to forgive my dad. So to lie for him when I was trying to like him again felt even worse. She should've told me. We could've handled it together. But no.

Fuck. My chest ached.

I walked toward the hockey house, desperate to find something to do instead of going to Audrey's dorm or home. Hell, I didn't want to see either Audrey or my dad, so I could crash at the house. Maybe have a few drinks and work through these fucked up emotions.

God, I was a mess. I'd played like shit, and all the trust I'd built up with Audrey and my dad was gone. I rubbed my hands over my eyes as I walked in. A few of the younger guys were already there, cups in hand and music blaring. I poured a beer and sat on the couch, my leg bouncing up and down with the unshed adrenaline. Girls showed up, dancing on each other and searching for their newest hookup. One eyed me, and I shook my head, ending whatever notion she had going on in her mind.

I was pissed and betrayed, but I wasn't an asshole.

My phone buzzed, and foolishly, I hoped it was Audrey. I wanted her apologizing. I wanted her to say something to make this better so I could just go to her dorm. Because even though I had a drink and was around everyone, I fucking felt alone and only wanted her.

Dad: please don't be mad at Audrey. She was thinking about you. It was also my new therapist. If you need to be mad, be mad at me. Not the girl who was trying to protect you.

A new therapist?

Did I believe him?

I did. He told me he was searching for one to help him work through the changes in Mom. I'd never shared that with Audrey because it slipped my mind. I tried not talking about him with her because it brought me down, but if I'd told her, would she have done this?

Wait. Protect me? My dad was on her side. That was confusing as fuck. A part of me liked that he was protecting her. She was amazing, but then the loss of the game and her blatant lie soured my thoughts.

"Scoot over."

I glanced up and found Quentin staring at me with a

different expression. He seemed upset. I didn't move one inch. I didn't wanna deal with him today. Unless something had happened to his sister?

"Is she okay?" I asked, voice dry as a desert.

"You mean after I walked her home so she wouldn't be alone? Or after you made her sob?" His words were sharp.

Fuck me. The pain in my gut intensified. She shouldn't be upset *at me*. She would feel guilty. "I—"

"Sanders, we've had a fucking journey together this semester, but let me make a few things clear. I figured out you two are together, and honestly, I dig it. My sister needs someone to take care of her and be there for her because no one else in her fucking life does. Everyone abandoned her, and I'm working on making that right. You can't be someone who leaves her too."

My jaw tightened as his words washed over me. I knew all this. Of course I knew and hated it. My hand clenched with the urge to punch him. "I didn't do anything wrong, Quentin. She kept something from me."

"About what?"

"Doesn't matter. She lied, and that's not fine with me."

"No. It does matter. Because Audrey will lie if she thinks she's protecting someone she loves. Given the choice to hurt or upset someone she cares about or hide the truth, she will hide it every time. She hid my dad's symptoms for years because they upset me. She told me it was fine or just a normal appointment so I could keep playing hockey normally. I had no idea my dad was barely hanging on. So yeah. She lies for good reasons, so I'm gonna ask you again. Why did she lie?"

I was gonna tear this pillow to shreds. His words made sense. They fit Audrey perfectly. She'd protect those she loved. But that clashed with my angry feelings about her and how her *lie* made me play like shit. "She hid something my dad did and confronted him in hopes of hiding it from me. Then, I played like shit."

"Okay, we all have bad games. It's a marathon, not a sprint. But that's not what matters here. She *confronted* your dad? Are you fucking with me right now?" Quentin glared at me. "Audrey cannot stand confrontation. It makes her throw up. Just think about how hard that had to be for her to *confront* your dad? She had to be shaking with nerves, and she did it to protect *you*. To shield *you*. And you left her? Just walked away without a word? Fuck you, Sanders. You're a better man than that, and Audrey deserves better."

Quentin's arguments made my stomach sour, and guilt clawed at me. Audrey totally hated confrontation. She cried for hours after she confronted her brother, and I was there for her then.

Was she alone in her room right now? My gut churned.

"You called me out when I was being an idiot, and you were right. But now, as your teammate and the brother of the girl you're with, I'm calling you out. Get out of your head. Get over this. This is forgivable. You'd be fucking stupid to let this ruin whatever you had because I can tell you for sure, my sister has never been this happy. Being in Audrey's life is a gift, Theo. Don't ruin it."

"I kinda wanna punch you in the face," I mumbled.

"Yeah, well right back at you. But my sister matters more than my feelings toward you, so if you hit me, I won't hit you back."

Damn. Quentin's words sobered me up real fast. This punk ass kid who was unbearable to be around like two months ago was showing more maturity than me. I kept thinking about Audrey in her room, curled in bed crying, and it physically upset me. She was protecting me in her own way. It made sense. I had to find her.

I never handled loss well when I didn't perform to my standard. Hockey was my escape, my future, so when I let something get in my head and fuck with my game, I lashed out. The loss and the lie blended together.

A new fear gripped me. Audrey always assumed the worst when we disagreed, and she'd never had a relationship, so she didn't know arguing was normal. Maybe I shouldn't have stormed off, but I'd needed to collect my thoughts. And fuck, if Quentin wasn't helpful.

"I gotta go talk to her." I stood.

"Yeah, you do." Quentin's face was grim. "It'll be tough, okay? She carries more burden and guilt than anyone else. But please don't hurt her."

My eye twitched. "I never have, Quentin."

"You did tonight." He shoved his hands in his pockets. "Good luck."

He walked away, leaving me to my own fucked up thoughts that didn't feel good. *You did tonight.* Why did that sentence cause a physical pain to shoot through me? I hadn't hurt her. I was just upset. I was mad at her.

But she's flighty. She'd always looked for ways out, and I gave her the perfect one. She was probably convincing herself we were over. I didn't want that. Fuck. I really didn't. I loved seeing her at the game. Hell, she was my person.

I loved her. I loved the hell out of her. So why had I run?

Goddamn it.

I ran my hands through my hair, pulling on the ends. Had I misplaced my anger at my dad to her, like she was the one cheating? Maybe. Or was it the fact my dad lied and kept things from me and my mom, so her lying felt like a betrayal? Throw in the loss of the game, and man, I was a mess.

I jogged toward her dorm as Quentin's comment hit me

again. She hated confrontation. I'd seen it firsthand, yet she'd done it to protect *me*. Fuck I was an asshole.

I needed to talk to her right fucking now. I had to. The longer I waited, the harder it would be to convince her we were okay. It was only ten pm, and someone left her dorm as I snuck in.

Banging on her door, I waited. "Audrey, can we talk?"

No answer.

I pressed my ear against the wood, listening for the shower or sniffles or the TV. It was silent. "Audrey, baby, are you in there?"

Nothing.

Okay, where the hell was she?

I texted her, but the message wasn't delivered. What the fuck?

Had something happened to her? Oh my god. No, Quentin said he walked her to her dorm, but she wasn't in her dorm now. That was an hour ago. Was her phone off? Why though?

My body felt like it was falling through ice, not balanced or coordinated. My chest pinched, and sweat covered my skin as a million scenarios raced through my mind. She was hurt. She went to a party without me. She was with another guy. She left town. She moved.

Each one was more absurd than the next. I needed to be logical.

Audrey was upset. Where would she go when upset?

The library.

The answer came to me fast, and I took off toward there. I shot off another text to her in case she turned her phone on. *I'll come to you, baby. I'm sorry.*

I was glad I wore joggers because I was sweating my ass off as I ran toward our library. It was pitch dark outside, and I didn't like the idea of her walking here alone this late, even though she did it all the time.

I shoved the doors open, and it was a Saturday night, so there weren't a lot of people around. Ten people here and there as I checked the first floor. Then the second and third. The familiar panic worked its way up my chest again when I didn't see her auburn hair. If she wasn't here, I had no idea where she was.

I had to call Quentin and the campus police. Holy shit. I left her, and something like this happened? I couldn't breathe.

"Theo?" A small voice penetrated my spiral.

I spun around so fast I almost tripped on my feet. Audrey sat at a table for four, but her books covered the top. She wore yoga pants and a worn crewneck sweatshirt. It was one her dad gave her—she'd told me that. Her hair was piled in a messy bun on top of her head, and a few curls escaped by her face. Her eyes were a little red, but she looked beautiful. Fucking perfect. And safe. And mine.

"You're safe." I closed my eyes and took a deep breath. For about fifteen minutes, I hadn't been certain. I gripped the back of the empty chair and waited a few beats before meeting her gaze. She frowned at me. The wrinkles on her forehead were adorable.

"I'm okay, yeah." She chewed her lip and glanced at her papers instead of me. "Why are you here?"

"To find you." My heart pounded against my ribcage to the point of pain. I hated how she wouldn't look at me. I hated it so fucking much. "I went to your dorm and texted you, but when you didn't answer, I worried."

She swallowed, still not looking at me. "Oh. My phone died a little bit ago. I'm charging it now."

Her phone sat right in front of me, the charging signal bright and clear. What she said made sense. "Why are you at the library?"

"Studying. It helps me." She rubbed her thumb and pointer

finger together over and over. She flicked her gaze to me for a beat before her face reddened, and she looked down. "Did you need to talk to me?"

"Audrey, you're killing me right now." I plopped into the chair across from her and almost smiled at her cute notes. She had amazing handwriting and organized her thoughts in such a cool way. I loved seeing her process and asking her questions, but that wasn't for now. "Can we talk please?"

She shrugged. "Sure. What did you want to discuss?"

"Baby, why are—"

She flinched at the use of baby, and my heart fucking broke. She paled and gripped her pen so tight her knuckles were white. She was hurting because of me, and I hated it.

"Auds, I'm sorry." There, I said it. She had to know how I felt.

"I know. I'm sorry too. For keeping information from you about your family." She frowned and studied the end of her pen like it was the most interesting thing in the world. It was a basic black pen. What was so fucking cool about it?

"I know you were trying to protect me." I reached over and covered her hand with mine. She stilled, and her eyes widened. Why was she so shocked I was touching her? I didn't get it. "Why—"

She pulled her hand back and placed it in her lap.

What the fuck was going on?

"I was wrong. Your dad was seeing a therapist to help him cope with having a wife who was injured. I looked her up, and she's legit. Your dad is keeping his word and working on himself, which is great." She glanced at me and offered a small, barely there smile before masking her face to indifference. "I shouldn't have kept that from you regardless of any reasons. I know why you're upset."

This was the ice queen I met *months* ago. It was starting to piss me off.

"Why are you acting like this?" I barked, not caring we were in a library.

"Like what? I don't know how I'm supposed to act, Theo! I've never broken up with someone before, okay? I don't know the protocol! I'm just trying not to break down right now, okay!" She closed her eyes and took a deep breath, her jaw trembling.

She thought we were done, and that was my fault.

"Honey, we're not broken up." What we felt for each other was deeper than one argument. It was so much more.

"Yes, we are."

"No, no we're fucking not."

She opened her beautiful green eyes, and a flash of anger was in them. "Theo. I lied to you. That's... unforgiveable. You left m-me at the game. How... how else should I take that? You didn't come over like we planned and left me alone. How are we still together?"

She truly believed those words, and it made my stomach twist with legit anxiety. If she thought that, she might not believe how I felt about her. "We had our first fight. All couples do that."

"But do they leave each other?" Her lip trembled. "Do they keep things from each other, like I did to you?"

"No. They don't." I ran a hand through my hair and sighed. "I'm not your brother or mom or dad, hon. You can't lie to protect me like you did for them. You're not my caretaker or responsible for my emotions. You're my partner, so I need an equal."

She nodded, and tears spilled over. "I'm sorry I lied to you. I'm so sorry. I was worried it mess with your game or you'd be upset since you and your dad were getting close again."

"It did mess with my game." I took her hand and this time, she let me. That was a relief. "I played like shit because I was worried about what you were keeping from me."

She closed her eyes as her jaw trembled even more. "I shouldn't have lied to you. I'm sorry, Theo."

"I shouldn't have stormed off like I did either." My voice was raspy, raw. "You were trying to protect me in your own way, and I know that had to be hard. But I'm telling you now, I need you to share everything with me. No more hiding to protect feelings."

"Okay." She swallowed loud and met my eyes.

"And I won't leave you. If I'm mad, I'll be mad with you, and we can talk it out. I let my temper from the game and anger at my dad and you all blur together. I'm sorry for that."

"It's okay. It's totally okay."

"Audrey, I plan to be with you forever, so no, it's not okay. You should call me an ass for walking away instead of talking it out."

"Forever?" Her eyes bugged out.

"We had our first real argument, which happens with couples. But you and me? Baby, we're it." I smiled, all the parts of my soul settling into place.

She opened her mouth but closed it. Uncertainty clouded her eyes.

Quentin's warning that it would be tough flashed in my mind, and I was willing to lay it all on the table. I had no ego here. I just wanted Audrey. Never thought I'd thank that punk ass, but I owed him for saving this. She expected people to leave her, and I'd followed the pattern. Not anymore.

"Auds, I love you. I fucking love you so much it's all I think about most of the time. There are two places I feel at home. On the ice and when I'm with you. I should've told you that a month ago when I realized it." I kissed her wrist, noting her pulse raced as fast as mine. Her expressive eyes stared back at me, wide and filled with hope. That hope was something I vowed to never kill.

"You love me," she whispered, her voice watery and filled with emotion. "You love me?"

I nodded, a grin splitting my face. "Yes, baby. I do."

She closed her eyes as a huge fat tear fell down her cheek. I wiped it with my thumb, and she leaned her head into my hand. "I love you, you know. So much. Too much. It terrifies me."

"It scares me too, Auds, but it's you and me. It always will be. Come here."

She walked around the table and sat on my lap, wrapping her arms around me. She smelled like vanilla and home. I breathed her in and rested my chin on her head, my heart finally settling down from all the worry. "I'm sorry I hurt you, Theo. I'd rather hurt myself than you. I know that's not healthy, but I haven't had a lot of normal relationships. I'll learn and be better for you."

Her voice cracked and was muffled against my chest. The pain in her words *hurt* me because she meant it. She truly, without a doubt, meant what she said, and I hugged her tighter. "Baby, I—"

She lifted her head and stared into my eyes. "I will *never* lie to you or keep things from you again. And will *always* pick you first."

My heart swelled. "I like the sound of that. And I will never walk away mad again. We'll talk it out."

"You also feel like my home, Theo. For someone who hasn't had one in years, it's the most reassuring, safest feeling in the world, and I'll do whatever I can to protect it. If that means living in Minnesota with you, then I will. If it means doing distance until we figure stuff out, I will. I always thought my future was just surviving, but since you came into my life, I have new hopes."

"Yeah, like what?" I ran my hand up and down her back, so fucking happy we'd worked through this.

"Living together. Wearing your jersey to games. Being with you all the time."

"Mm, yeah, I really like hearing that. We could also travel

together, do all the things we wanted to in my off season." I played with the ends of her hair and loved how she hummed in response.

"We could take your siblings, too." She beamed and my heart damn well beat out of my chest. She would think of my siblings. She was perfect.

"So glad I got paired with you this semester, Auds. Feels like my life finally makes sense." I kissed her softly, letting my lips linger. I tasted happiness again, and I'd protect it at all costs.

She shuddered and dug her hands into my sides. "I feel so safe with you," she whispered.

"Mm, I like hearing that. Tell me how you feel about me again."

"I love you." She swallowed, and her cheeks turned pink. "I've never said it to anyone else before you, and it's a lot. That's a huge emotion for me. But I truly love you, and none of the reasons have to do with hockey even though it's amazing watching you play."

I pushed a piece of her hair behind her ear and sighed in complete content. All the worry disappeared. We were okay. We'd be okay. "So, about that living together thing..."

27

M*ay, post-graduation*
Audrey

I stood in the center of the quad, staring at the library and nursing buildings. Central State had been good to me. I didn't get the college experience shown in movies or TV shows, but I had one unique and good to me. I was set to take my NCLEX-RN exams in a few months and had applied to the traveling nursing agency. With our clinicals in the ICU, I focused on that space to specialize in. It had the chaos and fires that I thrived in. Once I heard back from the agency, I'd have to see if the states I could live in would take my license. Not all of them participated in the Nurse Licensure Compact. Theo would head to training camps this summer in Minnesota, where he'd either make the Acorns full roster or play in their farm system in Iowa.

Wherever he ended up, I'd go. Smiling, I enjoyed the feel of the sun on my skin, warming me up. If it weren't for this place, I wouldn't have met Theo. I wouldn't have fallen in love with him and his family, and I certainly wouldn't have fixed my relationship with Quentin.

Speaking of my brother...

"Congrats, Audrey." He held a huge bouquet of flowers, all yellow and purple, and handed them to me with a bag. "It's a new pair of scrubs, only there are hockey pucks on them."

"Couldn't wait for me to open it?" I snorted. "Thank you. This is kind."

"You're done with this place. That's wild to think about. And you're going to be traveling with Sanders. We haven't been that far apart before, Auds." His mouth was turned down in a frown, and his eyes were sad.

"You're totally going to miss me." I punched his shoulder and got him to laugh. We'd hung out often after our showdown last fall. We actually *liked* each other. We were into similar things, and I even got to know his friends. "We can FaceTime once a week, and you know you can always visit."

"Do you know where you're going to live yet?" He scratched his head. "There's an extra spot in the hockey house that's always open."

"No, thank you." I'd rather eat glass. I kept that comment to myself but appreciated the offer. It was genuine, which was so different than how we used to be. "We found an apartment in St. Paul to rent for the summer. I still don't have my license to practice there yet, so I might be here just to work. His dad offered Theo's room at the house, which might be nice."

"His family is awesome."

That was the other amazing part about this past year. Quentin had sort of been adopted into the Sanders household, where he had come over to join Theo and I for dinners. Daniel thought he was hilarious, which went straight to his head. I also liked the idea of Em, Daniel, and Penny having an extra set of hands around if needed. Em would be attending Central State next year, living on campus, so she was close if Daniel or Penny needed her, but she deserved to have fun, not be a parent. Not like Theo and I had to deal with.

That was the one thing I wasn't excited about: leaving the Sanders kids. Leaving them felt like missing a part of my heart, but Quentin promised to check in on them. Plus, Theo's mom was almost ready to come home. She showed vast improvement and had really grown during therapy.

She was even planning on flying out to visit us this summer. I couldn't wait.

"I'm gonna miss this place. Dad would've loved coming here." I sighed, and Quentin pulled me into a half hug. It was the anniversary of his death this week, and it seemed so fitting. Like life had gone full circle. I was a shell of a person when that had happened, and now I had so much more joy.

"He'd be so proud of you. I am. I'm really fucking proud of you." Quentin cleared his throat and released me. Emotions were still hard for him, for us, but we were getting better. Still awkward though.

I never asked about our mom, but Quentin hinted she was going to therapy to work through some things. That made me proud of her, but it didn't change the fact my life was so much better without contact from her. One day, if she worked on herself, we could talk, but that was ways away. My family had tripled this year with Theo and his family, and with Quentin back as my friend, I was good.

The guilt of letting my dad down ate at me from time to time, but Theo always talked me through the feelings and agreed cutting people off could be the right choice.

"Thank you. I do think Dad would be proud right now, but I'm proud of *both* of us." The sun disappeared behind the clouds just as my phone buzzed.

Theo: Where ya at, babe? Thought we were leaving in ten minutes?

Audrey: Meet you at the car in five.

"We're heading out now." My own throat closed up, the

weight of saying goodbye hitting me harder than I expected. My future was with Theo, but this was my brother. The person who'd been in my life the most.

"You get everything packed okay?" Quentin and I both stared at different buildings and not each other. "How long of a drive is it?"

"About twelve hours. I found a podcast on the latest nursing—"

"Boring." He chuckled and pulled me into a bear hug. "I'm gonna fucking miss you. Damn. I wanted to hold it together."

"I'm gonna miss you too." My eyes stung, and I squeezed my brother, willing to make sure we stayed in contact. Families did long-distance all the time. "Be good, okay?"

"No promises." He sniffed and ran a hand over his face. "Let me know when you get there, okay?"

I nodded. I glanced around the quad one more time, and a heavy lead weight grew in my feet. I was so excited about the future, my life with Theo. But leaving was shutting this chapter of my life, where I found myself again. I learned what I liked and didn't and who I was without the grief of losing my dad. I discovered how to have healthy relationships with people and that hope was okay. My mouth trembled just as a familiar figure walked toward us from the parking lot. *Theo.*

My heart skipped a beat seeing him. His looks were the first things people saw. His chiseled jaw and dusty light hair, always styled and perfect. And his eyes. I was a sucker for his eyes. But it was his heart that captivated me. The way he cared for his family, for me. How he'd sacrifice himself to help those around him. I couldn't believe that we'd found each other, and I made sure to show him how much I appreciated him every day.

He loved head scratches and bowls of cereal with color-changing spoons. He hated leftovers but was obsessed with flavored popcorn. Seeing his mom always upset him the day of, but his steps were lighter the rest of the week. His siblings made him laugh the most. But seeing him with his dad was the best. Having a relationship after heartbreak or betrayal was precious. We coached each other through it, me with Quentin and him with his dad. Love was still possible after hurt.

"There you are, woman." He grinned as he neared, and my breath caught in my throat. The sun glinted off his blond hair, and his blue eyes glistened. "Hey, Q, you say goodbye?"

My brother nodded. "Drive safe. Take care of her." He held out a hand, but Theo yanked him into a hug.

"Visit soon. There's so much to do in the city. It's gonna be unreal." Theo slapped my brother on his back before he cupped my face and kissed me. It didn't matter how many times we had kissed, every time I levitated just a little bit.

"Okay, chill, I'm right here."

Theo laughed against my mouth and wrapped his arm around my waist, holding me tight against his chest. "Can't help it."

"Ugh. You guys are gross. I gotta head out before I have a meltdown, but let me know when you arrive in Minnesota, okay?"

I nodded and met Quentin's eyes one more time. My own filled with tears, and I threw my arms around him for one more hug. "I love you, Q."

"You too, sis."

He passed me to Theo, who held my flowers and me, as I let a few tears fall. He kissed the top of my head, squeezing me tight. "Are you sure you want to move with me? You could stay here, and I can visit every weekend."

"No. *No.*" I stood on my toes and gripped his chin. "I want to be where you are. We've discussed this. I'm just having more feelings than I anticipated."

"Well, we know big feelings are okay to have." He arched a

brow. Penny went through some big feeling moments where she was terror, and it became our little catchphrase. Big feelings were hard. "We can leave whenever you're ready. Take your time. I just want you with me. That's all I need."

"Are you nervous?" I whispered.

"About moving to another state with you? No, baby. Not even a little. I'm fucking excited. They have two incredible hospitals that are hiring, and I even talked to my agent about making a connection for you. They also have two public libraries we can visit. They also have a bunch of activities for the partners of the players, like there's a picnic next week. I can't wait to go to all of that *with you*. I'm pumped to play hockey, sure, but starting my life with you is more exciting."

I swallowed down the ball of emotion. This man was everything. "You looked into the hospitals?"

"Of course, I did." He chuckled. "We're doing this together. You're my home, Audrey. You're my girl. Soon to be fiancée I believe."

"Theo." I blushed and swatted his chest. "Don't just throw around that F word."

"Why the hell not?" He tickled my side, making me yelp. His gaze softened, and he kissed me softly again. "Do you *not* want to be my wife someday?"

"I mean, sure, yes, of course." I gulped. "What is going on? Are you—you proposing?"

His eyes gleamed. "Not yet, no."

"Why do you look mischievous?" I sucked in a breath, and my skin prickled with awareness, like someone stared at me. "What's going on?"

"You should look in the bag." He held out the gift my brother gave me.

"The bag from Quentin?" I tilted my head. My head spun. Was this heatstroke? Had I drunk water? How warm was it outside? Throwing around words like fiancée and wife and *not yet*. "Theo. Theo." I breathed hard, my pulse erratic. "I-I-I don't understand."

"You will soon." He winked. The bastard winked and jutted his chin toward the bag. "Look in it, please."

With shaky hands, I pulled out the scrubs my brother referenced. Then, there was a small box at the bottom of the bag. Oh my. My eyes about bugged out of my face. We had never talked about marriage. I mean, we did in the middle of the night after having sex, but like, that was a fever dream.

Hell, last week, we talked about wanting kids someday. Someday, like ten years from now. Not. Now.

"What... Theo."

"Audrey Hawthorne, sweetheart." He got down on one knee and set the flowers and the scrubs on the ground. He opened the box and pulled out a vintage ring, one with a beautiful pink diamond. I gasped, my mind forgetting how to function. Breathing was supposed to be easy, but each pull of oxygen took effort.

He's proposing to me.

"You are the best thing that's ever happened to me. You are my best friend, my fucking rock, the most brilliant and sexy and kind woman I've ever known. I love you, will always love you, and don't want to wait another second before putting my ring on you. We're about to start the next chapter of our lives, and I need you in it. Please be my wife. Be my other half in every way. I'll promise to take care of you and make you laugh. We can take our time picking a date, but I really just want to be yours, forever."

I blinked back tears as I stared at the gorgeous man kneeling before me. "How did the b-box show up in the bag?"

He laughed. "That's your thought right now?"

I nodded.

"You never make it easy, and I love it." He kissed the back of my hand. "How do you think? I asked your brother for permission to marry you, and he said yes."

Fuck. I cried fully now. Big, fat, juicy tears. "Oh."

"Mm, that *oh* better be *oh, yes, I'll marry you* because my knee is hurting right now, and I should probably get up."

Like he always did, he made me laugh and pulled me out of my head. I grabbed his hands and lifted him up, not that I did much. But he pretended to let me, and I ran my hands over his shoulders, then his strong chest. "You don't think we're too young?"

"I honestly don't fucking care." He cupped my face, dragging his thumbs over my jawline. "I know what I want, and that's you baby."

Nodding, I kissed him hard. "Yes, okay, yes, let's get married. Holy shit."

Laughing, he picked me up and swung me around. Peppering me with kisses on my neck, I freaking floated. Engaged? Me? Unreal.

"Okay, I need to put the ring on you now." He set me down and slid the ring on my fourth finger. His eyes watered as he stared at it. "My mom gave me that ring to give to you."

"What?" I gasped, the weight of it feeling a thousand pounds. "This is *her* ring?"

Theo nodded. "Yes. And it looks perfect on you." He kissed my finger and stared at me with so much love my heart skipped a beat. He was perfect. My fiancé was perfect.

"I love you," I whispered, hoping he knew all the unsaid things behind those words. "I can't wait to do life with you. Let's go."

"Ah, so the thing is..." He gripped the back of his neck, and his cheeks pinkened at the top. "This was all kind of planned, and well, everyone is waiting for us behind that building."

I whipped around, and sure enough, his dad, Em, Daniel, Penny, and Quentin all stood there with huge smiles.

"What did she say?" my idiot brother yelled.

"I said yes!" I held up my hand, and they all ran up to us, swarming us in a hug. I had never felt so content in my entire life. As they all took turns eyeing the ring, Theo just stared at me with a small smile on his lips.

I might've started college alone, unsure about my life, but now? I had a whole family, and I was about to marry the best man in my life. I couldn't wait to start that chapter, but it'd have to wait until after our celebratory dinner. I didn't mind. These were the people I loved most in the world.

Things happened for a reason, and I didn't spend too much time thinking about *how* we got to this point, but I was gonna enjoy every second of it. Especially my future husband.

THE END

ACKNOWLEDGMENTS

Will this part ever get old? I'm not sure. Writing a book always takes a team of people. This story wouldn't have happened without Mikaela Brown or Rachel Rumble. I had TWO separate text threads going on brainstorming ideas and Mikaela was all "make him the best book boyfriend ever" and Rachel was like "I want to cry my eyes out" (ha, jk, Rachel doesn't have emotions). But for real. The start of this story was such a fun moment.

Rachel, Nurse Rachet, thanks for giving me all the medical insight and crying at how good this story was. Your tears moved me. I'm also CACKLING writing this. For real though. Thank you for cheering me on and loving on Theo and Audrey, telling me where things could be better. I love knowing I have you in my corner. I love how you've turned to "my one reader friends" to "royal rumble" to "Rachel." I talk about you so much, and text you WAY too much, you're a part of my life now. Sorry, not sorry.

Mikaela, thank YOU for dealing with my manic texts where I have a million ideas that don't always make sense. You are always so kind and creative and fun working with.

Katherine McIntyre, you brilliant badass editor. Thank you for always taking my drafts and kicking my ass. It is so reassuring to know I have you and you'll call me on everything, while also cheering me on. Let's keep doing this? Please?

HALEY WALKER, you magnificent, beautiful butterfly. LOVE that we get to do this together. Love that our energy matches. Love that we're just getting started. I appreciate you and our friendship so damn much.

My family will never read this, but JUST to put it on the record, my parents and brother are great. Nothing like this story.

Lastly, I want to thank nurses. If you are one, I wish I could hug you.

ABOUT THE AUTHOR

Jaqueline Snowe lives in Arizona where the "dry heat" really isn't that bad. She prefers drinking coffee all hours of the day and snacking on anything that has peanut butter or chocolate. She is the mother to two fur-babies who don't realize they aren't humans and a mom to two perfect rascals. She is an avid reader and writer of romances and tends to write about athletes. Her husband works for an MLB team (not a player, lol) so she knows more about baseball than any human ever should.

To sign up for her review team, or blogger list, please visit her website www.jaquelinesnowe.com for more information.

ALSO BY JAQUELINE SNOWE

Central State Series

The Puck Drop

From the Top

Take the Lead

Off the Ice

Central State Football Series

First Meet Foul

The Summer Playbook

Scoring Forever

Holiday Rom-Coms

Snowed in for Christmas

Christmas Sweater Weather

Cleat Chasers Series

Challenge Accepted

The Game Changer

Best Player

No Easy Catch

Out of the Park Series

Evening the Score

Sliding Home

Rounding the Bases

Shut Up and Kiss Me Series

Internship with the Devil

Teaching with the Enemy

Nightmare Next Door

Standalones

Holdout

Take a Chance on Me

Let Life Happen

Whiskey Surprises

The Weekend Deal

Made in the USA
Middletown, DE
11 August 2024

58939832R00159